We'll Always Have Poison

ALSO BY BJ MAGNANI

The Queen of All Poisons

The Power of Poison

A Message in Poison

We'll Always Have Poison

A Dr. Lily Robinson Novel

BJ MAGNANI

Encircle Publications
Farmington, Maine, U.S.A.

Hardcover ISBN-13: 978-1-645990-525-8
Paperback ISBN-13: 978-1-645990-524-1
eBook ISBN-13: 978-1-645990-526-5

Encircle editor: Cynthia Brackett-Vincent

Book and cover design by Deirdre Wait
Cover images © Getty Images

Published by:

Encircle Publications, LLC
PO Box 187
Farmington, ME 04938

info@encirclepub.com
http://encirclepub.com

In memory of my beloved daughter Knina,
who saw the world in all its beauty—and with all its faults.
Though she rests now with the blue-green jewel of the universe,
Mother Earth, she will remain in my heart—forever.

CHAPTER 1

THE NORTHEAST COAST OF AUSTRALIA

Mountainous clumps of staghorn coral littered the seafloor like remnants of an exposed grave. The diver edged along the reef. He remained focused. Determined to capture the growing destruction, staccato flashes from his underwater camera reflected off the remaining bright purple sea fans. Delicate air bubbles floated above while he photographed the masses of stark white 'bones.' Closer to the shore, waves crashed over adjacent brain coral without effect. The coral sat unmoved; their pale fissures lifeless, devoid of thriving soft polyps.

Diving off this isolated stretch of beach had once been wondrous—all varieties of colorful aquatic life captured by the camera lens. Gone were the majestic manta rays that swam at his side, their broad wings flapping as they searched for zooplankton. Only a few remaining ornate butterflyfish, glorious in their brilliant orange-yellow stripes, darted in and out of the coral in search of polyps.

The change was undeniable. Bleaching had progressed. How could the Great Barrier Reef come back from this latest insult? The diverse ecosystem he had documented over the last fifteen years continued to collapse. He stopped. His fins fanned through the water, stirring the sand below. The ocean gasped for breath.

Tiny coral polyps had taken fifty million years to build the reefs. By comparison, human impact took less than two hundred years to unravel Mother Nature's work. If these bastions of marine life died, the world would lose fifty to eighty percent of its oxygen emitted via plankton and photosynthesizing bacteria. A quarter of the planet's marine life would lose their habitat, as coral reefs provide food, shelter, and protection for spawning. And, as lower organisms disappeared, those higher up the food chain, too, would be threatened.

The discouraged diver headed back to shore, lost in thought, believing the Great Barrier Reef was on the precipice of death. Only the sounds of his breathing filled his ears. Soon, he planned to meet with the Climate Council and deliver his report. What he would say would turn the world upside down. He made a mental note to call the Council Chair and request the presence of a security service at the conference.

Another diver hid, and watched, within the mounds of bleached coral. Her mask and snorkel allowed her to see the seafloor yet stay undetected—no bubbles to give her away. Strapped to her left leg, a diving knife remained ready. She took a few shallow breaths and waited. When her target stopped to remove his fins so he could step the remaining yards through the shallows, she made her move. The pouch at her side writhed in undulations. Using a set of snake tongs, she pulled the sea serpent from the bag, and with her own fins beating like a dolphin's tail, she swam silently to the unaware diver and positioned the head of the snake at his exposed ankle. The bite was swift. The snake, agitated from its journey in a blind pouch, squirmed and lunged with a second bite. The man stumbled. Gravity pulled him face-first into the water, his mask slipping off the top of his head.

The woman returned the snake to the pouch, grabbed her victim's camera, and swam along the shore with the deftness of a water ballerina. When she reached a dense cluster of orange mangroves, she rose from the ocean like a sea creature adapted to land. Hidden behind a tree, she dropped the writhing bag onto the sand and loosened its opening. In one swift gesture, she sliced off the serpent's head. A spurt of dark fluid missed splashing her face—the turn of her head, too quick. Picking up the still wriggling pieces, the lithe diver cast them into the ocean, knowing the fish would finish off what she had started.

Damp, blond tresses curled in ringlets spilled from under her diving cap as she prepared to change. She took a deep breath and, with some difficulty, stripped off her dive skin to expose a royal blue print bikini. Gathering her things, the shapely diver waited for her contact's arrival and thought, *one down*.

Back down the beach, gentle waves pushed the man's body toward the sandy shore, nudging curious ghost crabs in its path. Their scurrying etched tiny trails in the sand, defining their movements. Overhead, squawks from silver gulls filled the quiet as they eyed the lifeless form below. Circling blowflies landed on the salt-soaked corpse, depositing eggs in the eyes, nose, and mouth. By now, the sky was a glorious red with streaks of purple, blue, and gold. Polluted air created a spectacular sunset as particles of smoke and dust reflected beams of brilliant light. And when the bright was replaced with the dark, only a ribbon of stars lit the heavens.

CHAPTER 2

BOSTON

My name is Lily Robinson, and I'm on the upside of my recovery from a gunshot wound suffered at the hands of a terrorist. Remnants of my past stay with me, plague me, tangled in what's to come. It's the past I now hear knocking at my door. And maybe the future, too.

Rose and Kelley stand before me—young, hopeful, hand in hand.

"Oh, Dr. Robinson," Rose says, her tight hug engulfing me, "I'm so happy to see you."

I let her arms linger, and when we break the embrace, my daughter is beaming—a full smile, rosy cheeks, and dark hair tucked behind her ears. Her coat covers the navy sweater that drapes her slim frame. She seems happy. But would her smile disappear if I told her my secret? Our secret—that I'm her biological mother.

"So good to see both of you." I take their jackets and hang them in the closet. "Let's sit." Her wide-legged pants appear to float across the living room as Rose enters while Kelley, my former fellow, gets us some drinks so Rose and I have a few minutes alone.

"Rose, you look well." Yet her downturned eyes and brief parting of the lips tell me otherwise. "How does it feel to be back in medical school after your leave of absence?"

"Fabulous." She shifts in her seat and pulls at an imaginary thread on her slacks. "I'm loving every minute."

Kelley appears handsome today—his dark hair clipped at the sides, the slide of his shoes across the tile heralding his entrance. He casts a sideways glance toward Rose, his tight grip and steady hand tells me he grasps the situation. He hands us our drinks. "Thank you, Kelley."

"You're looking well, too, Dr. Robinson," Kelley says before taking his seat.

We make small talk about the university and our colleagues, and after a bite to eat, Kelley is eager to hear my thoughts about the string of recent overdose deaths filling the morgue. Once a student of mine, he now takes his place as a full-time physician helping run the toxicology service. My university job dwindled to a trickle when my knowledge of poisons became more than academic as the U.S. Government demanded more of my time as a covert assassin.

Kelley settles in his chair and spills a medical case he's been working on. "I want you back on service full-time, Dr. Robinson. We need you."

He waits for my reaction, and all I do is stare, knowing that I've been consumed by a clandestine sideline job that has vexed me since my daughter Rose went missing from my life more than twenty years ago.

Kelley starts again, moved by my silence. "Here it is. A twenty-six-year-old male, found down in one of the local eateries in Boston. When EMS got there, they gave him naloxone, assuming it was a drug overdose. He responded poorly, so they gave him multiple doses to reverse the opioid effects. But he seized and started flailing about; now he's in our Neurointensive Care Unit."

"I can almost anticipate how this will end," I tell Kelley.

"I'm sure you can," he says, nodding. "When he regained consciousness, he told us he had used cocaine, but when we tested his urine, it showed he had taken cocaine, and fentanyl."

"Of course. So let me guess, prolonged hypoxia caused Lance-Adams syndrome?"

"Exactly." Kelley nods, and places both hands on his thighs.

Rose leans forward and interrupts. "Okay you two doctors. I'm not following. What's Lance-Adams syndrome?"

"Sorry, Rose. Lance-Adams is relatively rare, but sometimes after a person has a cardiopulmonary arrest and is resuscitated, they develop myoclonus and even dysarthria." I pause at the puzzled look on Rose's face.

Kelley jumps in before I resume. "Look, heart and breathing stop. The brain gets no oxygen, and if the time interval before the patient is revived is too long, they can develop uncontrollable jerks called myoclonus after the heart starts pumping again."

I raise an eyebrow at Kelley. "That's what I said." Turning to Rose, I continue, "the muscle jerks interfere with motor functions, so limbs move uncontrollably, darting in all directions, sometimes hands swinging in the air, punches landing on the face. The patient also has trouble speaking, that's dysarthria, and some short-term memory impairment."

"Oh, I see. That sounds awful." Rose scrunches up her nose and shifts in her chair.

My voice softens. "What's awful is the aftermath. How long the person is deprived of oxygen before the brain damage makes coming back worse than the original problem, in this case, drug use."

Kelley captures my look and nods. "Our hope is he'll regain some of his function."

On cue, Rose frowns, her arms crossed in front of her, her fingers blanched. "So, it's more about the lack of oxygen rather than the drug use, per se," Rose says.

"Yes."

Her eyes glisten. A young woman still coping with her own depression, and trauma. I put my arm around her. "Rose, there'll always be those cases with bad outcomes. All we can do is our best."

She nods, her lips pursed, and her green eyes look past me. It's hard to read her thoughts, and I won't pry.

Rose and Kelley stir in their seats and make plans to leave. Kelley grabs my elbow, the pressure of his fingers anchoring me. "Come back," he says.

"I'll be back at the hospital soon. I need a little time off to reflect on my life," I tell him.

"Reflect on your life?" Kelley tilts his head to one side, his eyebrows close together. "What's to reflect on?"

I laugh, give them each a big hug, and kiss Rose's cheek. "I'll see you both soon." My hand brushes Rose's arm, and she doubles back for another hug. I feel her warmth against my body, and the floral scent of her hair jostles my memory. Does she sense our blood connection and, like me, choose to remain silent?

* * *

Rose was a rare bloom, the child of an indiscretion between a research fellow and her older professor. While I gave Rose her dark hair and green eyes, she had the shape of Charles's mouth and his stormy view of the world—even as a toddler. I wasn't in love with Rose's father, but I did love him. At least twenty years my senior, he was my mentor, and in some ways, I was his.

The nurses were supportive when I went into labor. 'Take a deep breath during your contraction, and slowly let the breath out,' they said. I felt the impending birth. I had to push. Sounds from the fetal monitor rang in my ears—fast-paced tapping—*thump*, *thump*, *thump*, *thump*.

"Lily, I can see the head crowning. Just a few more pushes," the doctor said. His gray hair spilled from under his surgical cap, his green scrubs fresh in the morning light.

"Good job, keep going. Almost there, Lily. That's it." The nurse spoke her words of encouragement, held my hand, and rubbed my back.

I gave one final push.

"It's a little girl, Lily. And she's perfect," the doctor said. His excitement bounced off the walls, turning the delivery room's tension into joy.

The nurse's face beamed. I pulled at her elbow before she took my baby aside, and she laid her upon my chest—Rose's eyes barely open, her pink skin mottled from her struggle to leave the watery environment and trust one with air. I stroked her damp hair, and a sweet odor—an intoxicating newborn smell that lingered for months—filled my senses. I searched for the right words, words Charles might have said if he were in the room with me. If he hadn't died. A covalent bond came to mind, the strongest chemical bond in our world. "My little love, our connection is an unbreakable bond." I felt the surge of endorphins kick in, a blinding euphoria sweeping away the remainder of childbirth.

I held her tiny hand in mine. A love forever. Yet in one fleeting afternoon when Rose was just three, she disappeared in the jungles of Colombia. Only images of a red-soaked earth and the smell of death in humid air stayed with me, waiting for me to regain my memory. For more than twenty years, I couldn't remember what had happened. Or maybe I just didn't want to. It's hard to know where the truth lies.

Those early days, I found myself going through the motions of life.

Not living life, just pretending. I was a passenger, not a driver. Brain fog inhabited my mind like the June gloom in a California spring. I squelched the overpowering guilt I felt while waiting for the clouds to part. Buried it. My logical mind and supreme focus blocked my emotions. I thought I would never love again. I could never love again.

It's hard to shake that way of life. Living less in the moment, guarded and suspicious. But then, that makes me who I am—the Queen of All Poisons.

CHAPTER 3

WASHINGTON, D.C.

A car hit the brakes just as a ball rolled into the street. The man with wispy brown hair ran out, picked it up, and threw it to the wide-eyed boy before turning into a white stone building. The sign out front read *Society for Climate Intervention,* the cover name for the team's headquarters, while the inner door required a retinal scan to enter. Inside, men and women, computers at their fingertips, monitored potential global threats.

Chad Jones stroked his chin and settled behind his desk. The call he'd just received had stoked more than concern. It had planted the seeds of a plan to get his frayed team back together. A scientist, Daniel Williams, found dead on a beach off the northeast coast of Australia, had been expected to speak in front of the Climate Council in Brussels. According to his known itinerary, he first planned a trip to South Africa to meet with Graham Harmon, another scientist, before going to Belgium. Yet, he failed to connect with his assistant to review the last-minute details the day before his departure. So, his staff looked for him in all his favorite places. And they found him.

His bloated body clung to his wetsuit. Intact diving gear and air tanks, two-thirds empty, indicated the scientist was likely on his way back to the beach when he died. When Chad had asked about the cause of death, his contact reported there had been some speculation the man may have encountered a sea snake. And although Chad knew little about these underwater serpents, he knew they were poisonous. Lily Robinson came to mind.

A knock at the door jostled Chad back to the papers on his desk. He arranged them in a neat stack before he shouted, "one moment," combed his brown hair with the tips of his fingers and straightened his blue-striped tie. Then he rose from behind his desk and got the door.

"Right on time," Chad said to the middle-aged man standing in the door frame. "Come on in, JP, and take a seat."

They shook hands, and Chad thought JP's hair had gotten even grayer since their last meeting. Jean Paul, or JP as they all called him, had sported a thick head of dark hair not all that long ago. But Chad knew full well that the stress of the job took its toll. He had worked with JP for years as his director and recognized him as one of the best field operatives on his team—a team primarily responsible for suppressing terrorist threats by any means. A controversial position, yet one with global acceptance within the consortium of those charged with overseeing world order.

"*Merci*, Chad. Good to see you again." JP scanned the room, eyed the ticking clock on the shelf above Chad's desk, and checked his watch hidden by his cuff. "*Alors*, what have you got for me?" He sat in the chair opposite Chad and observed the orderly pile of papers, then brushed the pleat in his charcoal slacks.

Chad cleared his throat. "Ha. No small talk. I should know better. You come right to the point." He evened out the corners of the pile. "We'll get to that in a moment. First, have you been in contact with Robinson?"

"I thought we agreed to let her be for a while. She almost died after taking a bullet on our last mission." JP sat back in the chair and let the held breath escape his chest.

"Yeah. A shit show." Chad shook his head. "But I'd like to speak with her." He drummed his fingers on his desk.

"*Et,* why is that?" He raised a single eyebrow, the crease in his cheek deepening. "She is not the only expert on poisons if that is your objective."

"Well, yes, I do have a poison question. True, there are others, but Robinson's one of us, JP. Not that she chose this business like you and I did, but we sucked her into it. At least Pixie Dust did. And Pixie partnered her up with you. That woman was like a black hole. You get too close, and you disappear."

JP closed his eyes and imagined the woman with the pink streak in her hair, her striking blue eyes, her full lips. "*C'est vrai, mais,* she is the past. What is going on?" JP said after leaving the image of Pixie Dust behind.

A woman gently pushed open the office door carrying two steaming coffee cups. JP thanked her and took the dark roast, black, no sugar. The scent of hazelnut rose from the other cup, and Chad gave the mixture an extra stir, ensuring the uniform merge of light and dark. The woman left the office and shut the door behind her.

"Okay, we'll get back to Robinson later. Now, my contacts in Australia alerted me to the untimely death of a climate scientist. A well-known, high-profile researcher named Daniel Williams. Outspoken and controversial." Chad pulled a folder from the top of the pile and opened it.

JP leaned in closer. "Perhaps he irritated the wrong people."

"More than irritation." Chad raised an eyebrow. "His team cataloged the slow death of the GBR, and he was expected to share his data at the Climate Council conference. The U.S. has a stake in that."

"The GBR?" JP took a few sips of his coffee, testing to see if it had cooled.

"The Great Barrier Reef off the northeast coast of Australia. For years it had been a magnet for tourists, but the corals are dying with all the pollution dissolving into the ocean. The Australian tourist economy has been floundering." Now Chad sipped from his cup.

"Was Williams murdered? A terrorist connection, perhaps?"

"Not a hundred percent sure, but we think so. He was scuba diving and supposedly documenting changes to the coral. But his camera never turned up with the body, and his team is certain he had it with him."

"Someone killed him and took the camera? *Mais*, surely one day of photos would not change the world."

"Of course." Chad shrugged his shoulders. "But if his camera was taken, it could mean he found incriminating evidence someone didn't want exposed. And we have no idea what he planned to say at the Council meeting." He took another sip. "Look, I get it. Climate change catastrophes are daily news stories. But I'm sure you wouldn't be surprised to learn powerful interests want to keep fossil fuels alive. Money talks; in the end, it's all about greed."

JP nodded. "*Et*, how did he die?"

"Well, that's where it gets interesting. Forensics found two startling clues. First, at the left ankle, which would have been exposed when Williams removed his fins, were puncture marks."

"A needle mark, perhaps? Someone shot him with drugs?" JP put the coffee cup on Chad's desk and waited.

"Not quite. No drugs were found in his system, and the air tanks were clean."

JP stared at Chad.

"Well, here's the thing. In addition to the puncture marks on the ankle, a single fang was found embedded in the leg of the wetsuit."

"A fang? A tooth from an animal?" JP's shoulders stiffened, his chin pointed upwards.

"Yes. Staff at the Australian Museum recognized the syringe-like fang to have come from a sea snake."

"You are telling me he was bitten by a sea snake and died in the water. An accident for sure, *oui*?"

"Not an accident. The fang belonged to the banded sea krait, and from what I'm told, that snake is not commonly found off that stretch of the Australian coast. And they generally don't attack people randomly. It's a strange set of circumstances, to say the least."

"*Mais oui*, now I see why you want to speak with Robinson."

"Look, JP, of all of us, you're the closest to her. You were there at the beginning. Just run a few things by her and see what she says."

JP laughed. "Ah, afraid to enter the poison garden, Chad?"

"Not at all. I may be the director, but I don't have your touch." Chad's pointer finger poked the table as he stared at JP.

"*C'est vrai, mon ami*. I believe she is either in Boston or at her cottage. Nothing like a trip up the coast."

"Thanks, JP. I'll get more details for you so you have some hard facts when you sit down with her."

"*Et*, Chad. What do *you* think?"

"Daniel Williams acted as a spokesperson for some prominent climate scientists. It could be related to the Climate Council business or something else. Washington is concerned." Chad lowered his voice, his eyebrows drawn together.

"*Et*, it is now the problem of the *Society for Climate Intervention*." JP's smile broadened.

Chad laughed. "So much for the name of our headquarters. But seriously, JP, we need to find out who's behind this killing and stop them before the work of the Climate Council is derailed. And, of course, we need to find out what Dr. Williams planned to reveal."

"*Oui*. If it is murder, the killer likely represents the interests of someone who wants to protect their investment. I agree with you—possibly oil, coal, and gas companies."

"How this plays out is anyone's guess. Right now, I'm finding out who sits on the Council and who plans to present data." Chad pushed a folder across the desk.

JP opened the file and scanned the contents. "The Council prepares an assessment of climate change based on scientific, technical, and socio-economic reports. Williams was planning on presenting some scientific data."

"That's correct. Scientists on the Council identify the risks for global warming and look at ways to mitigate future damage."

"These experts are from all over the world and plan to contribute the latest scientific knowledge on the various ecosystems—ocean, polar, mountain, and so on."

"Right. The earth depends on it. As for Robinson, please, check in with her. I'll call her too. She can do a little snooping from the confines of her home. You boys can do the dirty work. As I said, I'll work on getting more information about the Council, and then we can flesh out the plan. When are you going to see Parker?" The furrows on Chad's forehead deepened.

JP stood and brushed off his slacks. "When I leave here."

"Good. I thought I saw him earlier this morning. He's probably downstairs." Chad patted JP's shoulder as they ambled to the door.

"*Merci.*"

Chad stopped before reaching the door and turned. "JP, we need to find the killer before he sends the world into environmental chaos or worse."

JP took a breath and smiled. "*Oui.* Chop off the head of the snake." He shook Chad's hand and left the room.

*   *   *

Jean Paul Marchand left Chad Jones and returned to his office in another part of the building. He and Parker used two small offices near each other in the team's headquarters. He called his partner. Parker had always been Parker; there was no other name for his friend. He was a good ten years younger than JP and sometimes referred to Jean Paul as ol' man, which was the only sore point between them. They had worked together for several years and felt at ease in each other's company. Able to anticipate one another's responses during a mission and provide cover in more ways than one, created a solid bond between the two men. JP considered that Parker might suspect he and Lily Robinson were lovers, but it wasn't something they ever talked about. The quiet Frenchman remained a man who rarely shared anything about himself. Even with Lily.

A rap at the door caused JP to rise from his desk.

"Hey, hey, boss. I heard you were looking for me. How was the little break? Did you pop over to France?" Parker looked trim in his dark khakis and tattersall shirt. He pushed his wavy hair out of his eyes and shook JP's hand vigorously.

JP smiled and clasped both of Parker's hands. "*Bon. Merci*. Time is a luxury we do not have."

"Right. I should know better now than to ask you for any details." Parker smiled. "So, what's Chad got in store for us now?" He sat in the chair by the small round table near the window.

"What is your understanding of climate change, *et,* specifically, the Climate Council? Several scientists are scheduled to speak before the Council and present data on the severity of the current conditions."

"Not much, really. Only what I read in the papers. Why are we involved?"

"A scientist named Daniel Williams was presumably murdered off the coast of Australia. He may have discovered something in the course of his research."

"I see. So, scientists who give it to us straight on how the world is going to shit are in danger. Or there is another reason Chad would get us involved." Parker shifted in his seat.

"*Oui*. Something like that. Intelligence suggests this death could be related to a terrorist plot to keep oil, gas, and coal interests afloat."

"And why do they think it's murder?"

JP related the story of the sea snake to Parker as he took a small bottle of fizzy water from his office refrigerator. "You want a glass?" he asked.

"No thanks. So, you're saying this guy was bitten by a rare sea snake. Are those things poisonous?"

"According to Chad, it is. He wants me to contact Robinson." He twisted in his chair. JP found it difficult to speak about Lily as if they only had a professional relationship. He'd last seen her at the cottage, where they professed their love for one another.

"Shit. I thought we said we'd back off for a while. Is she still recovering at her cottage or back in Boston?"

"Unknown, *mais,* I plan to call her and set up a meeting. Meanwhile, see what you can find out about the scientists on the Council's agenda. Chad gave me a few names to start." He handed Parker the folder Chad had given him earlier.

"Do we have any idea what Williams was going to say?"

"Not yet. *Mais*, the head of the Climate Council is Hans Lundberg. He has been Chair for the last five years. Daniel Williams may have told him what he was planning."

"I've seen him on TV. Older guy, maybe early seventies, with an enviable crop of white hair."

"*Oui*, that is him. The Council headquarters is in Brussels. So, we will see him when we get to Belgium."

"Great. I can finally see *Manneken Pis*." Parker laughed, knowing he could get a rise out of JP.

"Ah. You are a man of the world. Not enamored of the Atomium *mais,* rather a bronze of a small boy peeing in a fountain." JP shook his head, well aware of the 'Little Pissing Man,' a famous fountain sculpture in the heart of Brussels.

"I guess I'll leave that stainless steel goliath for you." Parker laughed, propping his hand on the back of his head.

"First, we will travel to South Africa to see Graham Harmon, who also is scheduled to present before the Council. Chad is getting more details on him. Then we head off to Sydney to talk with Williams's people. What was he working on? What did he know?"

"Why not start in Australia?"

"Let us start with the living."

Parker scratched his head. "Around the world once again. I wonder what it would be if I added up all the miles."

"*Beaucoup, mon ami, beaucoup*."

CHAPTER 4

SYDNEY, AUSTRALIA

Decisions. Decisions. Would it be the ocean-blue contact lenses, the deep violet ones, or the rainbow, and invite the stares? Bored with her brown-eyed issue, marine biologist Dr. Holly Miller liked to poke the bear and make life interesting. Her colleagues were used to her eye-catching provocations. But occasionally, Holly caught someone off guard who couldn't help but stare. Some mornings, she knew what to wear— her mood dictated her choice. On other days, Holly wasn't sure how she felt. Even a pin jabbed into her skin would be no more than a dull sensation. Hidden beneath colorful eyes and a steely surface, her mind swirled with unsettled business—abandonment, revenge, and intellectual challenges.

Holly finally settled on the rainbow contacts, brushed her blond locks, and dressed in slim-fitting cream slacks, a tan blouse, and stylish low-top multicolored sneakers with a jumping puma emblazoned on the side. She grabbed a quick cup of coffee and avocado on toast before heading to the aquarium. Marine World Down Under was the largest aquarium in Sydney, and behind the multiple exhibits, conservation efforts consumed many dedicated scientists.

Holly parked her white SUV around the back of the aquarium and entered through the employees' entrance. Already, the crowds were queuing up at the front, eager children squirming to take the long traverse through the water tunnel as fish and sharks swam by, wondering what sea creatures the tide pools held. Holly made her way to the second floor of the building and into her office. She had just removed her jacket and hung it on the hook behind the door when she heard a loud knock.

"G'day, Holly. How was your weekend? Are you going to that talk on corals this afternoon?" Sara fired, staring at Holly's eyes.

Her enthusiasm woke up Holly's quiet introspection. Dr. Sara Wilder was already in her rubber boots and anxious to get to her penguins. Older than Holly and unmarried, the aquarium and its contents occupied most of her days. And nights.

Holly reeled from the bombardment. She rolled her eyes. "Possibly. If I have time. It seems like you're off for some wet work." She eyed Sara's pant legs tucked inside tall waterproof boots.

As the marine veterinarian, Sara dealt with various sea creatures, from fish to fowl. "Yes. Another long day. We have a couple of sick penguins and a sea turtle in bad shape. I was wondering if you're free for lunch. I wanted to ask you what you thought about that whale that washed up in North Narrabeen. I heard the director wants to get a more complete necropsy." Sara rearranged her headband and pushed her curly brown hair away from her face.

"I think so. My experiment this morning shouldn't spill over into lunch hour. I'll be hungry by midday."

Holly wanted to find out what Sara knew about the carcass. After it had washed up on the shore, the town had called a company to remove the dead whale and take it to a marine station for further study. The surrounding beaches had been closed due to the increased shark activity.

"That's great. I brought a sandwich with me. Do you need to get anything?"

"I can pop by the café and pick up something. I'll see you around 12:15." Holly managed a smile.

"Sounds good. By the way, love your high ponytail look. Wish I could do something with this frizzy mess," Sara said, running her fingers through her wayward curls. "And oh, I see you wore those hideous rainbow contacts this morning. Freakish." Sara laughed. "I still don't understand why you do that, Holly."

Holly smirked and shook her head. She'd noticed Sara's stares. Her colleague always made a thing about her eyes no matter what color lenses Holly chose. Which is why Holly provoked her. Sara usually gave her the talk of the eyes being the window of the soul and all that. If it was, why did Sara find Holly's eyes so disturbing? Was there a dark stain on Holly's soul, visible through the prism? Did Sara feel she needed to save Holly from herself? Holly didn't know. Or maybe Sara just liked her hair—always sleek and under control no matter the weather. Sara, self-conscious about her own looks, viewed Holly with envy.

"Ha ha," Holly bluffed. "I sensed a swirl of color this morning. And besides, rainbow matches my sneakers. See you later." Holly's voice prickled.

And Sara felt it.

"You got it." Sara closed the door behind her.

Holly looked down at her buzzing phone and answered it. "Yeah, I just got in. No, I haven't started yet. That annoying vet was in and wants to meet me later for lunch. I'll get back to you this afternoon after reviewing the data." She swiped off her phone, pulled a folder from her bag, and set it down on her desktop.

Then Holly Miller took the key out of her purse and unlocked the bottom drawer of the tall gray filing cabinet. She removed the camera and placed it on her desk. After double-checking that her office door was locked, she sat down, turned on the camera, and ran through the digital photos again.

CHAPTER 5

THE COTTAGE

The light forms dapples on the ground, and tiny cat's paws dot the water. Further out, white curls on the gray sea appear like tabby cat stripes while I peer through the spotting scope, looking for ducks and egrets in the grass by the shore. The cottage, secreted along the Massachusetts coast, is my place of solitude, a place where thoughts intermingle with nature, and the pace of life is just a little slower. I'm expecting JP to arrive with news. Of what I can only imagine, but I'll be happy to see him, nonetheless.

While I wait, I think about the woman who brought us together. An operative who became a legend in an alternate world. Was she aware of my sorrow and overwhelming guilt? Strange to think back on it now.

One morning, more than twenty years ago, I received a most unusual phone call. A woman left a message on my office phone. She identified herself as an employee of the United States Government, wanted to meet me regarding our national security, and suggested I call the CIA to verify her story. So, I did. The Agency knew of her and told me it would be my choice if I wanted to help my country. They couldn't force me. At the time, I suppose I thought I had nothing to lose. Later that afternoon, a youngish woman, maybe around thirty years old but clearly older and slightly taller than me, showed up at my office door. The smile on her face felt warm, and she greeted me as if I were a rock star.

"Hello, Dr. Robinson. So nice to meet you," she said, taking my hand in hers for a firm shake. Her eyes sparkled, and the brightness in her manner filled the room. I couldn't help but notice the dazzling pink streak in her hair. "My name is Sophie."

"Please, have a seat." I directed her to a minimalist chair with a black mesh backing parked in front of my sleek white table I call a desk. "How can I help you?" I asked.

The woman with the pink streak in her hair leaned forward and spoke quietly. "I'm an operative with a small government team whose job is to keep the balance of power in the world. We are interested in preserving democracy and eliminating terrorist threats." Sophie paused, looked at her lap, and brushed her black skirt with her hand, her fingers devoid of adornment.

Instinctively, I twisted the ring on my right hand, momentarily confused about her visit to see me. "I see. And what do you mean by eliminating terrorist threats?" That seemed to be the phrase she emphasized, so I asked. She sidestepped the question.

"We like to keep our ear to the ground. Sometimes academic scientists hear things, or you, as an associate editor of a toxicology journal, may come across some interesting articles on new toxins. Perhaps from the Chinese or the Russians?"

It's true. At that time, I traveled in a small circle of scientists, and occasionally, we did hear things through our grapevine. The medical examiners in Vancouver, Denver, and Tampa, and the toxicologists in Philadelphia, Minnesota, and Utah all talked with each other—

we still do. We've always shared our unusual findings—surprises that appear as unexpected peaks on our tandem mass spectrometers.

"No, I haven't picked up anything unusual," I had told Sophie. "Was there anything specific?"

"I wonder if you've heard about chemical weapons being used in the Middle East?"

I hadn't, but those were not the circles I traveled in.

"No, do you suspect something?" I had asked.

"I'd like to show you a series of photographs, and perhaps you could tell me what you think." Sophie had opened her sizeable purse and pulled out a folder. She placed it on my desk, turning the contents to face me.

The first few pictures were aerial views of what appeared to be desert in the Middle East. The next series of photos showed bodies—many dead bodies. Women and children, not just men. Shocked, the nausea crept up to the back of my throat. I still feel the same way. Not too long ago, I saw pictures just like those. Death hasn't stopped.

She blinked. "I can see that you find these photographs difficult. So do I."

I remember I sat for a moment, a queasy feeling in my gut. The sheer number of bodies triggered something I couldn't quite put my finger on. A lingering memory.

Sophie watched my face. She pushed her pink hair behind her ears and waited. Then her slender frame pitched forward, waiting for my response.

"Dr. Robinson? You're no stranger to death; you're a pathologist."

"I'm sorry, Sophie. I got caught up in a moment. So how can I help you?"

"Based on what you see in these pictures, can you make an educated guess about the cause of death?"

Crumpled figures soaked in their own body fluids filled the frame, and pink foam seeped from their nostrils and mouths. Organophosphates came to mind. "It's possible that these people were killed with a nerve agent. Perhaps some kind of cholinergic compound."

"We think so too," Sophie had said, collecting the photographs and putting them back into her case. "I'd like to come back and visit you regularly to pick your brain if that's okay with you. You have a unique skill set, Dr. Robinson. From what I've read, you have an encyclopedic knowledge of poisons and toxins."

Her admission surprised me. "I… I do have a photographic memory for scientific detail, and most of my research revolves around various toxins." I shifted in my chair, my uneasiness apparent. Parts of my past were blank—important details escaped me at that time in my life.

"You're still working in the laboratory of your old mentor, correct?" Her eyes darted around my office, looking for clues to my personal and professional life.

"Well, yes and no. Dr. Charles Powers passed away several years ago, but his work continues with other scientists who were collaborators on the grant, and me, of course."

"Good to know. Look, here's my phone number," Sophie had said, handing me her card. She stood up to make her way to the door. "Thank you again, Dr. Robinson. I'll be in touch."

With a graceful exit, the striking woman took her leave, and left me wondering when she would return. Holding her business card, I noticed the American flag in the shape of the United States, a phone number, and two words—Sophie Martin. She changed my life forever.

JP is here.

"Lily," he says, kissing one cheek then the other, "you are looking well."

I pull his face into mine, and we kiss like the lovers we are. No one is here to observe the formality, so I expect us to behave recklessly like those who have missed each other. He's so dashing—his graying hair, interspersed with dark strands, and ever-deepening wrinkles surround his blue-green eyes.

"Jean Paul, you have no idea how happy I am to see you. Chad said—"

"Shush, my Lily, let us sit down." His finger touches my lips.

He leads me to the soft cotton couch, and we sink into the white—me curled up next to him while he strokes my hair.

I trace his chin with my fingertips. "I'm so glad you're here. I've missed you. I'm not one for sitting around and waiting for my wounds to heal."

"You needed time."

JP and I catch up on our personal lives. I tell him about Rose and Kelley, and he shares almost nothing. I expect this now. He doesn't say if he's had a little time to travel to France but has heard his cousin, Adrienne, my Rose's adopted mother, is still rehabilitating from her car accident. Rose told me as much, so I'm happy for her. And maybe a little envious. Then, in an abrupt one-eighty, we jump from personal to work. I've missed the drama.

"I assume you have news from Chad. He called me this morning and told me to expect you. Something about a murdered scientist. What's going on?"

JP tells me about Daniel Williams, the climatologist from Australia.

"What an unusual poisoning. A banded sea krait. Also recognized as the yellow-lipped sea krait, *Laticauda colubrina*. Slightly off course, as they are more commonly found in the eastern Indian Ocean and Western Pacific around the coast of India or Southeast Asia, if I recall. Its venom is neurotoxic and produces convulsions, paralysis, cardiac failure, and of course, death."

He chuckles. "You remember more than most, Lily Robinson." His finger traces along my jawline as he smiles.

"Did you ask to have some specimens collected from the autopsy that I can send to John Chi Leigh's lab?" John is a friend and brilliant chemist I have collaborated with in the past.

"*Mais oui*. The concern is someone or some organization is trying to silence the Council members who are to report their findings in Brussels."

"When is that meeting going to happen?"

"In a few weeks."

"And your plan is?" I get in his face with my chin out and a smile.

JP fills me in. South Africa, then on to Australia. "A long journey, *mais,* we need to understand the context."

"You mean, what's the endgame. What do they hope to prevent from being shared on the world stage?"

"*Mais oui*. We leave for Cape Town in two days."

I listen to every word JP says and see a way out of my boredom. Cape Town has memories for me. The hospital doesn't expect me back to work for a long while, and I feel well enough to travel. I want to get back into the action. I *have* to get back into the action.

"JP, I was wondering if I could come along. Yes, you and Chad wanted me to step down for a while, but I need to feel a part of something. Dr. Kelley is running the tox service at the hospital now, and I'm idling in neutral without direction. It's not enough to fill my day. I've just been sitting around here thinking about the old days." I pause, watching his face.

"Ah, Lily. That was our hope, but Chad and I agreed that you would have to be the one to initiate it. It is your intellect we require." He pushes a strand of hair behind my ear.

I feel a sense of relief. I'm back on the team. My body moves deeper into the cushion as my breathing slows.

"JP, this pause in my life has stirred up so many memories of the past. It's hard to imagine that all these years later, I would still be doing this, still connected with you. Do you ever think about that?"

"*Oui*, sometimes. But time has washed away much for me. So many missions over the years." JP pauses. "*Mais,* the ones with you have been memorable." He kisses my forehead and then sweeps his lips over mine. "You have become philosophical, *oui*? Wondering where you would be now if you had taken a different path."

Yes, a different path. I go into the kitchen and pour the coffee into our special cups—his says, LOVER, and mine says, SWEETIE. I return, balancing the cups on a tray.

"Would you take a different path? You did not say." He takes his cup and touches the word LOVER with his fingertip. "Come. Sit here." He pulls me next to him.

"I was just thinking how I punched you after that first… first poisoning. I hated you at that point. And I hated Sophie Martin."

An eyebrow raises. "Sophie Martin. I have not heard anyone say her name in many, many years. She will always be Pixie Dust."

"I know. I do know. I find myself reliving parts of my life, questioning my choices."

"*Et,* did you find your answer?" He moves another strand of hair behind my ear, his fingertips gently brushing my cheek.

My eyes close for a moment, my throat tightens. "An answer? Despair hijacks our hearts, and brains, and leads us down paths we least expect." Tears collect in the corner of my eyes and begin their fall.

JP blocks their path with his thumb. "My Lily, *ma chérie*, you must be in the moment. I have always told you this."

He has. Dozens of times. He leans in closer and kisses me deeply. I smell an earthiness about him. My heart quickens, and my breathing follows. So does his. Desire grabs hold. Now clasped in one of the Fates' tapestries as she spins, intertwining our lives—past, present, and future, we move along the thread of life. We abandon our coffee, and I take his hand and lead him to my bedroom—soft sage greens with plush down and fur-like throws. JP sits at the edge of the bed, and I straddle him, sitting on his thighs, toes touching the floor. His shirt buttons are easily undone, yet I take my time, distracted by the feel of his moist lips on my neck. His breath is hot. My silky camisole is pulled down to my waist by thick hands—they're smooth, but not so smooth as to think he's never used them to move earth, hold a gun, or shake my world.

Now undressed, we lay naked in each other's arms. I trace my finger over the scars on his chest, and I'm reminded his job has always involved danger. Will it ever end? Will the two of us ever be enough? He lifts my hand and kisses the palm, and our lips find each other in the light. No shadows here. Blue-green eyes hold my gaze, and I feel him—the heat of his body, the firmness of his manhood—as we stir the chemistry between us. He is warm and delicious, and we dance the dance we have for so many years. Unspoken words. Fleeting promises.

Our bodies shudder in waves carried by an ocean of feeling, of passion, knowing full well each time we make love could be our last. Risk has always been part of the equation. So, our lovemaking is not quick. It is long and tender, and we know how to give and take. It is our romance.

After, we linger, neither of us eager to get back to the real world. We finally relent and return to the kitchen. Life's pleasures must be satisfied, and our empty stomachs wait their turn. I always play it safe and have fruit, cheese, and a baguette so that JP can have a taste of home.

"I'm so glad you're here, JP," I tell him again, brushing the outline of his lips with my fingers. "I'm going to get my things together and go overseas with you and Parker." I smile and see his eyes brighten.

"*Mais oui.* In addition to your favorite shoes, you may want to pack a poison or two. This is a case where we do not have the information on who or what we are dealing with. No dossier with a medical record where we can find the Achilles heel."

"The medical record. How Chad always manages to get the goods, I'll never understand. Pixie Dust had it for the first case. I was scared and maybe impressed, too. I can't get that first mission out of my head for whatever reason."

"What I remember is a nervous doctor vomiting over my shoes as we stood by the Charles River. You were someone Pixie Dust thought would make a good addition to the team. I had my doubts that night. *Mais*, over the years, you have managed to change my mind." He gives me a broad grin, cheeks bulging. "*Et*, you have become a little more subtle in your methods."

"Very funny. That was a very rough night."

"For me, too. I have marks from the punches." He laughs and pretends to pull up his shirt.

"Seriously, do you ever wonder about the collateral damage we cause?"

"No, I do not, nor do I want to. You have to learn to let it go, Lily. You cover your emotions, but underneath that clinical coat, you feel deeply. Is that why you chose to become a pathologist? Your patients remain anonymous. All you have is their name, date of birth, and hopefully, some medical history. You rarely see them in the flesh. You do not have to watch their eyes fill with tears when you tell them no cure exists for what ails them. You remain protected beneath your intellect. *Et*, you wear it like a cloak."

"Stop, okay, I get it."

"*Mais oui*, of course you do. That is who you are. Now, before our trip, we have homework. Chad is working on identifying the members of the Council and their current positions around the world. If you are going to travel with us, we need to plan. I will inform Chad so he can make the arrangements."

"Hmm. Another global tour. Will we go to Brussels too? You and I completed a mission together to save NATO. You must remember that."

JP takes his pointer finger and taps his head. "*Oui*. You replaced albuterol with brevetoxin in the inhaler of our target."

"Yes, it was a messy luncheon, as I recall, but the General was pleased. Sorry, I was getting lost in that mission."

"You are rambling. You feel you are well enough to travel, *oui*?"

"Stop. I'm fine, JP. My brain is just happy being stimulated again." I shoot him a look he catches at once and change the subject. "Say, I have a friend in Sydney who works at the famous aquarium, Marine World Down Under. It's an amazing facility. The complete package: marine animals, educational programs, research, and they even care for injured sea creatures. I'd like to see her when we're there. She may have some thoughts about banded sea kraits sighted in the area."

"It could be useful if you do not create suspicion."

"No, just two colleagues catching up while I'm on a walkabout." I smile. More memories. "I look forward to catching up with her."

"*Oui*, you can travel under the pretext of scientific inquiry and visit colleagues in places from your past."

"Great. I'll tell Kelley I'll be away, and he can inform Lisa. You remember Lisa." Lisa was my assistant at the hospital for years. Smart, and always provided defensible cover for me when I was with Chad's team. "Maybe I'll just call her to say hello."

"*Bon. Et*, thoughts about South Africa?"

"Sorry, JP. That one is personal." I give him a kiss on the cheek. I'm going to start packing.

JP leaves, and we plan to touch base later. Look at me. I'm back in the game.

CHAPTER 6

SYDNEY, AUSTRALIA

Holly paced her office while waiting for news of the necropsy from her colleague Sara. The veterinarian had performed the initial workup on the whale carcass after it washed up on the beach. Attracted by the smell, sharks had swarmed close to shore, and the beaches had to be closed. While the marine world was anxious to understand what killed the huge beast, the merchants didn't care about the cause of death—they only wanted the beaches open again. The rest was academic.

Holly was part of the aquarium scientific team working on ascertaining the mitochondrial genome of the Antarctic krill, *Euphausia superba,* sea organisms that lived at ocean depths of 100 meters (328 ft). Species identification using mitochondrial genes was well established and, specifically, Holly's focus. Krill, tiny crustaceans, are a powerhouse food source for marine animals such as whales, seals, penguins, and others and are considered a rich source of the omega-3 fatty acids EPA and DHA.

Unraveling a genome with 42-47 gigabases was fundamentally intimidating, but not for Holly. She had joined the aquarium about a year ago, having gained experience working in the laboratory of a notable genetics researcher at a much larger facility. Even with her move, connections with former colleagues continued, and they shared current discoveries while attending scientific meetings. Her methodical mind proved eager, and when a close friend asked her to provide contract work for a tech company—under the table and secret—she said yes. The money she earned in this venture more than adequately made up for the small wages from her visible job—money she could stash away until she could escape the Australian continent. The aquarium provided an excellent cover for her more clandestine work and allowed her legitimate contact with prominent scientists in the field.

Holly had reviewed all the photographs on Daniel Williams's camera and found several problematic. From what she could determine by the dates associated with the photos, they appeared to be clustered around two excursions: the most recent pictures were from a trip off the GBR, and earlier ones taken in the Southern Ocean. Most of the images from the northern coast of Australia documented the bleaching of the coral—areas of dead polyps devoid of fish and worrisome new spills from the interior coal mining project. As far as she knew, those spills were not acknowledged and would have caused a furor if they had been. The guardians of the oceans had eyes everywhere. A report to the Climate Council would reveal the devastation.

However, two photographs, clearly not from the GBR, showed what looked like a small, submerged pen behind a female humpback whale. Holly surmised that the camera may have been sent overboard to capture the whale's movements. She wasn't certain if Daniel Williams was aware of the faint outline of the enclosure. Located just beneath the ocean surface and camouflaged, the pen was unlikely to be detected by air but could easily be seen underwater. However, part of the camouflage net had been pulled away. Holly recognized its significance. Had Williams shown these photos to anyone? She returned the camera to the bottom drawer of her locked file cabinet—only a short-term solution.

At lunchtime, Sara begged her for some company and asked if she'd meet her in the cafeteria. Holly reluctantly agreed and said she would come down as soon as she wrapped up her morning bench work.

"Holly, over here," Sara's hand waved vigorously.

Holly took a deep breath and headed to the table.

"So glad you could make it today. Lots to talk about." Sara took a bite of her veggie sandwich and looked at Holly with open eyes. "Aren't you going to get a sandwich, salad, or something?"

"I'm not really hungry right now. Coffee will do. So, what's up?" Holly squeezed her lips together. The last lunch had been a one-way conversation.

"Well, I made an interesting finding. You know I've been working on the whale that washed up. After the necropsy, I examined its stomach contents. Krill."

Holly perked up but kept a neutral expression. "Oh, that's nothing new. Whales eat krill." She took a sip of her coffee.

"But not these krill. I'd like you to take a closer look at them. You've been working on the mitochondrial genome. Maybe you can tell me more definitively what this whale had in its rumen."

Sara had Holly's full attention. She would be most interested in taking a closer look. The rumen was the first stomach compartment in the whale, whose digestive system was similar to cows. It broke down the krill by mechanical muscular movements before moving the pulverized mass to the cardiac stomach. There, enzymes digested the chitin contained in the krill's shell.

Holly answered with another subtle deep breath, "Of course, I'd be happy to look. Are you going to share your thoughts with me?" She leaned across the table and stared directly at Sara's face.

"No. I don't want to bias you. See for yourself. Maybe I'm just imagining things. But I want your professional opinion."

Sara, who had leaned in to meet Holly halfway across the table, now moved back into her chair and finished her veggie sandwich while Holly gently shook her head and, without a word, drank her coffee.

"So, Holly, if you're free now, why don't you come to my lab and look at the stomach contents."

"Sure, but first, l need to take care of a few things. I'll meet you in about fifteen minutes. Okay?" Holly shifted in her seat and bounced her knee up and down under the table.

Sara stood up. "Good. See you soon." She pushed her chair into the table and left Holly sitting alone.

Holly pulled out her phone once Sara was out of sight and sent a text.

Our krill could be on the move

The reply came back quickly enough.

You tell me

Holly curled her fingers into the palm of her hand and left the cafeteria. She chewed on her lower lip until it hurt. Once she returned to her lab, she grabbed her white coat and flew down two sets of stairs until she reached the necropsy suite. Sara's lab and office were located adjacent to where any postmortem evaluations of animals were conducted.

"I'm here. What have you got to show me?" Holly clenched her jaw and forced a smile.

"Come on in. I removed some of the krill from the whale's rumen, and they're under the dissecting scope."

Holly moved to the lab bench and pulled out the stool to sit comfortably while looking through the stereomicroscope. She could see a single krill on the stage plate, moving slightly. She recognized the problem. This organism was twice the size of Antarctic krill. It looked a good twelve centimeters long. She positioned her eyes at the ocular lenses, turned the focus knob, and poked at the crustacean.

The krill under the scope was not *Euphausia superba*. Holly's heart beat a little faster. These Antarctic krill were modified. An increased number of bioluminescent organs, more than the usual pair found on the eyestalk, the thoracopods, and where the swimming legs were attached to the abdomen, were apparent. These were Holly's krill. She didn't need to look at the DNA from this crustacean to grasp that.

"Well, what do you think?" Sara's hands were firmly on her hips, and she hovered over Holly's right shoulder.

Holly raised her head and took a breath. "I think this is an unusually big *E. superba*. Normally, they grow to about six centimeters or 2.4 inches, and as you can tell, this one is probably closer to twelve and a half centimeters." Holly pushed Sara's ruler aside and turned back to the scope.

"Is that all? I thought it looked like they had more bioluminescent organs. I checked a couple of reference books to be sure. In the dark, they glowed more than I remembered."

"Maybe. But why are you interested in krill? That's my department. You're just the vet looking after the animals. Not the scientist."

Holly's tone was sharp, and Sara took a step back.

"I'm interested in anything that could explain why this whale died. We don't just house marine life here; we try to understand what's happening in their natural environment." Sara's frown expanded, and she felt the heat creep into her cheeks. "And just so you understand, the rumen was full of these krill. This is not a one-off. I've collected those still alive and put them in a tank to study later. If you're not interested, I'm sure I can find another scientist who is." Sara shifted in her white coat and returned the small plastic ruler to the breast pocket.

"No, no. Sorry, Sara. I didn't mean to offend you. How about I take the tank of krill to my lab and see if I can learn anything more." Holly wanted to control the evidence and thought it better to appease Sara than run the risk of her calling in other scientists who would undoubtedly be interested in these unique Antarctic krill.

Sara softened. "I'll get one of the lab techs to put the tank on a cart and bring it up to you." She turned to indicate that Holly should leave. "I've got a King penguin with a limp."

Holly took the stairs two at a time and raced to her office. She shut the door behind her and got out her phone. A text with the emoji of a face gritting its teeth filled the message box.

Our krill are out. The vet has the live organisms in a tank. The tank will be moved into my lab. Next steps?

The typing bubble appeared on Holly's phone, the dots undulating, then disappeared. She waited. And waited.

CHAPTER 7

CAPE TOWN, SOUTH AFRICA

A mountainous wall reaches up out of the blue ocean. Cape Town. The sights from my plane window bring back memories. The last time I was here, I was with Rose's father and my mentor, Charles.

Charles taught me about the nature of toxins. Hours in the lab, first dissecting out the nerves we needed, then carefully placing the specimen in a chamber, bathed in various solutions, with electrodes ready for stimulation. How would the toxin modify the behavior of potassium or sodium flowing through the cell membrane that we'd come to expect? On more relaxed days, we sought out microscopic organisms from the sea to understand how environmental poisons changed the world around us.

Charles was already the recipient of his Nobel Prize by the time I went to work in his lab. He had the kind of logical brain I admired—one that saw things clearly, where possibilities existed outside the box, and focused only on his work and not his emotional well-being. His demand for excellence made him a difficult taskmaster, and few graduate students survived the pressure. Yet, I found myself enamored of his intellect and caught up in his puppy dog stares and personal lectures. Benchwork in the laboratory mixed with field trips to the

Cape Cod marshes collecting algal cells that we would later immerse in poison-saturated seawater. We would buy lobsters for sucrose-gap experiments using the long nerves from their walking legs. Summer outings left us wet and hot, and later filled with desire.

Stripping down to our bathing suits, we showered at the marine station to rinse ourselves of coastal marsh muck and sulfur smell and discovered that a bar of soap became an erotic object. Charles's tanned hands, covered in soapy bubbles, rubbed my back and then my legs, sending dirt circling the drain. I reciprocated, washing him off, and couldn't help but notice the growing bulge beneath his shorts. Gifted with a thick head of wavy silver-gray hair, now slicked back by the water, his ruddy face had striking blue eyes that looked at me longingly with only gentle crow's feet alerting me to the vast difference in our ages. Charles told me he liked my long hair, straight to my waist, and the hoop earrings that danced against the dark background. An inappropriate fleeting kiss passed between us as the water skipped off our heads. Afterward, he stood in front of me and used his hands to squeegee the water off his legs and arms before wrapping me in a towel, rubbing my back, the drips sucked into loops of terry.

One steamy August afternoon, Charles asked me to lunch at his place, a cottage on the ocean. Summer gardens were just at their peak, and marsh grass had left its bright green behind in favor of a golden tinge. Kale and cheddar soup were on the menu, along with crusty French bread and a salad of butter lettuce, cherry tomatoes, and diced cucumber. Beyond the kitchen window, a gray ocean broke noisily on a sandy beach, leaving beige bubbles and froth behind while filtered sunlight lit my mentor's face. Charles's quiet laugh percolated our conversation, filled with detailed stories from his heady days in science. When he put his hand on my knee, he told me he wanted to sleep with me.

It's not as if I didn't see it coming. All the signs were there. A woman knows when a man wants to go to bed with her. A longing look, a touch on the hand, hours together that stretch from dawn to beyond dusk are the signals that mark the way, not to mention the kiss in the shower. I didn't feel coerced or sexually harassed, and I didn't expect that having sex with him would fundamentally change my role in his laboratory. But what I didn't plan on was getting pregnant.

* * *

The flight attendant reminds us to put our seats into the upright position and prepare for landing. My thoughts keep drifting to the past before getting bounced to the present. How strange that my life had a different path when I was here so many years ago. How I long to tell Rose of her beginnings and share a life with the daughter that was taken from me.

Parker took a different flight and will meet us later at the hotel. JP is on this plane, but we did not sit together. He flew coach, and I added some dollars to my ticket so I could fly first- class. First-class comes with additional perks, useful if you're still recovering from having a piece of your liver removed thanks to a terrorist's bullet.

Cape Town, South Africa's capital, has a rich and troubled history. European settlers landed in the late 1600s, and the slave trade exploded. Remnants of that time exist through museums and monuments, and I'd paid my respects to this difficult period during my previous visit here with Charles. A cable car brought us to the top of Table Mountain. Over a thousand meters above sea level, the view from this flat top peak was stunning. The South Atlantic draped the west, while

Cape Town occupied the north. Further north, we could see Table Bay and the former home of political prisoners, Robben Island, named after the Dutch word for seals.

JP and I arrive at our classy pink hotel near the coast at the foot of Table Mountain. We have connecting rooms, while Parker has a room on another floor. But he's no dummy, and I'm sure he senses that JP and I are more than colleagues. The hotel itself is magnificent, with views of the outdoors that bring in lush greens and blues, while crystal chandeliers are suspended from an elaborate striped ceiling indoors. Cream-colored drapes hang from the twenty-foot ceiling, rods tucked under ivory crown molding decorated in Victorian times. Potted palms soften the edges of the room. I can imagine its beginnings in the 1800s when weary visitors stopped in awe of the beautiful surroundings. Verdant gardens with sweet-smelling roses bring back memories of Charles. Coming to this country again stirs my thoughts and makes me question my life choices. My mind needs to free itself from the past.

I read some scientific papers on global temperature before I left Boston. Data show that the rise in sea level is occurring fastest on the East Coast. That's due to global warming. The earth's temperature has risen by 0.14°F per decade since the late 1800s. However, the rate of warming has doubled since 1981—to 0.32°F. When I think about the size and heat capacity of the Earth's oceans—it takes an incredible amount of heat energy to raise the Earth's surface temperature—even this seemingly small amount. Yet that almost marginal rise in temperature is shrinking sea ice, reducing snow cover, and rearranging the world's habitats. All of Earth's creatures are scrambling to find their new niches—if they can. Apparently, Dr. Graham Harmon produced some controversial models indicating that at the current rate of global warming, precipitation across the planet will increase by as much as 1-3% with each degree of warming. Where the precipitation will fall is unknown. Some places will have more and some less. Imagine countries with insufficient rain to raise crops or areas where flooding will only destroy plantings. The planet will consist of the haves and the have-nots when it comes to food and habitats. It's a troubling thought.

JP knocks on my door.

"Hi, JP. I was going over some notes I made on Dr. Harmon's findings. Tons of data there with all the work climatologists have been doing. Between reports on the bleaching of the coral from Williams and more detailed modeling on temperature increases in the oceans by Harmon, this planet is headed for an uncomfortable future if we can't act as a united front."

"*Oui*. It is hard to imagine a world where short-term greed rather than long-term gains prevail."

I look at him with a disgusted look. "Really? I have no problem imagining that because that's the status quo." I shake my head.

JP puts both his hands on top of my shoulders. "What was I thinking, *oui*." He laughs and draws me into him.

Once I pull back, I look into those blue-green eyes. "Are we going to see Harmon now?"

"*Oui*, Chad has made the arrangements."

We leave the room. Parker still hasn't arrived, so we'll connect with him later.

A car waits for us outside the hotel, and JP takes the helm. We are headed to the Marine Research Centre at the University. The drive along the coast showcases wispy clouds over a deep blue sea, and my mind drifts, thinking of Charles again.

Our affair had started that late August afternoon and continued for several months. I'm not sure what I imagined, but given that my father had died when I was only five and my mother passed away when I was just entering my teenage years, I saw Charles as an older man who could provide more than an academic mentorship. He was a crush, an infatuation, but over time, I realized how much I cared for him. I had had many lovers during my university years, but nothing everlasting and with men not as old as Charles. As a young woman, especially for one who entered the university system as a gifted student, I had much to learn. My brain skipped far ahead of my chronological age, so I quickly learned how to handle boys and men who desired me.

I found Charles shy and less experienced in bed than I, even though he was older. It surprised me, but then he was a man of science, not a practiced lover. His life focused on his work, not romantic relationships. Nonetheless, I discovered him to be a willing pupil, eager to engage in oral sex and positions other than the missionary. My gusto in providing a reciprocal education undoubtedly led to my lax precautions, and within six months after we started the affair, I had a new life growing inside me. Based on my calculations, I realized we were in South Africa when I had become pregnant.

I remember our conversation when he learned the news. He was surprised but delighted at the same time.

"My god, Lily. I don't know what to say." His mouth opened, forming a circle, and sparkles of light filled his eyes. "Actually, I do. It's fabulous," he said, reaching out to touch my belly. The smile on his face, bigger than a slice of the moon, lit up the room. As a researcher, he had made many remarkable discoveries during his career and created novel experimental tools, but he had never created life.

"You're not the only one surprised," I told him. I never had doubts about keeping the baby, but even then, somewhere deep down, I must have known Charles wasn't the love of my life. I recognize the difference now.

"Lily, perhaps we should get married so the child will have a real father. All my life, I've wanted a child but never found the time to marry."

He didn't understand that the child would have a real father, just not one married to the child's mother. "Charles, I can't marry you. I care about you, perhaps even love you, but I'm not in love with you." That's what I remember telling him.

I could see the disappointment of rejection on his face. I didn't want him to think I didn't care. I touched his hand. "I'm not ready to be married to anyone." I wasn't.

Nonetheless, he offered to be a part of our baby's life—and mine. Would he still be in my life today, in Rose's life, if he hadn't made that second trip to Africa, where he died alone, pinned under a cart with no one to save him? What I could tell you, Charles, about our daughter, would stir your heart.

JP has reached our destination. I see the University dropped in front of the mountains in the most picturesque view. Red rooftops cover sand-colored buildings, and the setting stirs me. Dr. Harmon's office is on the ground floor and easy to find once we check in with security.

Once inside, I'm struck by the contrast of the green and blue outside. Harmon's office feels brown. Wooden furniture, distressed with time, fills the space, bookcases tower to the ceiling, and an old rectangular desk takes center stage. Ivory-colored walls, scuffed and uneven, surround us, and a single framed photograph of Dr. Harmon and presumably his wife and daughter resides on his desk. His salt-and-pepper hair is swept to one side, and his lower lip dips, revealing a warm grin.

JP extends his hand, his craggy smile defying gravity. "Thank you for taking the time to see us."

Harmon nods. "Good to meet you."

He points for us to take the two seats in front of his desk, and before we sit down, I take his hand in mine and greet him. Harmon's hand is firm, and his eyes are set deep within the wrinkles of his face.

"How can I help you?"

JP explains that we are working in advance of the Brussels Climate Council meeting and confirms that Dr. Harmon will also attend.

"Yes, Hans Lundberg called to say you would be here as part of security for the Climate Council. He asked that I cooperate fully. I will be presenting data on the changes in ocean temperatures and how they affect the weather."

We discuss some of his findings and his obligation to write the report with other leading scientists for the Climate Council once the meeting is concluded. A natural lull in the conversation allows me to bring up Williams. "I understand you knew Daniel Williams?" I start simply, knowing he's learned of Williams's death.

Harmon's eyes move past me, the corners of his mouth turned down. His fingertips form a tent, and his chest expands before he speaks.

"Daniel and I were colleagues and also friends. We were at university together." Harmon clears his throat and rubs the desktop with his hand. "His death was shocking." A pencil, caught by his fingertips, rolls, and rattles noisily.

"I'm so sorry for your loss." My eyes glimpse the red polish on my fingernails. I inhale. "We understand Dr. Williams was vocal about the global effects of climate change. Maybe he ruffled a few feathers. Could you tell us more about what he was working on?" I shift in my seat, able to read Harmon's face, his downtrodden eyes, and pursed lips reflecting his concern. But it's more than that.

"He documented dying coral around the globe. In the most sensitive areas. I'm sure you are already familiar with the destruction of these habitats. But it was a trip he took earlier, to Antarctica when the Southern Ocean was passable, where he found something else that troubled him." Harmon wrings his hands, stands, and walks to a small aquarium he has sitting on a sideboard, sprinkling in some fish food before circling back to his chair. The aquarium contains striking, colorful fish, sea fans, and rocks. I see a clownfish dart in and out of an anemone. Harmon settles.

I cock my head and lean forward. "Aren't coral reefs found in tropical waters? What was he doing near Antarctica?"

"Helping a friend tracking some whale pods." Harmon rolls the pencil on the desk, the grating sound mimicking the ticking of a clock.

JP straightens in his chair, shoulders back, and leans toward the desk. "*Et*, what did he find?"

"We planned to meet here before going to Brussels together for the conference. He was reluctant to speak freely on the video call. But he made a point of commenting on the whales feeding on krill."

"Nothing unusual about that. Is there?" JP moves back into his seat.

"No, nothing unusual. But he did have a few questions for me."

"Oh, and what were those? If you don't mind us asking." I flash my biggest smile.

"He asked me about *Euphausia superba*."

"Antarctic krill?" The pitch in my voice elevates, and JP's face registers the change.

"Exactly." Dr. Harmon tents up his fingers again and stares into my face.

"But your research involves changes in ocean temperature. So why was he asking you about krill? Unless higher water temperatures would either mean krill would have to adapt or die."

"That's correct. But Williams knew I had collaborated with the nearby shark institute and published some papers." He clears his throat and places his palms flat on the desktop.

JP takes another turn. "Can you please clarify what this has to do with the krill?"

"Those studies examined how the changes in ocean temperature will affect the cookie-cutter shark, *Isistius brasiliensis*, a deep-sea species that emits a blue luminescence."

My mind begins to spin as I see the connection coming. JP sits back and shoots me a look. I nod, indicating that I'm following the science.

"Let me explain," Harmon says. "The shark's photophores run along the ventral surface of the body, so when the shark is viewed from below, it disappears against the sky. During the day, the shark stays in the deep ocean while it moves closer to the surface at night. This adaptation allows the shark to swim relatively undetected."

"*Et* these sharks are threatened by the warming of the ocean?" JP asks.

"To some extent. Most marine life will be threatened if water temperatures rise. It won't just be the corals in harm's way."

I bring the conversation back to the krill. "Dr. Harmon, would it be fair to say that Dr. Williams was interested in the bioluminescent qualities of the krill?"

"Yes, he was. He felt that the species he saw were considerably bigger than expected, and he found that the krill's bioluminescence was far brighter than he had ever witnessed."

"And because you are not just colleagues, but friends, he wanted to speak with you. He trusted you and knew of your recent work on the cookie-cutter shark."

Harmon nods, reaches around to the bookcase behind him, and pulls out a generous-sized binder, a compilation of some kind—scientific papers?

"I co-authored a review article, and it was published last month."

He opens the binder and pulls out the print copy of a paper I'm sure I can find online. He hands it to me.

"Unique properties of the Cookie-Cutter Shark, *Isistius brasiliensis*: Stealth in the Ocean."

I look at JP, his jaw clenched, and the furrows of his face deepened.

"You planned to talk more about this with Dr. Williams before you flew to Brussels, but you never got the chance."

Harmon inspects the back of his hands and nods. "For two years, Daniel and I were roommates at university. He was the best man at my wedding. And even though we ended up on different continents, we saw each other at least once or twice a year. He was a good man and a first-rate scientist."

Dr. Harmon's eyes momentarily close, and I hear him breathe deeply. I sense that it's time for us to leave. "Dr. Harmon, thank you for your time. We are concerned about the security of the Council members such as yourself, so perhaps we can speak with you again after we learn more. We plan to travel to Sydney in the next few days."

Both JP and I stand up. I smile, and we say our goodbyes to Graham Harmon.

When we reach the hotel, Parker is waiting for us. We retreat to his room and sit at a sturdy wooden square table with a lovely view of the sugarbush in the garden.

"Dr. Robinson," he says with an upbeat tone and a bear hug, "I'm so glad to see you. You're looking well."

"Thank you, Parker. I'm glad to see you, too." I give him such a big smile, my cheeks hurt as they squeeze into rosy mounds.

The light is still bright as it pours into the window. Parker is wearing his usual dark khakis and pale blue shirt. "Let me just say I was stunned you wanted to work with us again. I mean, after D.C. and taking a bullet from Petrikov. Shit, doc, I was worried you wouldn't make it." He shakes his head and gazes at his shoes.

I squeeze his hand. "Thanks, Parker. I appreciate your thoughts. I guess I surprised myself, but all that time alone recovering made me realize that I'm loyal to our cause, and to you, JP, and Chad." I turn to JP and give him a wink.

"So, what did Harmon say?" Parker sits with a thump, and JP and I take our seats.

I start. "Apparently, he and Williams were close. They planned to talk more before the meeting in Brussels."

JP nods. "He recounted their work on the effects of increased global temperature on the oceans, *mais* added that Williams may have discovered something unusual. A relationship between krill and climate change."

Parker puts his elbows on the table. "I don't get it about krill, but Chad and I found information on the expansion of the coal port in northeast Australia. A controversial project that involves mining coal in Queensland's North Galilee Basin and hauling it by rail to a port near Bowen off the northeast corner of the coast. Once the coal reaches the port, it's shipped through the GBR to other countries, India being one. Now, we think an accident may have occurred at the existing operation, and it's possibly being covered up. They can't afford to shut down."

"You think Williams was going to talk to Harmon about coal spilling into the reef?" I kick off my snakeskin stilettos, smooth out my navy blue skirt, and take a deep breath.

JP's eyebrows narrow. "*C'est possible.* Coal mining exists in Queensland. A government approved expansion in the Galilee Basin, just as climate scientists call for an end to fossil fuels in favor of wind, solar, and other renewable resources, creates conflict. From a government perspective, a large coal mining project would mean more jobs for Australians. Williams could have been a target if he uncovered something that would interfere with that economic goal."

"Maybe he found evidence of coal dust spills around the GBR when diving and took some incriminating photographs. His camera is still missing." Parker strokes his chin. "Do we have any coffee? I could use a cup."

"I can get some room service, Parker."

"Please, doc. That would be great. It was a long plane flight. I need more speed."

I pick up the phone and order coffee. We could all use a cup.

"Done. But what troubles me is why Williams wanted to talk with Harmon about the krill."

"A bellwether species?" JP asks.

"Not sure." I shake my head. "According to Harmon, Williams said the Antarctic krill were unusual. Could they have been affected by the change in water temperature? We should consider several possibilities for Williams's death. He was slated to present his findings as a climate scientist at the Council meeting. His research documented the slow death of corals in the Great Barrier Reef, and while he and other coral scientists have been shouting about this forever, few outside that circle have been listening."

JP nods and picks up my thoughts. "*Et* from what Parker just told us, Williams worked in a country where coal mining is thriving despite the call to reduce fossil fuels. Perhaps he was killed by someone trying to protect those interests. But Chad must suspect something more. Something that impacts world order." JP glances at Parker.

"Supplying coal to overseas markets is big business, JP. It's a geopolitical global marketplace. Intel points to a much more organized and sophisticated group."

"That makes sense to me. If you're the regular run-of-the-mill climate change denier looking to shut down a voice sounding the alarm, would you go through all the trouble of making Williams's death look like an accident? And with a sea snake? No, my gut says this is more complicated and more sinister," I argue.

"Robinson, we are grateful your intuition is with us once again." JP flashes a smile.

I know it's a bit of a dig, but who cares. The truth is, these guys need me, and more than for my knowledge of poisons. Years of buried feelings have allowed me to develop an intuition that reaches deep from within—like a Spidey sense. The therapist who helped me uncover repressed memories said the trauma I suffered in the Colombian jungle heightened my suspicion of people and situations. This played havoc with my personal life, making me more guarded and sensitive. And vulnerable. Even so, I've managed to forge a relationship with these men over the years. Yes, they need me. A puzzle to solve. And it's been a very long day.

"Why don't you two have dinner together, and I'll just have a snack in my room." My shoulders ache, and I want to lie down. They agree, and JP and I leave Parker to return to our respective rooms.

Before I open the door, I squeeze JP's hand. "I'll look forward to your visit in the middle of the night."

Thinking back on it, I saw no particular forewarning from my initial meetings some twenty years ago with Sophie Martin, and she and I had met many times during those early months. Her visits followed the hollow I felt after I had lost Rose. Months could never fill the emptiness, and Sophie became a welcome distraction. She'd show up to my office, sometimes with flowers, and ask me about strategies for chemical warfare and untraceable poisons. Eventually, the government had me fingerprinted as part of their background check, and Sophie had me sign a document that swore me to secrecy. But one day, it all changed. A day when my grief—and guilt—over the loss of my child had been overwhelming. The mirror that morning told me I looked worn; red rims circled my green eyes, and my pale complexion, flush. Inside, my heart hurt, and though the wound was invisible, the pain felt real. I dragged myself to the laboratory. Sophie had been waiting.

"Dr. Robinson, given your expertise in poisons, we have an unusual ask for you. Now, please hear me out before you throw me out." Her eyes narrowed, and her smile disappeared.

"Dr. Robinson, it's not widely known, but our government does conduct sanctioned assassinations. These targeted killings are part of our counterterrorism strategy."

I thought for a moment before I answered. The woman in front of me, dressed in a black sheath dress and wearing flats with a gold designer emblem on the top line, tilted her head and waited. "Yes, assassinations make the news. I've heard of them," I said.

Sophie looked directly into my eyes. "But I'm talking about those killings that don't make the headlines or any part of the public record. These are secret assassinations that help shape world politics. Different countries have different sensitivities to these kinds of actions."

I felt a breath trapped in my lungs, pushing against my chest wall. "What does this have to do with me?" I let the breath escape and debated whether to ask her to leave. A lump in my throat became troublesome. She must have sensed that.

"Dr. Robinson, our country has been betrayed by a man seeking vengeance. He shared the actual names of some of the operatives in Intelligence who work for us around the globe. Not only did he put them in danger, but their families as well. One of our people has already been picked up in Moscow, and another has been killed. We are concerned that the new technology he developed would expose all our encrypted information, and he's willing to sell it to the highest bidder."

"Why would he do that?" I could feel my hand tremble as I reached for the bottle of water perched on my desktop.

"His son was killed in what he felt was an unjust war. He wants retribution."

Sophie paused and bent down to reposition her shoe, keeping me on the hook. I found myself squirming like a worm.

"Sophie, I don't understand. If the man is a traitor, why can't you arrest him and charge him with treason?"

"Dr. Robinson, it's not that simple. Front-page headlines and trials bring information to the forefront. Information we do not want anyone, or any country, to realize we possess. But, on the other hand, if the man were to die a natural death, we could slip this incident under the rug." She pushed her hair behind her ears, never letting go of my eyes.

"What do you mean, a natural death?" My heart started thumping.

"Perhaps you could suggest a poison that might mimic natural causes." Sophie sounded casual, but I knew she could see the look of surprise on my face. "You would be providing a great service to your country."

I couldn't imagine she was serious. The idea that the U.S. Government would ask an academic for help with an assassination was beyond inconceivable. Panic filled my head as I shifted in my seat. Was this organization I agreed to help legitimate? Was this all a ruse by some rogue foreign faction twisting the facts? I had been seeing Sophie for several months now and felt we had developed a rapport. I bit my lower lip and reached deep in the drawer for antacids.

"Dr. Robinson, I can see your mind working in overdrive. I understand that you are in doubt. But you have to trust me. Believe me, we wouldn't ask you to do this unless we thought it necessary." Sophie's voice was gentle. A calmness permeated the office; no, more like the silence of a snowfall. Snowflakes absorb sound, so the world seems just a little quieter.

"You only want the information?" I asked. I felt shaky, sure I hadn't heard my visitor correctly.

"How about I share the man's medical history with you, and then you could tell me what you think?" She had reached for her oversized bag, pulled out a folder, and set it on my desk.

In front of me was a medical chart with a patient's problem history and medications. "How did you get this?"

"I'd rather not say. Let's leave it at intelligence gathering." Her blue eyes held my gaze as she waited for my response. "Dr. Robinson, you truly would be helping your country."

I started to thumb through the health record, my shallow breaths subsiding when I reached a page on the man's cardiac history. It looked like he was being treated for an arrhythmia.

"Why don't I leave this folder with you. I have another appointment now. I'd like to get you in touch with one of our team who will work with us on this case. His name is JP. I'm also going to leave you a secure phone," she said, putting a small cell phone on my desk. "I'll ask him to give you a call and set up a meeting. He should be able to quell your doubts."

"Just JP. That's all?" I didn't realize at the time that this operative, this man, would become one of the most significant persons I would ever know.

"Yes, just JP. I like to share as little as possible about my operatives. So, you will recognize him—he is about six foot one, dark hair, blue-green eyes, and a killer French accent. I think that's a good start, don't you?"

Sophie got up from her chair, nodded, and left me alone. I picked up the phone she had deposited on the desk. So very primitive to those we have today and very different from what I had at the time, a small squat candy bar design in lipstick red. She left a shiny gray metallic flip phone with an organic electroluminescent display—one of the original Motorola Timeports. I put my phone next to it and tried to spin it around, watching it as if it were a top. An image of Rose when she was just a toddler produced a fleeting smile as I thought about how we played together after I returned home from the lab. But the smile had turned to sadness, and guilt, like acid, burned the back of my throat. Only emptiness waited for me. Rose was dead and lost forever, and I blamed myself. Yes, I believe Sophie was aware of my swirling regret. Found me an easy mark. But I needed something to force me to think of anything else but Rose. Sophie's ask would do.

* * *

Sometime later, a knock on my door jostles me. I check my watch and see it's only been a few hours since JP and I parted. Once oriented, I realize it's at the connecting door and hear JP calling my name. He sounds impatient.

"JP, sorry, I'm still a little groggy. Is everything all right?"

He enters the room and closes the door behind him with a thud. I can see the furrows around his eyes, and his frown tells me all is not well.

"What is it?" My eyes feel as if grainy bits are lodged in the corners. I blink.

"Another climate scientist visiting Sydney was found dead. Dr. Omala Patel." He strokes his chin, and the crease in his cheek deepens.

"Oh, god. How was the second body found?"

"Scuba diving accident. However, this was a recreational dive. She was PADI certified and out with her husband. Both were found dead in the shallows. Similar to Williams."

"Is the camera missing? Were their fins on or off? How similar to the Williams case?"

JP shakes his head and throws up his hands. "The PM is being conducted now. Unexplained circumstances surrounding the deaths mean we leave for Australia tomorrow. I suspect there may be a connection to the murder of Dr. Williams."

"God." I plop back onto the bed, shaking my head. "You think they were murdered?"

"The authorities assume it was an accident, *mais*, you would say otherwise."

"I understand. We need to make sure we get postmortem specimens I can send to Dr. Leigh before they cremate the body, or something."

"Get some sleep. We have an early flight. Meet Parker and me in the lobby."

He sweeps me into his arms and hugs me tight. One of those reassuring hugs, so I don't want to let go. Did Daniel Williams and this woman scientist know each other or have overlapping research? If the Council meeting doesn't go forward as planned, they can't generate a report for policymakers. Dollars from supporting nations will be lost, and setbacks on climate initiatives will be incalculable. Is an assassin killing off the Climate Council members and witnesses to their work?

JP hears natural causes, and he thinks of me. That's how I like to work. I'm the assassin who leaves them dead without a trace.

Assassin. What a loaded word for a directed kill. Eliminate the person or persons who get in the way of one's objectives—a world leader, a prominent spokesperson, a military commander. In my case, I'm asked to eliminate evil in this world—threats to the greater good. That's what I tell myself. The good of the many outweighs the good of the one. My head falls back onto my pillow, and I shut my eyes and drift. I see Charles's face through the mosquito netting, and I'm back at the safari camp twenty-five years ago.

CHAPTER 8

BRUSSELS, BELGIUM

This mercantile city of northern Europe evolved from its Stone Age beginnings to a thriving metropolis that embraced twenty-first-century politics. Its rich history stemmed from the influence of many European nations, and both French and Dutch are spoken here. At its heart is the Grand-Place, a stately cobbled square dating back to the twelfth century surrounded by guild houses—Bakers, Greasers, Carpenters, Boatmen, and the Oath of Archers—City Hall and the Maison du Roi. As the hub of Europe, Brussels is the home of the North Atlantic Treaty Organization, the European Parliament (the Hemicycle—the center of debates and votes), the European Commission, and the Climate Council. A thriving city of multinationals and private enterprises.

The Climate Council was located near the Museum of Natural Sciences off Rue Vautier, just south of the European Parliament. The office of the Council Chair hid behind tall, ornately carved mahogany doors that opened into a spacious, brightly lit space with east-facing windows. A dark wooden desk sat at its center, and two overstuffed armchairs were positioned in front, their feet firmly anchored on a Chinese silk rug.

Hans Lundberg viewed the agenda on his desk. Light poured

through the window behind him and illuminated the two pages outlining the critical topics the Climate Council needed to address. Unfortunately, there were more items than time would allow. Lundberg paused. He dragged his fingers through his white hair and raised his bushy eyebrows. All the submitted data had been reviewed to date. The names on the agenda were those scientists he had asked to give a formal presentation at the meeting in addition to their written reports. As Council Chair, it was his prerogative. With a single stroke of his pen, Lundberg crossed one name off the list. He placed the pen perpendicular to the paper and took a deep breath.

Daniel Williams had already forwarded his data and planned to speak to the group. Lundberg had anticipated a one-on-one meeting prior to the conference. Dr. Williams had already been scheduled for a formal presentation to the organization. His work on coral bleaching was well known, and many organizations used his data to launch initiatives to save coral reefs worldwide. Man-made restoration strategies utilized artificial substrates, or cultivated more resilient corals that could withstand hotter water temperatures and ocean acidification like those in waters off the Florida coast. Underwater nurseries existed where thousands of coral fragments were grown to help seed the oceans while mass-produced coral larvae would hopefully reinvigorate damaged reefs.

Lundberg had been shocked and devastated by the news of Williams's death. He'd already reached out to Dr. Graham Harmon to present Williams's data since they had collaborated on the ocean and cryosphere changes that would affect coastal communities and small islands.

Lundberg stood and shuffled to the bookcase on the far side of his office. The bookcases rose a good ten feet, and a ladder rolled along the top of the bookcase so all books would be within his reach.

Many of the volumes were about geology— several he had authored or coedited. Metamorphic rocks were his primary interest. How these rocks transformed over time, influenced by heat or pressure—changes in environmental factors—had been his life's work. Though mostly retired, he still lectured at his alma mater, Stockholm University.

Lundberg's assistant knocked gently on the door even after explicit instructions requesting the professor be left undisturbed. The knocking was insistent.

"Yes, please come in," Lundberg said.

A waif-like woman entered the office, immediately swallowed by its vastness, and planted herself before the professor.

"Professor Lundberg. I have an urgent message for you from Dr. Patel's office. They said they need to speak with you now."

Although India had not historically contributed to greenhouse gas emissions, Dr. Patel's research on the ocean's chemical changes was critical to the Climate Council's efforts. Her work investigated the acidification of the ocean. As more carbon dioxide was produced in the atmosphere, more dissolved into seawater. This lowers the pH, a scale that measures acidity, alkalinity, or neutrality. The ocean had maintained a slightly alkaline pH of around 8.2 (on a scale of zero to fourteen) for millions of years. Dr. Patel demonstrated that the pH had dropped to 8.1. And although this seemed like a small change, marine life was affected as the oceans became more acidic. Shells were made of calcium carbonate and dissolved under more acidic conditions. Some organisms adapted and survived by producing thicker shells, but this took more energy.

Lundberg felt the small hairs on the back of his neck rise. He was already revising his agenda due to the unfortunate death of Williams and hoped Harmon and Patel were ready to present their part. He had his assistant transfer the call to his office.

He listened intently to the story about the scuba diving accident. Both Dr. Patel and her husband had drowned. Hans Lundberg said little. His hand shook when he put the handset into the cradle. As soon as his heart stopped pounding, he would call Graham Harmon, who would surely have more information. Two startling accidents. His eyes darted back to the agenda, and he squinted, trying to get it all in focus. The agenda. The deaths. He debated whether to contact Ilse Knight.

Ilse Knight still had a strong grip on the members of the Council, having been Chair before being replaced by Lundberg. She had been instrumental in shepherding nations to work together for climate change. Her previous experience in politics in her home country of Germany had been critical in her landing the Council Chair post when Hans Lundberg initially retired, giving her insight into global political struggles. But after only a few years, she stepped down from the position, and Lundberg was asked to assume his old post. Although asked many times what influenced her decision, she only replied that it was for personal reasons.

Several months after she left the Climate Council, she assumed the role of CEO for a small start-up technology company. NovoGeneOne had several divisions, and each one operated in a silo. Ilse liked the idea of separate research departments. All reported to her. She attended only weekly conferences with individuals to assess each group's progress. The lack of organization-wide meetings suited her. If she felt there should be any cross-collaboration on a project, Ilse saw to the pairing herself.

Ilse Knight looked younger than her sixty-eight years, and her pale blue eyes were nicely framed by gray hair cut in a stylish bob. She had lived alone since her divorce, and her only child had been dead for more than twenty-five years. She grieved as any mother would and worked longer hours to avoid the pain. The doctorate she obtained in physical oceanography set her on a research course studying the properties of seawater—temperature, density, pressure—and its movement as waves, tides, and currents. Successful in her scientific career, she entered politics as a minister for the environment, wanting to make a difference, and later became a member of the Climate Council. After serving as a Council member, three years later, she was asked to assume the position of Chair.

As a former Chair of the Climate Council, Ilse Knight expected to be invited to the upcoming conference as a professional courtesy. Although she worked in the private sector, she still followed the discoveries of several scientists she had known from the beginning of her marine science days, including Daniel Williams, who had recently called her asking for advice. His death would leave a vacuum in Australia. And the recent news that Dr. Omala Patel died unexpectedly in an accident was also baffling. Dr. Patel was an experienced recreational scuba diver, along with her husband. So many scientists who worked on the oceans were accomplished divers and frequently mixed pleasure with their work. Occasionally, at the smaller scientific meetings, they would charter a boat and dive together, enjoying all the gifts in the ocean—its fish, coral, sponges, and waving sea fans. Ilse had obtained her certification years ago and only recently retested to update her proficiency. She had planned a trip to Australia, but the timing was uncertain.

Ilse had prepared to hear more about the changes in the ocean's chemistry from Omala, but her untimely death meant a change of plans. She made a mental note to call Hans Lundberg. She entered her office and plugged in her electric tea kettle, ready for a break. The slice of tea bread was neatly wrapped in foil and remained on her desk inside a paper bag. She sat down, opened her meeting book, and found the list of scientists who were scheduled to speak at the conference. She crossed off Williams and Patel and checked to see who else was working closely with them. She stopped at Graham Harmon's name, bouncing her pointer finger repeatedly. He was far more interesting than Williams and Patel. She remembered that Lundberg said they were working together on a joint presentation.

Ilse Knight pulled a folder from her file drawer at the side of her desk and took out Harmon's recent paper he had published with the Shark Institute scientists. She made a note to contact Harmon and see what information he could share with her, particularly about the progress his Shark Institute partners had made since the article's publication. Keeping an eye on potential collaborators and competitors was essential.

Steam whistled through the kettle spout, and Ilse looked surprised, forgetting she had planned to make a cup of tea. She poured hot water into the cup, dangled a tea ball into the wet, and waited. The saucer from the cup served as a nice plate for the gingerbread, and when the tea had steeped long enough, she removed the ball by its chain.

While the tea cooled, she picked up her office phone and dialed her assistant. Within a few minutes, a young woman entered the office, a smile on her face.

"Yes, Dr. Knight. How can I help you?"

"Bring me any files on Drs. Williams and Patel."

"Were these your files from the Climate Council?"

"Yes."

The assistant raised her eyebrows and twisted her head. "I'll get those for you right away." She turned on her heels and left the office.

The tea had cooled, and Ilse took a sip before nibbling at the corner of the gingerbread. Her assistant soon appeared at the door carrying a small stack of files in her arms.

"Here you go."

"Just put them on the edge of the desk. That will be all."

The assistant did as she was told and left the room, pulling the door behind her. Ilse took another bite of her bread and opened the top folder. Her mobile phone rang.

"Yes, I got the news earlier today. Both Omala and her husband. Shame. She was a good oceanographer and chemist. I'm reviewing her and Daniel's files now."

Her voice remained flat and unhurried. She took a sip from her cup and nibbled another corner of the bread while she listened on the phone.

"All right, I'll give you a call later. We can discuss it then."

She swiped off her phone, then picked up a remaining crumb on the napkin, and put it on the tip of her tongue. Her eyebrows knitted together when she noticed the framed photograph across from her desk was tilted slightly. She pushed her desk chair aside and strode to the wall. The picture, taken long ago, showed a group of men and women with children on the deck of a large marine research vessel, the James Cook, named after the British explorer. Captain James Cook had sailed the Pacific in the late 1700s following the movement of Venus across the Sun.

Ilse pushed up the bottom left of the picture until she was satisfied it was straight. This research vessel had sailed out from Woods Hole, near Falmouth, Massachusetts. The colors on the photograph were slightly faded, and the faces somewhat grainy, but they were all there. Time had been unkind to those peering back at Ilse. Many were gone, and the few that remained were either too old or too bitter. Ilse didn't feel old.

CHAPTER 9

SYDNEY, AUSTRALIA

I'm wrung out from the almost sixteen-hour trip to Sydney. We took a short flight to Johannesburg before catching a longer one to Australia. It's been years since I've been to Sydney, but I remember it well—the magnificent curves of the Opera House on Bennelong Point, the lush Botanic Gardens, and, of course, the iconic Harbour Bridge. Our route to the hotel takes us past the Royal Botanic Garden and to our well-situated hotel near the Circular Quay. JP, Parker, and I need to check in and get something to eat. The appointment to see the body of Dr. Omala Patel is scheduled for later. We'll meet with the forensic pathologist who performed the autopsy, and I'll ensure the proper specimens were collected for toxicological analysis. Those will be shipped to Dr. Leigh's laboratory in Hong Kong.

After a quick snack, we drive to the morgue located in the western part of the city and meet with forensic pathologist Dr. Jim Hamilton. He's a stand-up guy, a transplant from the U.S., and a friend of Logan Pelletier, a medical examiner I met in Washington, D.C.

"Nice to meet you, Dr. Robinson. Logan's had a lot of nice things to say about you."

"Please call me Lily. Good to meet you, too. I only wish it could have been under different circumstances."

"Welcome to my world. Come on, follow me."

After exchanging pleasantries and information, we brave the chill of the morgue to take a closer view of the body. I slip a white Tyvek jumpsuit over my clothes, booties to cover my heels, put on a mask, and take a pair of surgical gloves, just in case.

Dr. Hamilton, wearing his personal protective equipment too, pulls out the deep draw containing Omala Patel. "I found no obvious signs of trauma on the body—no bruising, broken bones, that sort of thing," he says, pointing to the head, the torso, and extremities.

I give him a nod. "And internally?"

He's already performed the autopsy—the expansive stitches holding together the Y incision that runs from each shoulder to the pubic bone are evident.

"I can show you the photographs of the case in my office. There was some generalized hemolysis and seawater in the lungs. I've listed the official cause of death as drowning. However, as for contributory causes, I'll wait for the toxicology report."

"And the heart?"

"There could have been a fatal cardiac arrhythmia and heart failure. But I couldn't see anything that looked like an infarct. And the husband had similar findings. Also, water in the lungs." He points to another drawer in the mortuary cabinet.

"Thank you, Jim. We have permission to take some samples of the specimens you collected for further analysis." I've got the necessary paperwork to authorize the transfer.

We doff our protective gear, and I meet Jim in his office to review the autopsy photos before we box up all the specimens going to Hong Kong. Dr. Leigh is expecting the bits of tissue and whole blood.

The formidable Dr. Leigh. He's noted for his association with a well-regarded clinical laboratory whose primary business is to look for drugs in the urine of racehorses. Yet his private research laboratory is a clandestine place for detecting and synthesizing exotic toxins. I have been there many times as we have collaborated on various scientific projects. He's a gifted chemist who has identified rare toxins that were the cause of death in many of my most challenging cases. To my surprise, he revealed to me only recently that he has an undercover role for an international consortium tasked with keeping world order. He's well aware of what I do, both academically and for the U.S. Government. Our bond, our friendship, and our struggle for the truth became only stronger when I learned how his family was connected with mine—our grandparents were young lovers before each married someone else. John became my Guardian Angel when he learned of his grandfather's ardor for my grandmother when she was in Hong Kong. The ring I wear is a witness to that love.

I leave Jim Hamilton, and JP and Parker are already in the car with the engine purring by the time I get there. We sit idling and talk before driving back to the hotel.

"You all set, doc? Too much gore before lunch?" Parker asks with a smirk on his face.

"About what I expected."

"You don't think it's natural causes, do you?"

"I don't think so, Parker. Not if we have two people dead on the same dive. But we should wait to see what Dr. Leigh turns up. If it was murder, the killer must also be an accomplished scuba diver. They had access to Williams and maybe Patel and her husband, too. This is not a coincidence."

JP shakes his head. "How many scuba divers are there in Australia or around the world? *Beaucoup*. These scientists are connected through the Climate Council. *Et*, if we find evidence of residual toxin in Dr. Patel, then someone who dives also knows poisons."

"JP, I'd like to visit my friend at the aquarium. She may have some helpful information."

"*Oui*. You go, Robinson. Parker and I will give Chad the preliminary findings."

I stroll around the Wharf at Darling Harbour before walking to the aquarium. The MWDU is just as I remembered it—low and sleek next to the docks at the harbor's edge. When I reach the entrance, I text my friend, who says she's already waiting for me. I push through the crowds, and although it's been some time, she still looks the same, her curly dark hair held back with a headband, full lips, and hazel eyes that sparkle. She's wearing jeans topped with a floral patterned blouse. Sara Wilder's smile is broad, and her open arms embrace me without hesitation.

"G'day, Lily. It's so good to see you." Her Australian accent is thick and charming, and I realize how much I have missed my colleagues on this continent.

"Sara, so good to see you too." I hug her like a long-lost friend.

"Should we catch up at my office, or would you like to have lunch first?" Sara's voice sounds exuberant and upbeat. She touches my arm and smiles.

I haven't had much to eat since early this morning, so food is welcome. "Let's eat first if that's okay."

She loops her arm through mine, and we amble through glass tunnels surrounded by fish and seawater.

"Gosh, I'm so excited you're here."

"Me too. It's been too long. I'm sorry we lost touch." I feel sheepish that it's been ages since we last talked. I squeeze her arm.

"You're here now." She smiles.

So delightful to see her cheery face.

"Lily, are you still teaching at the medical school?"

"Yes, of course. But I've been on leave for the last few months. Wanted to catch up on some travel and visit with colleagues." I reach in my bag. "And I have my latest book for you."

"Oh, cheers, Lily." Her face lights up as she turns the book from front to back. "Beautiful cover. Toxic flowers?"

"Of course. The publisher thought it was a good choice for my second volume on toxic plants."

"I think I might have your first volume here." Sara winks, and we both laugh.

A pause ensues as we continue walking and reluctantly change the subject.

"Sara, I was sorry when I learned your mentor, Dr. Jackson, passed away. The last time I was in Sydney, I visited his lab and remembered his collection of cone snail shells. I still have the shell he gave me as a gift."

She casts her eyes at her hands. "Yes, he was a talented scientist. He encouraged me to go to veterinary college. We still have his collection of sea snakes, cone snails, and marine toxins."

How lucky that Sara brought this up without my asking. "That was a highly curated collection of poisonous creatures. And I recall he had some formidable toxins in his laboratory. Who has access to those toxins and snakes now that he's gone?"

"The professor's old lab was closed, but we kept all his toxins for research purposes in one of the -86° C freezers in the research wing. Poisonous marine life, like sea snakes, jellies, octopuses, and some deadly fish, is kept in tanks in the aquarium. Like the other aquatic animals, they are cared for by staff."

I nod. Are the marine animals' habitats tamperproof? Is there a logbook with the toxin inventory for the vials in the freezer? I wait to continue the conversation once we sit down to lunch. When we arrive at one of the restaurants in the aquarium, Sara recommends the fish and chips and, with a laugh, assures me the fish we eat are not aquarium specimens. I'm game.

"I hope this is all right, Lily. They do have a fancy restaurant that's like eating underwater. It's all glassed in." Sara tilts her head to one side.

"No, this is fine." Our table is far enough away from others so we can talk freely—not that I'm about to disclose any secrets. "Are you working on any exciting research projects?"

"I stopped doing full-time research years ago to focus on clinical work. However, I have a collaboration with some scientists studying whale migration and their diet. But my clinical load is heavy, so it doesn't leave me much time. Taking care of the animals at the MWDU is really a full-up job. And I also do necropsies on marine animals."

"That's interesting. Have you done any recently?" Sara and I used to share research interests in toxins, and now we examine the dead, looking for the cause of death.

"Just did one on a humpback whale."

"How unfortunate. What was the cause of death?"

"Tangled in fishing lines and drowned before he could be cut free."

I lean in closer to the table. "Oh. Sad. Tell me, Sara, what kind of krill do these whales eat?" I might as well bring up krill while I have the opening.

"Funny you should ask. This whale recently returned from the Southern Ocean, where it would have been feeding on Antarctic krill. But the kind of krill I saw in the stomachs were unlike any krill I've ever seen."

A chill moves over my body, and I feel the hairs on my arms rise.

"What do you mean?" I bend back in my chair, making room for the waitress to serve our fish and chips.

"I'm not the world's expert on krill, but we have a scientist here who is, and from what we could tell, the krill in this whale were twice the normal size and had many more photophores. The glow from these creatures en masse must be fierce." She picks up some fish with her fork and pops it in her mouth.

Harmon told us that Williams had commented on unusual krill. Could these be the same? "An expert at the aquarium? Who's that?" I'm nibbling at the edges of the potatoes and fish since fried food can only be eaten in small bites.

"Holly Miller. She can be a little cool, but she's very smart. Her work examines the DNA of the different krill for speciation. Knows more about those buggas than anyone. Funny, though, she was a little reluctant to admit these krill were out of the ordinary." Sara gazes off into space like she's thinking about what she just said.

"How interesting. I'd love to meet her and say hello." Holly Miller does sound interesting, and Sara's remark on her behavior makes me suspicious.

"She's not here. Not sure if she's home or traveling. She never wants to be disturbed once she leaves work. Very protective about her 'me' time. A bit of a prickle." Sara's nose wrinkles, and she gives me a lopsided smile.

"A what?"

"A prickle. You know, difficult, but sharp." Sara laughs.

It sounds like Holly is someone I need to talk to. She may be able to help shed some light on a theory I've been tossing around in my brain. We finish lunch, talk more about her old mentor, and stroll back to Sara's office. The walls are covered with pictures of her and her advisor, Dr. Jackson, when she worked in his lab. Sara never married or had kids, and I suspect she was devoted to him and their work. A couple of smaller photos show her with some penguins. She always loved the critters in her care.

"So, Sara, I'd love to see more of the aquarium, and if it's possible, just take a peek at Holly Miller's lab."

"Oh, sure."

Sara takes me behind the scenes of the enormous tanks with different aquatic environments. We also visit the penguins, and she *oohs* and *aahs* over the King and Gentoos. I decline to get down and dirty with her, especially since I'm wearing high heels while she's switched to rubber boots. It's clear Sara has a big heart for the animals in her care.

After the tour, we go to Holly Miller's lab. It's laid out as I expected. Various pieces of benchtop equipment, balances, boxes of small vials, and then the two tanks over in the corner filled with krill. One tank has krill that appear larger than those in the other tank.

"Holly is our research biologist, and as I told you earlier, she's been looking at the different species of krill. These in this tank," Sara props her hand on the tank's cover, "are ones I pulled from the dead whale."

"I see what you mean. They are bigger. Why do you think that is?"

Sara hesitates. I have the sense she wants to say something but holds back. "Not sure. Maybe a different species or a genetic variation. I'm sure Holly will sort it out."

A genetic variation, or a genetic modification?

Sara is excited to show me one of the krill under the dissecting scope, and I'm fascinated by the opportunity. "Lily, look at this," she says, turning off the light and pointing to the bioluminescence on the larger krill. "This is what I found so unusual."

I look through the scope and understand what Sara is talking about, but I realize that krill are not my strong point. "They look like small shrimp." Did Holly expect to see these bigger krill, and that's why she was reluctant to engage with Sara?

"They do. But these are no ordinary *Euphausia superba*." Sara puts the creature back into the tank and washes off the glass base.

I can't help but follow my hunch. "Could these krill have been genetically modified to enhance their bioluminescence?"

Sara folds her lips together. "Not sure. It's possible. I'd think Holly could answer that."

It's clear to me she's holding back something, but I don't press Sara. "Sara, this has been wonderful. I promise I'll see you again before I go back to the States. Oh, and I would love a chance to speak with Holly Miller. I found your krill discovery fascinating." I hug Sara and mean what I said about regretting we hadn't kept in touch.

I take one last look around Holly's lab. What I'd like to do is peek in drawers and file cabinets for any experimental notebooks. That isn't going to happen, but I'm tempted. My curiosity can be problematic.

After my visit, I return to the hotel to see what JP and Parker have learned.

The hotel room is bright, with a prominent window draped in a beige print overlooking the Opera House and the Harbour Bridge. JP and Parker visited with Dr. Williams's staff while I was at the aquarium. We squeeze around a small table with our cups of coffee and quizzical looks on our faces, ready to compare notes.

"Robinson, how was your visit with your colleague?" JP asks after he takes a long sip from his dark roast. He does look handsome in the light, the sunshine catching the silver in his hair. But I detect a serious tone in his voice that makes me wonder what he's thinking.

"Good. Sara is such a lovely person, and I'm sorry I haven't kept in touch with her more over the years. While it was a social call, I did learn something interesting. Sara recently examined a humpback whale that died and discovered unusually big krill in its stomach. If the whale had last fed in the Antarctic before drifting to the Australian coast, maybe that's where those unusually large krill came from."

Parker narrows his eyebrows, probably thinking I'll launch into another science lesson. "Why do you think that's a problem, doc?"

"Didn't we learn from Harmon that Williams asked him about krill?" I turn to JP, hoping he has something to add.

"Chad said Dr. Patel was scheduled to meet with Williams prior to the Climate Council conference. She would have seen him before he left to see Harmon in Cape Town. *Mais*, Williams was killed before he had that meeting. *Et*, Dr. Williams's assistant said he tried to call her before she left India, but Patel and her husband were already traveling and could not be reached. I don't think she realized until after she got to Sydney that Williams had died."

"So, she was expecting to meet with him. What was her specialty?" I ask.

"A chemical oceanographer. She monitored the pH of the oceans."

"Oh."

"*Mais*, the assistant also confirmed what we heard from Harmon. Williams seemed fired up when he returned from his Antarctic trip. *Et*, that was before he returned to the GBR. Williams, Harmon, and Patel planned to meet once they were in Brussels, most likely to coordinate their findings. Other than what we already understand about bleaching coral and more acidic water, we have no more information on what Williams wanted to share."

Parker perks up. "The question is, could their findings be enough to slow down or stop the coal, oil, and gas industry in Australia?"

JP nods. "It could. The Council takes all the data from the scientists and puts together a plan for policymakers. Strong fossil fuel lobbies would only want weak environmental laws."

"We can't overlook the obvious. I talked to an independent source who said one of the mining companies released coal-laden water into wetlands near the GBR. Politicians were paid off to look the other way." Parker takes a sip of coffee before continuing. "Now, if Williams found proof, someone could have knocked him off to keep it from coming out. Remember, we haven't found the camera, so who the hell knows what it contains."

I shake my head. "Keeping that information quiet is certainly a motive to kill whistleblowers. But I still can't get the krill story out of my mind. It's come up again. There's another story here, and we can't discount an assassin with an alternate agenda."

JP thrusts his shoulders back. "*Encore*. True, true, and unrelated?"

"Why not?" I put both hands on the table and stare at JP and Parker.

"Or true, true, and related." JP manages a slight smile.

Of course, he's right. I flick off my heels and stretch my toes.

Parker leans in. "So based on their findings, our scientists plan a drop mic presentation at their conference. And if that's not enough, another agenda we can only guess about will really shake up the world. Doc, all we have at this point are two bodies that perished in diving accidents."

"No, Parker. We have three bodies that died under unusual circumstances. Williams was bitten by the sea krait, and I'm sure Patel and her husband were also poisoned."

"Dr. Leigh should be able to answer that," JP says. He turns an eye in my direction with a downturned mouth.

"I get it. You both think I see poison around every corner. I do. That's my bias. It's like after buying a new car. All of a sudden, you see that make and model everywhere. But nothing's changed other than your awareness. Whoever this terrorist works for has access to poison. And the intel has suggested there's more." The last sips of coffee cross my lips, and, despite the caffeine, I feel gravity dragging me down. I could be on Jupiter rather than Earth—the pull is so strong.

JP and Parker exchange looks and nod quietly.

"What? What'd I say?"

"So, how about those new electric vehicles?" Parker laughs, easing the tension.

Best to keep your eyes focused ahead.

CHAPTER 10

CAPE TOWN, SOUTH AFRICA

When the plane landed, Holly jumped from her seat, grabbed her small overnight case from the overhead bin, and quickly escaped. Her legs needed a good stretch, and her stride lengthened as she exited the airport. The taxi to the Airbnb in Mowbray took about fifteen minutes, and after freshening up, Holly collected her backpack and set out for her hike while it was still light. She was already familiar with the town's layout and knew the address of the house she was looking for—a house with a beautiful backyard garden filled with flowering plants and a pool outlined in brick. Located near the Swartrivier, the house sat at the end of a cul-de-sac and could not be seen from the road. Once Holly jimmied the lock on the gate, she entered the property and ran down the long rose-lined path toward the pool. Devil's Peak loomed in the distance, and she worked quickly before Graham Harmon returned home.

Holly knew something about Graham Harmon's routines. Sara Wilder had told her. And what Sara didn't know, Holly's contact at the tech company did. While Sara had never met Harmon personally, she was friends with Daniel Williams, and he and Harmon were colleagues and good friends. The two men talked regularly. Williams had shared stories and pictures of Harmon's home with Sara, and she, in turn, shared the information with Holly. Chatty Sara found the stories made good lunchtime small talk. So, Holly knew that Harmon had a pool. Sara showed Holly pictures Williams had sent her of the house—its gray exterior, bright white trim, and a sequestered flower-filled backyard, free from the eyes of prying neighbors. Harmon's pool contained seawater, with a small spa at one end for soaking and jets for a vigorous massage. According to Williams, Harmon enjoyed a swim after work, and he and Harmon had spent many an afternoon talking science, feet dangling in the water. Holly banked on Harmon being a man of regularity.

Holly found the pump housing with the filter and reset the timer to start up well after midnight. She carefully unpacked the Thermos from her backpack, where she had concealed the concentrated toxin. It only had to be toxic enough to make Harmon lose consciousness. Then, hopefully, he would drown. The spa's lining was a mosaic of dark green and blue tiles of various shades that complemented the mosaic waterline tiles and a masterful design of turquoise sea turtles covering the pool floor. The still water didn't register a single ripple when she poured in the contents of the vial.

Holly counted on Harmon having small cracks in the soles of his feet like most people did. In addition to entering the systemic circulation through small fissures in the feet, the toxin would be dermally absorbed through intact skin. If he chose to turn on the jets, the toxin would aerosolize, and he would get a good dose into the lungs. From what she'd read, the amount of toxin added to the pool should be enough to kill him—if not immediately, then within a reasonable time frame. Or perhaps he would fall face-first into the pool and drown.

With the toxin delivered, she collected her backpack and left Graham Harmon's house the way she came. The trek back to her bed and breakfast took a while; when she reached her room, she had something to eat and drink. The shower felt refreshing, and afterward, she lay in bed and promptly fell asleep.

Holly dreamt of herself as a little girl, showing off for her father, reciting facts about the periodic table, and showing him drawings of a double helix with all the base pairs in a neat embrace. His smile took her in, and she climbed on his lap and nestled her head on his chest. The image dissolved into black smoke, and Holly shifted in the bed, waking in sweat. She closed her eyes and counted backward from one thousand, urging her brain to let go of ghosts, and willed herself back to sleep.

The next morning, she rose early and took an Uber to Devil's Peak. The driver dropped her off at the trailhead near Tafelberg Road, and she started the hike up to the Saddle between Devil's Peak and Table Mountain. Holly's calf and thigh muscles barely registered a burn, as she was in good physical shape between her daily runs and swimming. The journey felt exhilarating.

Sugar bushes and restios were abundant along the trail, and the lush scent of blooming flowers filled the air. She rested at a flat rocky outcrop and admired the view of Table Mountain and Lion's head. Bright pink sissies surrounded her. She removed her water bottle from her backpack and drank languidly to quench her thirst. After a short rest, Holly made the final climb to the summit. The view was worth it. Vistas of Robben Island and crashing surf interspersed between clouds, and the heat of the sun warmed her back. She stretched out her lithe limbs, closed her eyes, and turned her face toward the sky.

Holly expected that Graham Harmon was already dead. Since his house was secluded, she wouldn't be surprised if the body wasn't found for a day or two. Holly's contact had confirmed that it was this weekend that Harmon's wife would be away. And when Harmon didn't show up at his laboratory, his staff would call and investigate his absence.

After half an hour, she returned to the trail and headed back down the mountain, where she called an Uber for the ride back to her stay.

When she reached her room, she showered, washing trail dust down the drain, and planned for her departure to Sydney. She made a call first.

"Hi. It's Holly. I'm getting ready to catch the plane back. The weather's been beautiful here, and I almost hate to leave."

"And your task? Successful?"

"I'm sure of it. But it could take a day or two before we hear anything. In fact, you may hear about it sooner than I do." Holly heard the simple grunt on the other end, sighed, and hung up the phone.

The instructions had always been clear from the start. One by one, they would die, and the project would move forward to surprise the world. Holly pulled her hair into a high ponytail, picked up her carry-on, and pulled the door shut behind her.

CHAPTER 11

SYDNEY, AUSTRALIA

Holly returned to the MWDU on Monday morning and dumped her things in her office before going straight for the lab. Her shoulders dropped when she entered her domain until she eyed the krill tanks. Familiar with the minute details of her space, Holly couldn't help but feel her dissecting scope had been used. The position was changed from where she had left it.

She shook her head. Probably Sara brought in a creature she pulled off one of her pets. Sara had a way of coming into the lab to use some of Holly's equipment without asking. Holly cleaned off the scope and wiped the benchtop, tilting her head to see if the surface had any specks of debris. She jabbed at a small spot where seawater had left a ring and then walked around the lab, her eyes scanning for anything that looked displaced. She'd speak with Sara later.

Once settled into her office, Holly reached for her research notebook, hidden in her locked bottom cabinet drawer, and reviewed the data with the information she had saved on her thumb drive. Then she called her contact at the tech company, NovoGeneOne.

"Hey, I'm back. I haven't heard anything. Have you?" She caught her breath.

The reply was no, and after a pause, Holly jumped to the next topic, hoping to earn praise. "I've got the new sequence worked out for the larger photophores if you'd rather incorporate those into the new skin."

Cloning photophores from krill helped refine her scientific protocols on bioluminescence and allowed her to develop new techniques and experiment with photophores from different organisms—the most exciting from *Isistius brasiliensis*, the cookie-cutter shark. The work had been tedious, but after Holly submitted her findings to the lead scientist at the tech company through an intermediary, she was given a considerable cash bonus. Money meant independence. Holly's contact kept her informed of the project's progress and reassured her that together, they would enjoy a rich payout. Only patience was required.

Her news was met with resounding enthusiasm. Holly straightened up, thrust her shoulders back, and smiled—a big smile, until her cheeks hurt. Before coming to the aquarium, she had worked as a full-time researcher in a substantial basic science laboratory's discovery section. Pure science, for science's sake. The laboratory's lead rarely acknowledged her hard work, making advancement difficult within those walls. So, when the MWDU aquarium offered Holly her own laboratory to allow her to focus on speciating krill, she took the job.

Independence, marine scientist colleagues, and days at sea made work at the aquarium appealing. And yet, the MWDU position didn't offer what NovoGeneOne could—intrigue, excitement, and money. Initially, she wasn't privy to all aspects of the work at the tech company. All she had been told was that she would be part of a small team whose project would revolutionize the world. That had felt exhilarating. Holly begged to learn more. And when her contact, the Admiral, took her into his confidence, she did. All the prototypes created to date had succeeded, and the next big phase was underway.

Still jet lagged from her trip, Holly headed to the cafeteria for coffee. Sara was helping herself to a muffin when she saw Holly and flagged her over.

"G'day, Holly," Sara said in a loud, enthusiastic voice, "how was your weekend?"

Holly smiled weakly, and now that she was cornered, she decided to see if Sara had trespassed in her lab.

"Hi, Sara. Fine. I had some projects at home that kept me busy." Holly sat down and blew on her coffee while Sara stirred hers after adding a packet of sugar.

"Sometimes we just need those kinds of weekends, don't we?" Sara bit into her muffin, and a crumb stuck to the side of her mouth, daring Holly to touch it.

Holly tapped her finger to her mouth, telegraphing the message to Sara to please use a napkin. "By the way, Sara, were you, by any chance, in my laboratory while I was gone?" She sipped her coffee and stared at Sara's face.

Sara wiped her mouth. "I was. How'd you know?" Sara cast her eyes down at the muffin and picked off the remaining part of the muffin top.

"It's my lab, and everything has a place." She worked on keeping her tone even. More information could be had from Sara if she came across like sugar and not vinegar.

"Actually, I was bragging about you to an old friend from the States who came by for a visit. She's a doctor and very interested in science. I told her about the dead whale, and we got to talking about krill. She was fascinated and hopes to meet you." Sara pulled one entire side of the muffin and stuffed it in her mouth.

Holly felt her shoulders tighten and her neck muscles stiffen. Chatty Sara. How strange that Sara had a visitor asking questions about krill. "Did she bring up krill, or did you bring up krill?"

Sara stopped and looked into Holly's eyes. Today they were hazel, and she thought she saw her pupils change from round to slits, like a viper. She didn't quite understand Holly—one minute cool, distant with clipped emotion, and yet other times more collegial. Sara shuddered, fidgeted in her chair, and tried to let the feeling go. "I don't remember. But she said she'd love to meet you," Sara said.

Holly shifted in her chair and looked at the others in the cafeteria, debating what to do with Sara. When she made up her mind, she leaned forward, her elbows on the table. "Nice. Tell me, Sara, exactly what does your friend do, and where's she from."

Sara sat back, some of the tension draining from her body, and shared all the details she knew about Lily Robinson and her academic work. Holly listened intently. She was particularly interested in the part about Dr. Robinson's poisons.

After they left the cafeteria, Sara made her rounds on all the marine life in the care of veterinary services—the turtle with the broken leg, the seal who seemed to be off his food, and a tank full of fish with a bacterial infection. Holly returned to her office and did an internet search on Lily Robinson.

CHAPTER 12

CAPE TOWN, SOUTH AFRICA

I'm woken from a sound sleep. Deep within a dream. Someone's standing over me. I rub the grit from my eyes and sit up in bed. My watch says 4:00 a.m.

"Lily, wake up." JP's eyes look tired, and his face is drawn.

My heart's racing like it does when my pager goes off in the middle of the night. Startled awake, I get my bearings, and as my heart rate slows, I come to full alert. "JP, what's wrong?"

"Chad called. It is Harmon. He was found dead in his pool. We should get there as soon as we can."

I shake my head. "Oh god. Cause of death?"

"Presumably drowning."

"But you don't think so, do you? And neither does Chad." I slip into a pair of jeans, hopping on one leg, then the other.

"*C'est vrai*. It would be too much of a coincidence to have him die following the deaths of Daniel Williams and Omala Patel. Most likely targeted."

"What else did Chad say?"

"He requested that tissue and blood specimens be saved for you. I'm sorry, *mais* no conversation with the pathologist who performed the autopsy. With a third Climate Council member dead, Chad wants this under wraps. Let everyone consider it a drowning."

Not being present at the autopsy or being able to question the pathologist is like tying my hands behind my back. Talking through the process helps me think. But I'm betting on the toxicology report. "I'll be able to see the autopsy report and have those tissues sent to Dr. Leigh. Right?"

"*Oui*. You and I will go to Harmon's laboratory to learn more about his work. Perhaps we missed something. Parker will remain in Sydney to continue the review of Williams's notes. There may be something more about a coal spill."

Back on the next flight to Johannesburg, then on the short flight into Cape Town. I feel South Africa inhabiting me again. What was the African proverb Charles and I learned? "If you want to go fast, go alone. If you want to go far, go together." I close my eyes and relive the time Charles and I spent in Cape Town all those years ago. While the memories flash before me in only minutes, I feel the warm breeze in the gardens and hear the sounds that have lasted my lifetime. Our time after the World Congress was the true gift—the seed was planted for my darling Rose.

Charles indulged my love for botany, and we toured Kirstenbosch National Botanical Garden, at that time the National Botanical Institute, located on the eastern foot of Table Mountain.

"Lily, I'm so delighted you attended the conference with me. We get to see one of the most beautiful cities in the world together," he had said, taking my hand. His smile lit up his face, and thinking back on it, I could see where Rose got her lips—full lips that showcased her perfect white teeth, just like her father's.

Men with brains that harbored novel ideas waiting to be discovered were an aphrodisiac for me. I found Charles's brilliance intoxicating. And perhaps, I discovered in him a bit of the father I barely knew. But that must have been deep-seated because I didn't see it then. Instead, I focused on the lush gardens at our feet and the blue sky overhead.

"Look at these gorgeous proteas," I told him, pointing to the exotic flowerhead's pinkish-purple fuzzy pollen presenters. Sitting on the tips, curled, slender stalks, they formed a neat cup of delicate plant parts that looked like a wispy swarm of tiny spermatozoa. "Here," I said, pulling him along, "these are King Protea, *Protea cynaroides*, the king sugarbush, and the national flower of South Africa." I had done a little reading on the plants of Cape Town before we left Boston.

"My god, Lily, you do have a mind for facts." Charles touched the broad pink flower head after a Cape sugarbird finished its feed and flew to an adjacent bush. The bird had stood at the center of the flower, like a ballerina balanced on the top of a music box platform, surrounded by the showy pink bracts.

We left the gardens and the mountaintop and spent a day at First Beach in Clifton. White-gold sand and surprisingly cool, clear blue water set with mountains in the backdrop contrasted our experience in New England. Off our own Cape, Cape Cod, the ocean was always gray and cold, even in the summer. Collecting specimens from the North Atlantic sea for our experiments forced us to wear waders or a thin wetsuit to keep the cool water at bay.

After our stay in Cape Town, Charles and I flew to Kruger National Park. The flight took about two and a half hours, and my window provided a view of the landscape below. The contrast to the hardwoods of New England left me breathless. Dry savanna grassland was punctuated with dispersed trees; there were no closed canopies, so sunlight could pour onto the ground unimpeded. A herd of impalas was feeding, one or two of the group on alert, heads up, keeping a watchful eye for predators. I was excited to think we were going on safari, hoping to see the big five: elephants, rhinos, Cape buffalo, lions, and leopards. I remember thinking that being in the presence of any of these animals would be spectacular but could also pose a threat.

Charles had splurged for a luxury tented camp that, at first glance, transported us back into the 1920s. Located in the park's central region and set overlooking the Nwatswitsonto River, well-built canvas tents covered teak floorboards and beckoned us to enter. The main lodge was filled with rich brown oversized leather club chairs and a generous leather couch with thick rolled arms studded in brass nail heads. A wooden coffee table etched from history sat in the center, holding a lamp and several albums of safari photographs. Open to the outside air, the tent allowed the sweet smell of the Jackalberry trees to waft under the canopy. A deep breath flew from my chest and drifted toward the rafters, lingering until it dissipated. Above, lanterns hung from the posts, and we expected they would light the night with a warm golden glow.

Our bags were taken to our bedroom, a fully closed space under the tent with views of the river. A king-sized mahogany four-poster bed was center stage, covered by a canopy of sheer mosquito netting that trickled down to the floor. Charles brushed the wooden trunk at the foot of our bed with his hand, examining its nicks and indentations.

"I bet this ol' thing has a history. Maybe it traveled over the continent at the turn of the century," he said, taking off his shoes and letting his bare feet get acquainted with the sisal rug. "I wonder where it's been and what it's seen."

"This place is gorgeous. I had no idea. Charles, this trip is probably costing you a fortune," I said.

"Part of the travel is deductible because of my work at the conference. But I wanted an opportunity to get away and spend time with you," he said, tracing his finger over my lips.

Charles put his arms around me, and although not a romantic man, he was, as was I, swept up in the romance of the place. He took my hand and led me to the bed, where he unbuttoned my blouse while kissing my neck. I imagined myself in 1925 wearing a khaki-colored outfit—a long culotte skirt and a short-sleeved button-up shirt cinched at the waist with a thick leather belt. On my head, I'd have a pith helmet and be wearing exotic leather boots—maybe ostrich—on my feet. I admit I felt excited. Excited to be in South Africa with him and, by his attention. We made love on a backdrop of exotic bird calls and hazy sunshine.

Satisfied after our morning delight, we met with the tour group—only one other couple, and our tour guide, Bandile, in the main lodge. Bandile was Zulu, a handsome man with dark brown skin, a broad nose, and sparse hair secreted under a wide-brim hat. His smile was infectious, and his friendly demeanor kept the atmosphere light even during tense moments created by the wildlife roaming outside the camp.

"Make sure you stay within the camp's boundaries and do not go off the elevated boardwalks. Leopards frequently hunt at night near here, and I would not want to find one of you partially eaten the next morning." He laughed, made his point, and wondered if anyone in the group would be foolish enough to wander out on their own.

The afternoon brought more sunshine and views from the camp surroundings.

"Lily, get your binocs. You hear that mewing call of the black-headed Oriole?" Charles had been an avid birder in Massachusetts, and Africa was no different. He dragged me near a Jackalberry tree, and I caught a glimpse of a bright yellow bird with a distinct black head shooting off multiple staccato calls.

But the sound that haunts me to this day belonged to the White-browed Robin-Chat, whose multiple melodious songs let us know each morning that he was the master of his territory. A lovely bird with a robin's red breast, black cap, and a black mask covering his eyes, with a distinctive white stripe sitting above, giving him his name. My binoculars hung around my neck, awaiting a glimpse of any bird or wildlife wandering near our tented camp. We were in awe.

Later in the evening, Charles and I changed out of our modern khaki-colored safari clothes into something more elegant. Eager to reproduce the look and feel of yesteryear, Charles wore pressed tweed slacks and a matching suit jacket complete with suede elbow patches. With my dark hair pulled up into a twist, I chose a long pale blue sheath with mosquito-resistant leggings and an embroidered silk jacket. Both of us were slathered in mosquito repellant, hoping to ward off the carriers of malaria.

The first night of dinner was a feast. A rectangular table draped in a white linen cloth, and two candelabras sat on the surface, flames dancing above, with beaded crystal bling dripping from the arms. Silver place settings designated our spots, complete with fine silverware and crystal glassware. A sterling pitcher etched in floral filigree and filled with cool filtered water revealed beads of moisture on its surface.

With growls heard from our stomachs and not the surrounding bush, we eagerly anticipated the meal. Quail was served with mieliepap, sauteed spinach, and fresh-baked bread, following an appetizer of prawns—visually exciting and gastronomically satisfying. Ample champagne gave me a familiar buzz, and I found myself laughing freely and enjoying my time away from the laboratory. After the main course, Charles and I skipped dessert, only sipped cappuccinos, and then headed back to our room to get an early start on our safari the next day.

Eager to rinse off the mosquito repellent and confident that our mesh netting would keep us safe, we bathed in a generous slipper-shaped bathtub and rubbed each other's feet until the day's exhilaration faded. The water made lovemaking natural, a primordial sea from which life arose. And we created life that night. I'm sure of it.

JP gently shakes my shoulder. "Robinson, Robinson, we are here. You dozed off."

When I see his face, it startles me. Did I expect to see Charles when I opened my eyes? Bouncing back and forth between time zones creates havoc with my sense of time and place. One minute, I'm in the past, the next in the present. The following flight is quick, and once in Cape Town, we will stay at the same hotel we were at before.

A rest from travel is welcome before heading out to Graham Harmon's place. JP drops his bag in the room next door before coming into mine.

"My Lily. You have been so quiet on these trips to Africa. Why is that so?"

I reach out and stroke his cheek, eliciting a smile that warms me. He's not Charles. I've often said I was never in love with Charles, although I did love him. Now I know what all-encompassing love is. I didn't back then. JP is the love of my life. He excites me.

"JP, Rose's history begins in Cape Town, and I can't help but think of her father."

He listens intently, touches me ever so gently, and kisses my neck and lips as if they were fragile flowers. Our lovemaking does not stem from a graduate student's crush or a mentor's infatuation. We share a forever bond that goes deep, held together by chemistry and understanding. I want to feel the weight of his body, feel his skin brushing mine, feel delicate butterfly kisses. I want to feel alive and in the present. It's not too much to ask. My breathing deepens, as does his, and our ballet begins. He pauses at my center—my core—and fulfills my desire before he and I join. He is the love of my life.

After a short rest, we find our way to Graham Harmon's lab, and sadness creeps into my mind, thinking about the last time I saw him. I should have followed my instincts and urged him to seek protection. Or maybe we should have seen to it. Now, I can only hope to shed light on his death. JP assures me that the specimens from the autopsy have been sent to Dr. Leigh.

Security escorts us to the laboratory, and we have some time before one of Dr. Harmon's associates speaks more about their projects. We have free rein to view his data and laboratory notebooks.

Harmon's desk is piled high with papers. JP and I work at either end, sifting through pages. After a few minutes, I find something interesting. "JP, this looks like Harmon's notes for his talk at the Climate Council." We both stop to focus on the printed pages of his PowerPoint presentation.

JP scrutinizes a graph on one of the slides. "Remarkable. He had hard proof of the rise in temperature of ocean waters to about one degree Celsius."

"That's almost two degrees Fahrenheit."

"This slide shows what the global Sea Surface Temperature (SST) values are from several data sets, COBE1, COBE2, HadISST, and ERSST. I am not sure what those refer to, but they demonstrate that the most recent decade (2010-2019) had a higher rate of warming."

"Let's take a copy of these slides for Chad. He can show them to some of our experts on climate change. Maybe there's something in those data sets we're missing. It's common knowledge the oceans are getting warmer, so why kill Harmon over it?"

"*Oui*, they are fairly technical. Here is another slide about the acidification of the ocean."

"Dr. Patel's work."

"*Oui*. Harmon and Patel were going to present data that in addition to temperature changes, the ocean pH will continue to decline another 0.1-0.4 pH units by the end of the century."

My eyes wander to the picture sitting in the middle of the desk—a younger Harmon with his wife and daughter. Harmon never mentioned a wife or daughter. Who discovered his body? Chad will tell us when he gets more information. On the bookshelf, several more photographs are displayed. One appears to be a class picture with Harmon and Williams standing next to each other. They were so young. I snap a picture of the two photos with my phone as a reference for later.

My phone rings as I take the photo. It's Dr. Leigh.

"Ah, Lily Robinson. Nice to hear your voice."

"John Chi, will I see you when I return to Sydney, or do I have to travel to Hong Kong?" I give him a gentle laugh, always charmed by our greetings to one another.

"Not sure, Lily Robinson. But I am somewhat surprised to see you back in the shadows so soon after your unfortunate experience in Washington, D.C."

"I'm not. I missed the action." I hold my breath, waiting for his scolding.

"Lily Robinson, you should be teaching the next generation of toxicologists and not chasing down terrorists."

I laugh again. "John Chi, I've tried to do both." I let the pause linger before I speak. "New subject. What did you find in Daniel Williams's and Omala Patel's blood?"

"I confirmed Williams had sea krait venom, which was concentrated in the tissue around the ankle. I believe that is what the laboratory in Australia found, too. We assume the venom came from the bite of the sea krait since a fang was found in the wet suit. Patel was different. She had palytoxin in her system, and that was the cause of death."

"Palytoxin? How would she have gotten exposed to that? I assume her husband also had palytoxin in his body."

"Yes, both of them were poisoned with palytoxin. Could they have handled the Zoanthid corals while scuba diving?"

"I'm not sure of the range of these soft corals. But they were experienced divers who would have worn gloves. I'll check the report to see if they were wearing gloves when they were found. Could they have inhaled the toxin from their tanks? Even if the tanks were checked for gases, no lab other than yours would be sophisticated enough to pick up palytoxin."

"If you can get me air samples from their tanks, I will do an analysis."

"Thanks. I'll let you know what I can find out."

"One last finding, Lily Robinson. I did a preliminary analysis of the blood of Harmon. A peak, evident of palytoxin. A surprising coincidence for someone who drowned in their swimming pool."

This is unexpected. Yes, I believe that Harmon was murdered. And this is the proof. His death was no accident. All these climate scientists were killed with poison. Even if the ultimate cause of death was drowning, poison was the knife that sent them to their watery graves. Someone with a knowledge of marine toxins is stalking the Climate Council, and we need to stop them. I hang up with John Chi and find JP.

"That was Leigh. Both Patel and her husband died from palytoxin, and he was able to confirm that Williams was killed with sea krait venom."

"*Et*, I will ask if these are natural deaths. *Oui*?

"We've already discussed this. The snake that bit Williams was far off course, so I find that unusual for a natural death."

"*Et*, Patel?"

"Possibly, they were exposed to it naturally, but I doubt it. Any chance we could get our hands on their air tanks? I'd like to have them analyzed for palytoxin."

JP strokes his chin and squints. "The tanks may be gone by now, *mais,* I can check. What is the origin of palytoxin? Another sea snake?"

"Not a sea snake. Palytoxin comes from Zoanthid corals, which are soft corals, sometimes called button polyps. They look a little like anemones. Some marine enthusiasts keep them in aquariums. And, of course, cases of people getting poisoned handling the corals have been reported. Also, warming tends to trigger the release of the toxin, which can then be aerosolized." I look hard into JP's eyes.

"Interesting. *Mais*, there is something else, *oui*?"

"Yes, one more thing. Leigh only has preliminary results but found evidence of palytoxin in Harmon. That cannot be a natural death. Unless..."

Harmon's office has an aquarium. Yes, I remember seeing it the last time we were here. The bright orange and white striped clown fish darts about, and a royal gramma basslet, its vibrant purple and orange scales, catches my eye. Other fish swim back and forth with precision above the pebbly bottom. On a prominent rock, a daisy-like bouquet, with a blueish purple center rimmed in pink and outlined by greenish "petals," waves in the water. Zoanthid coral.

"Unless?" JP asks.

"Look in the tank." I point to the colorful cluster clinging to a rocky surface. "I'm sure this is a colony of Zoanthid corals."

"Are you saying Harmon's death could be an accident?"

I shake my head. "It doesn't make any sense. Harmon would've known how to handle these corals if he kept them in his aquarium. I don't believe this is an accident." I take another deep breath. "Can you get me a copy of Harmon's autopsy report?"

"*Mais, oui.* I said as much. We have three scientists dead who were about to speak of changes to the earth's climate. There must be more."

JP continues to rifle through Harmon's desk, now energized with new information, while I search the file cabinets.

"Robinson, this is a note Harmon made presumably while taking a phone call. It is dated after Patel's death."

JP hands me the note he found under a pile of papers. "I agree. It's got a name here, Ilse Knight and NovoGeneOne. Didn't you say she was head of the Climate Council at one point?"

"I did. She took over from Hans Lundberg as Chair and then stepped down after a few years. Lundberg leads the cause now."

"We definitely need to speak with her. You have Ilse Knight on your list of people we should talk with, right?"

"Let me see if Chad has learned any more about her before we go poking the bear, as you say." He laughs and raises an eyebrow.

JP pockets the note, and I'm reminded about Harmon's collaboration with the Shark Institute he revealed when we visited him last. I walk to the file cabinets and find the one Harmon took the folder from. I unlock the file cabinet using the key at the bottom of a cup holding a cluster of pens. A common ploy. In minutes, I locate the file.

"JP, look at this. The Shark Institute was working on photophores embedded in laboratory grown shark skin."

JP and I sit at two lab stools in front of the waist-high laboratory counter and look through the folder.

He nods. "Engineers have been working for years trying to mimic shark skin. They are the envy of those looking to reduce friction."

"Exactly. But it's more than that. Shark skin is made up of dermal denticles—tiny V-shaped scales that reduce turbulence and drag, so the shark is a more efficient swimmer. And remember, Harmon told us about a particular shark, the cookie-cutter shark, with photophores on the ventral surface. It seems like the Shark Institute had success in recreating the skin in a laboratory setting."

"*Et*, that leads us where? More aerodynamic planes, or boats?" JP runs his fingers through his hair.

"Not just more aerodynamic, maybe invisible."

JP gives me a stare. "What are you saying?"

"Bioluminescence is a chemical or biological reaction that occurs within an organism's body. I've seen it firsthand swimming off the Cape at night. *Jaws* fear aside, you can see the water glow in your wake. It's dinoflagellates, the small plankton that produce the beautiful glow."

"*Et*, krill are capable of that too. *Oui*?"

"Some krill. Not all. And I didn't know about the cookie-cutter shark before we talked to Harmon. The cookie-cutter shark produces bioluminescence from its belly that matches the sunlight's color and intensity above it. It's called counter illumination and can change with clouds and variations in the light."

"*Et*, it would be powerful to create an aircraft with those qualifications. *Mais*, this is far-fetched, Lily."

"Maybe, but Daniel Williams knew Harmon was collaborating with the Shark Institute. He must have discovered something more." I lean in closer to JP and whisper. "Perhaps their deaths had more to do with sharks than ocean temperatures."

CHAPTER 13

SYDNEY, AUSTRALIA

JP and I are back in Sydney to reconnect with Parker and fill him in on what we discovered at Harmon's lab. Sara's on my mind, too, since she is the link to the krill expert, Holly Miller. I have so many questions and feel the answers are here in Australia.

Now that I'm settled into my hotel room, I call JP and Parker to join me for a quick meeting.

"Doc, back again. JP's been telling me about Harmon's drowning," Parker says.

"And did he mention the palytoxin and the cookie-cutter shark?" My bag is on the cushioned chair, and I pull out Harmon's scientific paper. "There has to be a connection between the shark and the krill." I wave the article in the air.

"Not again, Robinson." JP shakes his head and sounds dismissive.

"I get it, JP. But Harmon told us the bioluminescence of the cookie-cutter shark makes it invisible when viewed from below. In essence, the bioluminescence provides a cloak. What if the research about photophores in these animals has led to the discovery of some sort of cloaking device."

Parker chuckles. "You think the Klingons are involved?"

"Very funny. I'm serious about this. Didn't you say Chad worried about powerful corporations looking out for their interests? Maybe there's a new technology we know nothing about."

"Doubtful. Corporations are more likely to cover up their mistakes and bury their secrets. Like unreported coal spills," Parker says.

"Why can't it be true, true, and unrelated?" I dig my toes into the carpet and continue. "Those krill taken from the whale that Sara showed me were definitely genetically altered. I'm sure of it."

"Yeah, that's definitely not the Klingons." Parker sniggers and shakes his head.

"Give it up, Parker, or I'll have Scottie beam you into oblivion." I shoot him one of my annoyed looks.

JP laughs at my interaction with his partner. "Let us focus on planet Earth. Where does this leave us?"

"I wonder. Sara mentioned an upcoming trip looking for whales in the Southern Ocean when I last saw her at the aquarium. That dead whale she examined may have come from there. Why don't I ask her if we can tag along? Maybe we can learn more about Antarctic krill. Changes in the ocean's temperature and salinity could have affected these food sources for whales."

"*Et* that may be something Williams and Harmon discovered."

"Possibly." I rub my temples. "I'll call and tell her we're interested in seeing whales in their native habitat. Who knows what we'll find."

"And how do you explain us?" Parker asks.

"Oh, just colleagues here for some work. JP will use his cover name, Dr. David Lavigne, and you, your journalist's cover. Tell her you're doing an article on whaling or something."

They nod, and I give Sara a quick call. She tells me she's leaving for a flyover to the Antarctic tomorrow morning and is thrilled to have company on her excursion, documenting whale feeding and migration patterns.

I turn to JP and Parker. "We're on. I need to get organized."

We are prepared for the thirteen-hour round trip. I introduce JP to Sara as Dr. David Lavigne, a scientist from France, and Parker as Jeremy Jones, a freelance writer doing a story on the Antarctic. No one has to go into too many details about their background since the trip is the star. Once on board, one of the crew, Eddie, gives us some background information.

"Cheers for joining us today. It's my privilege to have visitors with us while the MWDU aquarium searches for whale pods. Dr. Wilder is our senior scientist on board."

Sara does a little wave even though we all know who she is. Eddie starts up again.

"Antarctica is twice as big as Australia and is the world's driest continent. It holds about 70% of the world's fresh water. We'll be flying over the Southern Ocean, so keep a lookout for anything interesting below."

Sara jumps in. "I'm particularly interested in humpbacks, but fin, Antarctic minke, orca, and sperm whales have been seen here. So, shout out if you spot something."

Parker nods and takes notes, presumably for his magazine article. He raises his head. "Can you tell us about the food sources for humpback whales and orcas?"

Sara smiles, clearly excited to have Parker shooting some questions her way. "In these waters, killer whales eat seals, minke whales, and Antarctic toothfish. They are considered apex predators and eat other marine mammals, as well as cephalopods—"

"Cephalopods?"

"Squid, for example." Sara doesn't lose a beat.

Parker nods enthusiastically.

"Humpback whales, on the other hand, are baleen feeders. They eat squid, too, and small fish like herring and mackerel. But their mouths have keratinaceous baleen plates that act like a sieve so they can filter their meals, allowing them to feed on krill." She winks at Parker, his brown hair framing a rugged face.

Huh, I think those two are flirting. Sara tells us more about whales and their migration and mating patterns. Parker hangs on every word.

We've been flying over the ocean for several hours, and Sara's using field glasses to spy on the waters below. I hear her gasp, and she calls me over, pointing to a shiny reflection beneath the water's surface. I use my binoculars to scan the ocean and see what she's pointing at. Sara asks the pilot to circle the area as low as possible so we all can get a better view. Now JP and Parker are interested, and they break out their field glasses and start looking for the object reflecting the sun. Is it a submerged ship or plane, I wonder?

"Lily, it appears like an enclosure of some kind. And it's filled with krill."

Sara is excited, and even without the field glasses, I can see a reflective swarm of krill. "Why would they be in a pen?" I ask her.

Sara pauses like she's holding onto something. "No idea. It's very unusual. My guess is this is someone's research project. I should check with Holly when we return."

This is strange indeed. The oversized krill Sara showed me, taken from the dead whale, likely came from here. "Sara, maybe this is the source of those unusual krill."

She leans in closer and whispers to me. "You read my mind, Lily. And I wonder if that's why Holly seemed so reluctant to talk about the krill. Is she conducting some kind of experiment out here?" Sara writes down the coordinates of the enclosure in her notebook.

That's information I want for further investigation. I shoot a sideways glance at Parker. He nods. I'm trying to piece this all together. Why would someone want to grow big krill out in the ocean where hardly anyone could find them? I need to speak with Holly, too.

"Sara, I agree. We should talk to Holly when we return?"

Sara hesitates. "We? I will speak with her. Holly has seemed preoccupied lately. But she does clone their genes, and maybe she's working on a species that can produce more omega-3s, particularly since krill contain phospholipid-bound omega-3s. That allows krill oil in supplement capsules to mix easily in our stomachs."

JP and Parker are straining to hear us.

"I had trouble hearing you. What did you say about omega-3s?" Parker changes his seat so he's closer to Sara. Hmm, is Parker interested in omega-3s or Sara?

"From krill," Sara says.

Then he jumps up and shouts excitedly, "Thar she blows." He grabs her hand and squeezes, clearly caught up in the moment, "Sara, what kind of whales are they?"

JP and I look out the window and see a few whales traveling together. How glorious.

"Good eye, Jeremy." Sara cozies up next to him, and Parker doesn't seem to mind. "Those are humpbacks."

Sara makes more notes in her book while continuing to observe the pod. She and Parker are animated, and I see the spark in her eyes while they follow the whales and talk about who knows what.

Finally, back in Sydney, we disembark, and I overhear Sara asking Parker if he's free for breakfast tomorrow. She would love to give him a personal tour of the aquarium. Parker accepts. I hope he remembers to answer to Jeremy, and that he has some deep knowledge about any articles he's supposedly written. I hate deceiving Sara, but our deception is about keeping the people I care about from getting hurt.

Once we return to our hotel, JP, Parker, and I reconvene for a huddle. We get a couple of coffees and sandwiches and head back to JP's room, where we sit near the desk under the window overlooking the harbor. JP begins while slowly unwrapping his ham and cheese.

"This krill enclosure seems suspicious, no?"

I nod and blow on the coffee, hoping to cool it down fast. "Very."

"Graham Harmon said Daniel Williams asked him about krill. Could the changes in the ocean environment documented by these scientists affect this species? Could this have something to do with a pharmaceutical farming effort we are unaware of?" JP asks.

"Sara did mention something about the omega-3s and pharma, so that's possible. But then where does the cookie-cutter shark fit in?" I swallow a bit of my tuna.

Parker shoots me that quizzical look. "Doc, what is it with you and the cookie-cutter shark? You're obsessed." He pulls the tomato off his roast beef sandwich and takes a bite.

"You're right. I am obsessed. We should consider all the possible reasons for these scientists' deaths."

Parker and I glare at each other. Maybe these killings do have to do with pharmaceutical resources and who owns what parts of the oceans. Medicines are being made from the sea. Yet, I can't help but think there's more to it.

"Very interesting, doc. You may be on to something. Listen, I've got a breakfast date with Sara tomorrow," Parker says. "I'll find out more information."

JP and I both take a deep breath.

"Just relax, you two. I'm the nice writer, Jeremy Jones, just getting my story." He winks at us. "And besides, she's cute."

I roll my eyes but say nothing. Sara is a friend. A little older than Parker, I'm sure, not that it matters. I'm surprised she asked him to breakfast. Sara was devastated when her mentor passed away. She idolized him—I could tell—but stayed in the background and devoted herself to his, no, their work. Sara kept her distance, unlike me and my mentor. Young women are susceptible to falling into the arms of the professors they revere. So easily impressed and dazzled. Despite what most people think, it's not about sleeping with the boss to get ahead; it's more about wanting to be close to someone you idolize. Then again, from the man's point of view, well, it might be the excitement of getting into the pants of a young thing.

JP's phone rings. He mouths to us that it's Chad. Parker and I ask that he put the conversation on speakerphone.

"So, JP, you have the gang all there. I have some follow-up from the note you found on Harmon's desk. NovoGeneOne is a small start-up company located just outside Bruges and primarily harvests potential biopharmaceuticals from the ocean. But I didn't see any connection with Graham Harmon, and as far as we can determine, there's nothing suspicious about the company," Chad says.

"Interesting. So, we do have a pharmaceutical connection. Please send me the link, Chad, so I can read any details. They didn't have much on their public site," I say.

"Fear of competition?" Parker asks.

"Maybe. The literature on marine pharmacology is only growing. Did you know that Ziconotide was the first drug of marine origin to be approved to treat pain?"

"That escaped me." I swear JP rolls his eyes.

Chad ignores me, then says, "Seems that India's coastline is the latest to be proposed for a source of new drugs."

"Patel? Was she the connection?" Parker asks.

"It's not clear. You should plan to ask the CEO, Ilse Knight."

JP tilts his head to one side, his eyebrows raised.

Chad continues. "Ilse Knight is the CEO of NovoGeneOne. Remember, she was formerly a scientist turned politician before assuming the position of Climate Council Chair. Stepped down from that role maybe a year or so ago, and it reverted to Hans Lundberg."

"Sounds like we need to get to Belgium sooner than expected," Parker says.

"We do. And we said there are no coincidences." I bite my lower lip and think about the current Chair. "So, Harmon knew something about NovoGeneOne, or maybe Williams told him something about NovoGeneOne. Either way, these scientists were on to something."

Parker stuffs the rest of his roast beef sandwich into his mouth and nods. I make a face.

"Chad, does Hans Lundberg have security? We're facing an accomplished, calculated killer who's murdered three people."

"If so, Robinson, it's someone who can easily move between Australia and South Africa." Chad's breath is amplified over the phone.

"And someone with access to poisons," I add.

"It's time you got to Brussels. The conference will begin in a week, and we need to catch the assassin before he gets to anyone else."

Chad hangs up, and I brace myself for what's to come. I feel the vibration of my phone. A text message from Kelley. He wants to run a case by me if I can give him a quick call. I excuse myself from JP and Parker and step to the side.

"Dr. Robinson, good to hear from you. Are you enjoying your time off?"

"Yes, Kelley. A little R&R while I see some old friends." Another lie. "And catching up with some old colleagues. Before we review the case, how's Rose?"

"She's amazing, Dr. Robinson. She's finally emerging from the gloom and enjoying all her courses. Any time she feels too much pressure, I'm here for her to decompress."

"Wonderful. So, what's going on?"

"This case falls into the oddball category. A twenty-five-year-old male had drinks in the bar with a couple of his friends—guys and gals—and soon after had a burning sensation in his gut. He passed blood in his urine and presented to the ED with priapism."

"Priapism? An erection that wouldn't go away?"

"Exactly. The ED docs were able to help, and he's doing fine now. The toxicology service was contacted because they felt his drink might have been spiked. I ran a date rape panel looking for GHB, Rohypnol, ketamine, some of the drugs we normally see, but it came up negative, so I thought I'd ask what you think."

Kelley's right. This is an unusual case and makes me think we are dealing with something old, not new. "And you said he felt like his insides were burning. Kelley, see if you can find a lab that tests for cantharidin."

"Never heard of it. What's that?"

"Cantharidin is a powerful irritant that causes blistering and a burning sensation in the body, including the urinary tract. It's been known to cause a long-lasting erection, and that's how it gained a reputation as an aphrodisiac." Parker's ears perk up, and he walks over to where I am.

Kelley still can't place it. He's quiet. Thinking. "Why doesn't this sound familiar?"

"You would have heard of it as Spanish fly, notoriously used by the ancient Romans and Louis XIV. The Marquis de Sade was accused in the poisoning deaths of prostitutes he fed Spanish fly."

"Ouch. Our victim had a fly in his drink?"

"Not exactly. Spanish fly is neither a fly nor from Spain. I recall that the male emerald blister beetle, *Lytta vesicatoria,* is the source. People ground up the beetle and put it into food and drink, expecting remarkable things to happen."

"And the burning?"

"The toxin causes a loss of cellular connections allowing tissues to fall apart and, following oral ingestion, causes ulceration of the gastrointestinal and genitourinary tracts and electrolyte disturbances. GI bleeding and kidney necrosis can lead to death." This is really old school. "I would investigate whether someone bought this online and didn't realize how dangerous it could be. People have died using it."

"Thank you. I'll be sure to present this case at Grand Rounds." I hear Kelley sigh and expect he's thankful the puzzle is likely solved.

"Take care, Kelley, and give Rose a hug and a kiss for me." I let out a big, deep breath as I hang up. I do miss the tox service. I miss Rose.

Parker is hanging over my right shoulder. "Shit, doc. I never knew Spanish fly was a ground-up green beetle."

"I don't think many people do. Behave yourself with Dr. Wilder."

"I'm the perfect gentleman." Parker wrinkles up his nose and walks away.

The next day, we make the arrangements for Brussels. The conference is in less than a week. I called Sara to see if I could connect with her, and then Holly, before we leave Sydney. Sara wasn't sure Holly had come in for work but said she'd leave a message. She also said she's excited about having Jeremy Jones come by for breakfast. Oh boy. Parker left earlier wearing his best khaki pants, a light blue shirt, and a navy sports jacket for his date and tour of the aquarium with Sara. I have never seen this man fuss this much with his clothes. He is truly smitten.

What would it be like if Parker and Sara found love with each other? Parker has never spoken about his personal life. But then, none of them do. JP has been an enigma for all the years I've known him. A quiet man, but one I think, who harbors deep emotions. I remember our first meeting.

Newbury Street in Boston's Back Bay, with its beautiful 19th-century brownstones, was an old shopping haunt for me—shoes, fashionable clothes, and charming coffee shops. I first met the dark-haired man at a small café on Newbury Street, steps away from the Public Garden. A man whose essence would seep into my own, a man whom I discovered was a soulmate. He looked handsome, with blue-green eyes, gentle crow's feet, and a crease in his cheek that told of worry and loneliness. These characteristics have only deepened in the years we've known each other. A function of time and the constant surge of adrenaline that comes with danger.

Would I even consider Sophie's ask? I had reminded myself that, first and foremost, I was a physician sworn to do no harm, and yet there I was, being asked to conspire in a murderous plan. Shocked that my thoughts would even go there, I had pushed aside the folder and placed a heavy book on top, pretending it had disappeared.

I struggled to put Sophie's dossier out of my mind. That night, after reviewing the target's medical history, I came back to my Boston apartment and tried to remember the details of my last trip to Colombia, but I had no memory of it. My mind always drew a blank. I learned the truth decades later, and all of it just recently. But twenty-plus years ago—I was blind. It had been Sophie Martin who offered her sympathy over my daughter's death, and now I wonder if she covered up the actual circumstances of the massacre just to have me join her team. Given my despair, feelings of guilt, and loneliness, I had decided to help her with her cause, never realizing that once you cross the line, no matter how righteous you think you are, you are now on the other side.

Once I had agreed to help Sophie Martin with her dilemma, a wave of nausea swamped me—a feeling that continues to plague me during troubled times in my life. Yet, I rationalized. And rationalized. Sophie had told me that the Cambridge scientist had betrayed his country, which had cost innocent lives. I could only help.

"*Bonjour*, Dr. Robinson. It is my pleasure to meet you. Sophie has told me about you. I am impressed by your academic achievements," JP had said.

He had a twinkle in his eyes that sucked me in from the very moment we met. I do believe in love at first sight—that telltale tingle that fans over your body. "Nice to meet you, too. I confess I find it awkward talking to you out in the open like this. Aren't you worried you will be seen?"

"*Mais no*. I am having a cup of coffee with a beautiful woman. There is no crime in that." He smiled, sat back in his seat, shoulders relaxed, and sipped his coffee. The cheek!

Our eyes met, and I felt him flirting with me. "I got it. A meet and greet. *N'est-ce pas*?" I tried some French, thinking it could relax me, followed by a simple question. "You know about me, but I don't know anything about you. Who are you exactly?"

"Ah, it is better that way. I will only be JP to you. Your operative connection. Too much information is troublesome. If you have finished your coffee, we should walk along the Charles."

We left the café and strolled along the river, eyeing the Cambridge bastions of education, Harvard and MIT, on the distant bank. JP reviewed the motivation behind our mission. He echoed Sophie's story about the professor selling the key to the encryption codes used by our country, exposing our foreign assets, and seeking to avenge his son's death. JP wanted me to feel the betrayal as much as he did.

We rehearsed how the mission would take place. JP asked me for my suggestions for the meal, something that would make it likely to look elsewhere for a cause if there was any suspicion. I thought about foods that contain toxins that make us sick. If it would come to that. My hands shook, and my mind raced, thinking we were planning murder, but it was government-sanctioned, and I tried to imagine myself in hand-to-hand combat with a foe. 'But, your Honor, it was self-defense. I was saving the world.'

The lies we tell to keep us going.

CHAPTER 14

SYDNEY, AUSTRALIA

At the end of the date, Sara thanked Jeremy Jones for the visit. He had been an unexpected surprise. She pushed the hair off her face and took a deep breath before reaching for his hand. He pulled her into a hug.

"Come on. I had a great time. You're a fascinating woman. Great info on the aquarium's research scientists and their projects, and hey, the dead whale krill story—crazy."

She smiled. "Speaking of crazy," Sara paused and took a deep breath, "I don't want this to end." She twirled her hair around her finger. The tour of the aquarium was more than fun—it was exhilarating. Sara felt that dizzy buzz. Jeremy showed almost childlike enthusiasm and curiosity about many of the exhibits.

Parker smiled and touched her face. "It's not crazy. I feel it, too."

Sara felt a little purr inside her belly when she looked into his brown eyes and listened intently as he spoke. His face was pleasant, oval with a strong chin, and she could tell he had muscular arms under his shirt. She hadn't felt this way in a long time.

"How about we find a quieter spot to talk," Parker said, his voice low and sexy.

Sara felt captivated by his gaze, and a sudden hunger appeared. She hesitated. A romantic relationship had always been just beyond her reach. Too busy with science, veterinary college, and caring for the aquarium's menagerie. Yet, she yielded to that undeniable spark—let it consume her, and her pulse raced. Her time was now. Sara shed her logical, predictable self like a snake's skin and felt herself rise like a balloon ready to burst.

She chewed her lower lip. Sara didn't want to step on any toes. What was Lily's relationship with Jeremy? Lily would have said something if there was something to say. She would spill the tea on her handsome friend Jeremy Jones if Sara asked. Sara was sure of it.

"I'd love that. When do you have to be back? I could take the rest of the afternoon off." She rubbed his forearm and felt his strength.

Parker put his hand on hers and checked the time. "I suppose in a few hours. What do you have in mind?"

When Jeremy finally left her apartment, Sara took a deep breath. A most unexpected, glorious man had become part of her world. She'd fallen in love in a day. She shook her head and shimmied like one of her penguins. Then doubts sprung up. Her fingers curled into her palms. This could never work. *He lives in America, for crikey's sake*. Yet, they agreed to stay in touch, and she would try to make a trip to the United States, and he would try to get to Australia. He told her he traveled for his job, and they could always meet halfway around the world.

"Don't forget to send me any article you write about the aquarium. I'm happy to review the facts." She'd brushed his hair with her fingers.

He'd wrapped his hand around the back of her neck. "If I do write that article, I'll be sure to send it to you." His gaze moved from her eyes to the floor, and he shifted his stance. What wasn't he saying to her?

Sara wished the last kiss had never ended. Her hand covered her heart, and she finally took her head out of the clouds, ready to do some work now that she had returned to the aquarium. A big sigh left her chest, and she clicked open her computer to type an email to Holly. Then, the sound of her phone ringing made her jump.

"Oh, Holly. I was just about to email you about my friend wanting to meet you."

"Sara, sorry I missed you today. I wasn't feeling well and took the day off. Is this your friend you told me about earlier?"

"Yes, Lily Robinson. She was curious about krill. I told her you were the expert."

"Why is she interested in krill? I thought you said she was a toxicologist."

"Right, she is. But she's a bit of a science nerd and found them fascinating. Which reminds me, we flew over the Southern Ocean yesterday and saw something unusual." Sara was getting a feel for Holly's sensitivity around the subject.

Holly held her breath. "Oh?"

"Are you aware of a krill enclosure near one of the glaciers? At least that's what it looked like to me." Sara heard the silence on the other end but waited patiently.

"No, this is the first I'm hearing of this. I'd love to find out more about what you saw. Did you document the coordinates?"

"Of course. I was checking on the humpbacks when we saw the reflection from below. My guess is this is where those large krill came from." Sara bit her lip. Should she have told Holly she had documented the coordinates?

Holly measured the breaths moving in and out of her chest. "Sara, you said we. You mean you and the crew?"

"Well, yes, but I also had some guests on board to see the whales.

My friend Lily and two of her associates."

Holly had all to do, not to scream. "How about I come to your office tomorrow, and you can tell me all about it?"

"Sounds good. I'll talk to you then. Oh, why did you call?"

"Nothing important. Just wanted to see if I missed anything at the staff meeting."

"Not a thing. I've got to get going now, Holly. One more chore to do before I go home. That little bugga Sammy needs his meds." Sara hung up the phone.

Staff meeting? Since when did Holly call her about anything, much less a staff meeting, which was canceled. She wasn't sure about Holly's tone. Was she worried, angry, or surprised about the enclosure? Sara remembered the conversation she had had with Daniel Williams. He had asked about krill, too. Why not ask Holly?

Sara made a mental note to run a few ideas by Lily. She appreciated her analytical brain, and Lily did seem interested in the krill story. Yet, why was Lily so interested in krill? What was all this fuss with krill? Biopharmaceuticals? Sara scribbled a note in the margin of her calendar, pushed a pile of papers aside, and looked for her notebook. She wanted to hide it somewhere safe in case Holly snooped in her office. Sara sifted through the desktop piles but didn't see it anywhere. The notebook wasn't in the file cabinet drawer either. Sara would look for it tomorrow when her mind was fresh and not filled with thoughts of Jeremy. Sammy was waiting.

Sara grabbed her light parka from the closet in her office and prepared to head for the penguin display. She carried her rubber boots under her arm and waited until she got to the exhibit before slipping them on.

The immersive boat ride through the penguin exhibit (a short tour where children and adults floated along a watercourse and watched the penguins in a simulated habitat) was closed for the day. Sara entered the enclosure with the King penguins. The compound consisted of a small rocky cliff, outlining a snow-covered flat area that led to a pool deep enough for diving penguins. The snow in the area proved slippery at this time of day, but Sara carefully made her way down the slope holding a bucket filled with whiting fish. The air was cold, around five degrees Celsius, and she pulled up the zipper on her jacket to blunt the damp air.

She had already preloaded a fish with the antibiotic and now needed to locate the right penguin. Sammy was over by the rock cropping. She threw a few fish in the opposite direction to distract some of the other penguins and headed for Sammy. His green-colored wing band identified him as the correct bird. Males had their band on their left wing, while females had their band on their right wing. Each band was color-coded, making it easy for Sara to find Sammy in the group.

"Here you go, Sammy." She put the fish with the antibiotic up to his open beak.

Sammy happily swallowed fish and medicine and waited around for more. Sara patted him and then picked her way up the slippery slope to the changing room. Sammy followed. Sara turned and shook her head.

"You silly little bugga. You've had your fish. There will be more tomorrow." Sara laughed, one hand on her hip, the other still holding the bucket.

She checked her watch. The hour was late—well after closing time and she wanted to get back home and inhale any reminders of Jeremy Jones—the scent of his hair on her pillow. She smiled. The exhibit lights had already switched to sunset, mimicking the night and day cycle when she reached the door where the buckets were kept for the fish.

The King penguins vocalized in unison, sounding like tight strings on a violin, and waddled in a flurry. Sara turned. The hand in front of her came fast. She raised her arm defensively, blocking her face, then grabbed her neck. Her voice screamed out. Sammy made a loud shrill.

The bite was swift. Sara's legs went out from under her, and she hit her head on the side of the storage bin, the bucket falling out of her hand. Her limp body slid down the snowy slope to the flat landing. Sammy tobogganed after her and stopped when his beak hit her body. The small colony of King penguins waddled across the ice toward Sara and the bucket, looking for fish. Sammy stood up on his feet and shuffled in circles around her body. The bucket rolled. No more fish. He shimmied, then turned and dove into the pool.

CHAPTER 15

SYDNEY, AUSTRALIA

Parker is back from his outing with Sara. A lot later than expected. JP and I corral him, eager to see if he's gotten any useful information.

"So, Mr. Jeremy Jones, how was your date with Dr. Wilder?" With wide-open eyes, I poke Parker in the shoulder.

He hesitates. "Surprising, actually. More than I expected."

Parker casts his eyes to his feet, and I wonder if there isn't something more.

"Anything you need to tell me, Parker?" Hardly the Inquisition.

"We're all adults, aren't we, doc?" He slips into a chair.

JP shoots me a look but lets the comment go by. "*Eh*, what did you learn, Parker?"

"Aside from the many facts about marine life, doc," he studies me, "I'm used to science lectures now—thanks to you—I learned a lot more about projects at the MWDU. Sara is one knowledgeable lady." Parker has a brightness about him. Maybe a buzz.

"Like?"

Parker lays it all out for us.

"Well, for starters, she knew Daniel Williams. She said that his laboratory's work on corals was important to the aquarium, and he frequently met with some of the aquarium staff. One tank in their research section is dedicated to reseeding coral."

"What were her thoughts on Williams's death?"

"Very suspicious. She didn't know about the sea krait, and I didn't tell her, but she found it hard to believe he drowned. He was an experienced diver. She also said he was found on a remote beach known to only some local divers and Williams's lab. He frequently filmed that part of the GBR."

"Did she know Patel?" JP asks.

"Never came up. My guess is that she knew Williams because he was a Sydney native while Patel was initially on holiday from India."

"And Harmon?"

"No, not personally. But she'd heard many stories about him from Daniel Williams and was aware of his work on ocean temperatures, and on sharks. However, she did bring up Holly Miller several times when I brought up the krill enclosure."

My ears perk up, and JP stops writing. He's taking a few notes.

Parker continues. "I think Holly Miller is a person we need to look into. She came to the aquarium only about a year ago. Sara described her as brilliant, secretive, and extremely focused on her work. She's apparently an expert on krill and can sort them through their DNA. She's working on a big cloning project now. Sara said she's also a master scuba diver, and her big hobby is training for Ironman triathlons."

I feel a shudder travel down my spine. "I've asked Sara if I could meet with Holly, but we haven't been able to connect."

"*Oui*, this is someone we need to pay attention to. We are going to Brussels tomorrow, *mais* perhaps there is time to meet with Holly in the morning. Robinson, can you arrange this with Sara?"

"Like I said, I'm still waiting for Sara to get back to me. I expect she'll call me by tonight if she can arrange something for tomorrow."

"*Eh*, give her a call. *Merci*."

I call Sara, but there's no answer, and no email from her either. She must be busy.

JP made reservations for dinner at a posh restaurant near the Opera House. We have a quiet table overlooking the harbor with chandeliers comprised of silver globes reminiscent of the Atomium at our next stop—Brussels.

The food on the menu is fresh, and while I pick the salad with summer vegetables for starters and coral trout for my main course, JP goes for the mud crab congee and duck while Parker sticks with sashimi scallops and chooses the lamb for the main course. We opt for a cheese course and later chocolate crackle with five textures of Queensland mango with our coffee.

I lean in a little closer to Parker. "So, Sara seemed a little more than professionally interested in you when we were on the flight to Antarctica. Am I wrong about that?"

Parker snickers and then smiles. "You're not, doc."

"And how do you feel about that?"

He puts his napkin down, his eyes soft and a sweet smile on his face. "That's personal, Dr. Robinson," he pauses. "Maybe we can talk about it later. But I will say that I found her charming and interesting."

Parker's right; it is personal. And I've learned that these men never want to share too much about themselves. But if he were having this conversation with JP, would it be much more about his physical attraction to her? I wasn't blind to their body language on the plane. Nothing was secretive about that.

After dinner, we retreat to the hotel. I still haven't heard from Sara to see if she can arrange a meeting with Holly tomorrow morning before we leave for Brussels.

* * *

At breakfast, I indulge in the sunlight pouring in through the window. JP knocks at our adjoining room door. Parker will come up later.

"Any updates from Chad?"

"No, *mais*, when we get to Belgium, you and I will travel to Bruges to see Ilse Knight."

I nod.

JP pours a cup of coffee. "Have you heard from Sara Wilder?"

"Not a peep, and that's unusual. Let me call the main number at the aquarium and see if she's in this morning."

JP starts in on his eggs, grilled tomato and mushrooms, and smokey bacon. My avocado on toast is waiting with my coffee.

"Good morning. This is Dr. Robinson. I'm calling for Dr. Wilder. I'm her friend and colleague. We were supposed to meet this morning." I put my phone on mute and let JP know they're getting her. "Hello, yes, this is Dr. Robinson. Is Dr. Wilder there?" The person I'm speaking to is the head of the department. "I don't understand. You're telling me there's been an accident? I'm coming right over."

My hands and voice are shaking. I take three short breaths, and from the look on JP's face, he braces for what I'm about to say.

"My god. Sara's dead. They found her in the penguin exhibit this morning. They think she slipped on the ice and hit her head."

"An accident?" He throws his napkin down and stands up.

Heat creeps into my cheeks. "I don't believe it for one goddam minute. This is murder." I sink into the chair, guilt smothering me. I brought Sara into this, and now she's dead. Oh, shit, what have I done?

JP walks around the table and squeezes my shoulder. "You do not know that. Let us get the facts."

JP is right. I immediately think the worst.

I stiffen at the knock on the door.

It must be Parker.

I don't think I can face him. My heart strains in my chest.

JP nods and gets the door.

"*Eh*, Parker, have a seat." JP opens his hand and points to a chair next to me.

"Sure, boss. What's going on?" His eyes examine the room.

I wipe away a tear caught in the corner of my eye. Parker stares at me.

"Christ. It's like someone died." He pauses. "Oh, fuck. Someone died. Which climate scientist?"

"Parker, not a climate scientist. Sara Wilder. I am sorry."

The color drains from Parker's face. This is a man who has faced death and seen death many times in his life. But I believe he cared for Sara. I could feel something blossoming between them. I reach out and take his hand.

"I feel terrible. This is my fault. You both get how much I hate collateral damage. Sara was a friend."

"Robinson is getting ahead of herself. We have no proof this was murder. The director said it was an accident."

Parker inhales deeply. His jaw clenches, and he clears his throat. "I'm with the doc on this one. Sara was alive and well when I left her yesterday." He turns away from me, and I see a single tear in the corner of his eye.

I feel myself choking up. I squelch the emotion, staying in control.

His voice deepens and becomes more forceful. "We need to catch the fucking bastard who did this. And I want at 'em." Parker stands and moves to the door, then turns. "Are you coming? I want all the details of this so-called fucking accident." His face is red, and I see the burn in his eyes.

JP and I jump and follow Parker out the door.

I've already made a call to medical examiner Jim Hamilton. Sara's body was taken to the same mortuary as the Patels and Daniel Williams. I will meet with Hamilton later after JP, Parker, and I finish at MWDU. JP has secured permission from the authorities, so we have free rein.

A gloomy atmosphere lingers in the aquarium. None of the staff are smiling—the news of Sara's death has disturbed many. She was popular and well-liked. I introduce myself to the director, who remembers I am Sara Wilder's friend, a pathologist, and Sara's scientific colleague. She feels comfortable talking to me about the circumstances surrounding Sara's accident as I explain that I will be going to the mortuary a little later with my two colleagues to follow up on Sara's death.

"This is just so tragic and unexpected." I hold back the tears, but it's hard when I see tears in the eyes of the woman standing in front of me.

"Absolutely tragic. Sara was loved by everyone and all the animals she cared for." She shakes her head, and I can see her chin trembling.

JP pipes up. "So sorry, madame. We were also colleagues. Could you show us where the accident occurred?"

The director takes us behind the scenes of the penguin exhibit, which has been closed for the day. She explains that one of the King penguins, Sammy, required antibiotics, and Sara wanted to give him the antibiotic herself. Usually, the staff took care of that after Sara made a diagnosis and the prescribed treatment. The director told us how much Sara loved the penguins. Next to whales, they were her favorites. Out of the corner of my eye, I see Parker flinch. I know this is hard for him, but like me, he blocks most of his feelings and uses his version of clinical focus.

We see where the staff change and where the fish are kept. On the left is a dark space, out of view, where someone could hide.

"From looking at your key card access, can you determine who was in the aquarium last night?" JP asks.

"Yes, of course. The usual cleaning staff and a few scientists who worked into the evening."

That makes me think about Holly. "Did Holly Miller stay late last night?"

"She was out sick yesterday. I haven't seen her today either." She pauses and casts her eyes on her shoes before clearing her throat. "She and Dr. Wilder frequently had lunch together."

After we examine the scene, I let JP and Parker know I'll meet them back at the hotel.

Dr. Hamilton is waiting for me at the morgue. He's already completed the autopsy—he was asked to make it a priority—but allows me to see the body. I close my eyes and force my clinical mind. I will not fixate on the face.

The autopsy suite is cold. A chill moves up my spine when I view the body of my friend dressed in a shroud. I bite back the tears. Jim Hamilton is compassionate as he describes his findings, understanding Sara was my friend. He pulls back the cover. The 'Y' incision from shoulder to shoulder and down the entire front from the chest to the pubic bone looks like miniature railroad tracks on creamy flesh. The stitches are large, like those depicted on the Frankenstein monster in the film. There is no reason to make them small, so they will fade in time. Sara has no more time, and no one will ever see these scars. He lifts her head, and I can see where the scalp has been stitched back together after he examined her brain.

My breathing deepens, and I wonder if Hamilton hears it.

"Here's the thing, Dr. Robinson, the laceration you see on the back of the head probably occurred when she fell. But I found no hemorrhaging in the brain. No subdural either."

"So, the head wound didn't kill her. Then what did?"

"Take a look at this." He points to two small marks on the side of Sara's neck.

"Needle marks?"

"No, my guess is puncture marks from a bite."

My eyes widen, and I'm about to speak, but Hamilton cuts me off.

"Now I bet you're thinking snakes, right. No, not a snake bite. Believe me, I've seen plenty of those in Australia."

He sees the quizzical look on my face and once again jumps in before I get a word out. "I think this is a bite from an octopus."

"An octopus?" The pitch in my voice goes up a notch. "Sara was in a penguin exhibit at the aquarium. Are you sure?"

"See these faint imprints around the puncture wound?"

I strain to see what he's pointing to. A line of red marks that look like tiny octopus suckers stain the flesh. I know what this is.

Hamilton sees the recognition on my face. "I'd say someone would have had to put that sucker right up to her neck, no pun intended. It's the only way that I can see this happening."

This means that Sara was murdered. Hamilton has agreed to have specimens shipped to Dr. Leigh. I'm going to ask JP if I can stay behind and meet with Leigh if he can fly in from Hong Kong. Maybe I can find out more about Sara's last hours. JP and Parker can go on ahead to Belgium without me. Another change in flight plans.

Parker and JP are already at the hotel when I return. I give them an update on the findings from the autopsy.

"I'm sorry you have to hear this, Parker."

"Part of the job, doc." He examines his fingers before using them to comb through his hair. "So, could Sara have been saved if someone found her sooner?"

I feel as if Parker wants me to say this was a quick and painless death. The truth is, it probably was a painful death, but given the bump on the head and the cold, I pray she didn't suffer much. The bite from the blue-ringed octopus genus, *Hapalochlaena* is small and painless. These tiny octopuses—about 2 inches or 6 centimeters—have tetrodotoxin or TTX throughout the body, but they secrete venom from their posterior salivary glands. The poison immobilizes prey such as crabs and shrimp. Toxicity results in respiratory depression and paralysis—death by suffocation due to paralysis of the diaphragm. Had she been found sooner, and with supportive care, Sara would have lived.

"Parker, the air in the penguin exhibit was cold, and Sara was knocked unconscious, so I don't think she knew what happened." I feel a twinge in my belly. Is it a lie to comfort Parker as much as it is to comfort me?

JP clears his throat and turns to Parker. "Robinson wants to stay back and wait for Dr. Leigh, who will arrive in Sydney tomorrow. You and I should get on to Brussels."

Parker nods. "But the killer is right here in Australia. You said it yourself, doc. It's some crazy fuckin' Australian poison freak. Are we going to have to worry about you when we're gone?"

I've never seen Parker like this. He's letting his emotions get in the way. It happens to the best of us.

"I'll be fine. Leigh will be here tomorrow, and you two won't leave until later tonight."

Parker tells us he'll be working out of his room and taking his meals there. When the door closes behind him, I fall into JP's arms and shed some tears. He strokes my hair and whispers.

"*Ma chérie*, it never gets any easier."

The tightness of his arms around me helps quell the tears and bury my feelings of dread.

A knock on the door breaks our embrace and disturbs my inner thoughts.

Parker is back.

"I meant to tell you I found this notebook that must have accidentally gotten mixed up with my stuff when I met Sara." He swallows hard, then continues. "She and I spent some time in her office, and I put my notepad on her desk. When I picked it up to leave, I didn't realize her notebook was in the mix." Parker holds up an eight-by-ten slim notebook. He opens up to a page and turns the book around to show us. "These are the coordinates of the presumed krill pen we flew over during our trip. Chad needs to get his ass on this. Find some divers to check it out." He takes a breath.

I grab the notebook and give it a quick look. "You think Sara was murdered because she discovered something."

"We agreed she had information relevant to the other deaths."

Parker sniffs. "Yes, she had a lot to say about Williams's death. I think someone knew more about Sara than we thought. We need to talk to Holly Miller. The director told us Sara and Holly frequently had lunch together. There must be more."

"But she also said Holly wasn't at the aquarium yesterday."

"Fucking bullshit." Parker's face turns red again, and I hear the anger in his voice. "We all know people get into secured areas by tailgating. Holly could have slipped in behind someone else. I think her name is all over this." He slams his fist on the table.

"Back off, Parker." JP's voice turns dark.

"I won't, ol' man." Parker glares at JP and moves into JP's face. I see a flash in JP's eyes.

"Knock it off, you two. Sara was my friend, and I'm struggling to keep it together. I agree that Holly seems suspicious. She's local. So, who was in Cape Town? She would have to have an accomplice?"

"*C'est vrai*. Chad checked into that. No one named Holly Miller left Sydney and flew into Cape Town the weekend Harmon was killed."

Parker grabs the notebook out of my hand. "I'll go through every inch of this and see what I can find." He turns to JP. Fire lights Parker's eyes. "Let's make sure we're on that plane to Brussels. The killer may have already left Australia. Hans Lundberg could be the next target, or even Ilse Knight."

It's unusual to see this degree of fervor in Parker. And JP is quieter than usual. We are all drawn into our private corners. Waiting for the bell to ring before we come out fighting.

In moments when I'm alone, I still hear the buzz and chirping in the African night—soothing and not unlike summer crickets or tree frogs back in New England. But in Africa, another unfamiliar sound, like a low groan, percolated in the night. I always meant to ask our guide, Bandile, what he thought it was. Fear grips me.

Ready for safari, Charles and I sipped our morning coffee and inhaled the growing sunlight. Later, we gathered our cameras and binoculars, ready to see the elephants and the lions. Bandile had the 4x4 prepared for the road. Open sides with a canopy top allowed for fresh air, and Charles and I piled into the truck, eager for a day to view wildlife. The one other couple staying at the lodge chose to remain close to camp, enjoying reading their books by the gurgling of the river.

The dirt roads led us further into the backcountry. Bandile pointed out a herd of zebras and a solitary black-backed jackal hunting small rodents. A pride of lions, some sleeping and others restless, gathered near a watering hole. Bellowing calls alerted wary prey to their presence. Like house cats, the big cats rubbed up against one another, their heads bent down, brushing the shoulder of a comrade. With open mouths and flickering tongues behind their canines, females panted, perhaps hot, after returning from a morning hunt. Charles took many photographs, and I only took a few, too enthralled by the moment and satisfied to capture it in my memory for eternity.

On the way back to camp, we stopped to watch birds on the horizon when behind us, a lion emerged from the bush in a dead run and headed toward the truck. We stood our ground until a thundering herd of elephants stormed out from behind the trees in pursuit. The ground beneath us shook, and our guide told us that a bull elephant was likely leading the charge after feeling threatened. Elephants are the king of the African bush, not lions. With the herd—males, females, and young—getting closer as the bulky lion rounded our vehicle, we were caught in the middle of nature's altercation. Bandile turned the ignition key only to hear a sputter in return. He tried again but ran out of luck as the gray wall, ears flattened against their heads and trunks shaking, approached the vehicle, heedless of us, focused only on the lion. Bandile, a seasoned guide, and Charles and I, were caught between a rock and a very hard place.

Bandile grabbed his rifle, not to kill the beasts but to fire a warning shot and deflect the gray river from its inevitable course. Our truck spilled over. The gun went off. Our vehicle, now on its side, left us vulnerable to the wilds of nature. I remember my heart pounding so hard I thought it would rip through my chest. The fear of being trampled to death or eaten alive as I clung to the two men on either side of me, was a feeling I can still recall. Goosebumps sprinkle my arm just thinking about it. At the time, my mouth ran dry as the desert sands—I swear I could taste the grainy bits. An elephant crashed into our truck. My scream rang out. The elephant realized its mistake and stepped over us, barely missing our heads. We huddled in a tight ball, minimizing our external parts, our bodies pressed against one another.

Bandile radioed for help while Charles and I made loud noises to keep predators at bay. The afternoon light faded, ushering in a bright red expanse of sky. Hot colors blanketed the earth as night creatures began to stir. The rescue was slow in coming. None of us had any broken bones, but later that night, I can recall the sizeable bruises on my hip, and Charles' dislocated shoulder, which we yanked back into place.

That may have been the first time in my life that fear had gripped me with such force that I have a body memory of it, not just a mental memory of it. Now, when my heart races in the face of danger, I can smell the fear, feel the fear in my gut, and hope that my fear does not give me up. I have been careful not to let my adversaries kill me. Life has taught me well.

CHAPTER 16

SYDNEY, AUSTRALIA

Leigh should be here any moment. His flight landed an hour ago, and I'm standing just outside the customs exit area where international arrivals go. John Chi and I haven't seen each other since we were together in Washington, D.C. He was chasing down the Poison Tsar while I lay in a hospital bed recovering from a gunshot wound.

Here he is now, carrying a small leather bag. His hair is gray, almost white at the temples, and his dark-framed glasses settle delicately on the bridge of his nose. The classic navy sport coat balances out his tan slacks and light blue oxford. Similar dress to Parker. I lean in for a hug. Yes, we are at that stage in our relationship.

He pushes back and gazes into my eyes. "Lily Robinson, you are looking well. I assume you made a full recovery." His smile is shallow, no teeth exposed, as he is a contained man.

"Yes, I feel fine, John Chi. I'm glad you're here." I squeeze his hand. "I assume you haven't found the Poison Tsar, or we would have heard."

"Not yet, Lily Robinson. I suspect they are in Jokovikstan. The Markovic family is cunning."

Dr. Leigh refers to the twins Igor and Anastasia Markovic, the older siblings of Grigory Markovic, whom Leigh killed in South Korea. It seems Igor and Anastasia masqueraded as a single person—

the Poison Tsar.

Once we get to the hotel, he and I sit in my room to discuss our most recent case. I give him a quick update.

He squints. "I see. You have come up against another poisoner. Someone who has access and knowledge about various venoms from animals in Australia."

"And not anyone we would know either. This isn't one of the terrorist Markovic factions we are used to dealing with."

"You are sure of that?" He shifts slightly.

"Chad didn't seem to think so. This is someone who wants to stop the Climate Council—or something else—from moving forward with their agenda."

"Someone from a fossil fuel industry?" He leans in and looks me directly in the eyes.

"Maybe. Or it might have something to do with biopharmaceuticals. Or it could be something else altogether." I let out a big sigh. "But it just got more personal. They killed my friend Sara Wilder either because they found her, or something she uncovered, a threat. She had nothing to do with the Climate Council."

I give him the details about Sara's autopsy.

"A blue-ringed octopus. You said as much when you sent the specimens. I can understand the toxin, but using the animal as a weapon? Outlandish and not a sure bet."

John used to have a gambling problem. So, he understands more about betting than I do.

"True. It's about as crazy as a poisonous sea snake." I shake my head. "I'm very suspicious of Dr. Holly Miller. She's clever from what I've heard, and elusive. I've not been able to speak with her. Each time she's been away from the aquarium. She's the expert on krill, and, as far as I know, not poisons."

"Ah, Dr. Robinson, you know better than anyone that what lies beneath the surface can be deadly. Still surface waters hide the most venomous creatures below."

I nod in agreement.

Leigh pushes his glasses to the bridge of his nose. "My assessment is that you are not dealing with a professional assassin. Those assigned that function plan meticulously and use failsafe means—guns, drone kills, and, in your case, poison. Your delivery method depends on your skill, Lily Robinson, and not a creature like a snake or an octopus to carry out the deed. Animals are too unpredictable."

That's true. When given an assignment, I prepare, informed of the target's medical history and physiological vulnerabilities, and concentrate my poison for the most efficacious delivery. This is an amateur with some hidden agenda.

I think back to my first meeting with John Chi Leigh years ago. He was hired to kill me. Instead, he saved me from another assassin, knowing that our ancestors were linked by a bond of love. Since then, our paths have crossed many times, given his genius in creating derivative toxins and identifying the seemingly impossible ones.

"So, John, you should have no trouble detecting TTX. Yes?"

"Have faith, Lily Robinson."

Detection of tetrodotoxin, TTX, should be easy for him. This toxin has been found in many organisms in nature, like the blue-ringed octopus and the pufferfish, *Tetradon,* which also has a beak of sorts.

He pats his leather bag. "I brought you something." He smiles, this time showing his teeth as he dips his chin. "Before I go to my room, I want to give you this." He pulls a vial from his bag. I see powder along the sides and at the bottom. Leigh taps the vial. "Lyophilized TTX. Very concentrated. You know what to do."

I do. Just add water, shake, don't stir, and the crystals will go into solution. Kind of like a James Bond Martini, only deadlier. Leigh appreciates my love for neurotoxins that block sodium channels by interfering with how nerves work. TTX inhibits the propagation of impulses along the membrane of a nerve or muscle cell, resulting in respiratory and cardiac failure and, ultimately, death. There is no known antidote.

"Thank you, John Chi. Your gifts are truly special. But I did bring with me some other poisons." I give a nod and carefully remove the vial from his hand.

"Of course you did." He smiles, and we both let out a little laugh.

"I'll see you later. I'm sure you want to rest for a bit before dinner." I gently touch his arm.

"I will knock on your door, and we will walk to the restaurant together." He bows gracefully and retreats to his room.

We've dined many times together, and although John Chi is a man of few words, he relishes his meals. We'll eat dinner at the Customs House at Circular Quay and enjoy the views across Sydney Harbour.

I head back to the aquarium to see if I can connect with Holly Miller. The director greets me, calls Holly's office, then tells me there's no answer. So, I ask if I can sit in Sara Wilder's office for a while. She agrees, and soon, I'm sitting behind Sara's desk. The bulletin board has a few pictures of her favorite animals. There's one of Sara with a King penguin, maybe Sammy, and another of her on the deck of a boat with whales in the background. A postcard from Boston catches my eye. I take it down and flip it over. It's one I sent her years ago. I'm amazed she kept it. The chair suddenly feels hard, and I bury my head in my hands. I'm so sorry, Sara. I'm sorry I didn't keep in touch over the years and sorry that you died because of something I pulled you into.

Guilt follows me. JP is right when he says I should never tell Rose I'm her biological mother. I couldn't live with myself if anything happened to her. Few people are aware of the truth. Yet I want her to know who her father was, that she was loved even before she was born, and that her mother is still alive. I struggle for resolution. For peace.

The nooks and crannies in Sara's desk beckon me. Her calendar is open, and the lunch date with me and the breakfast with Parker are marked along with our trip over the Southern Ocean. I also see she had a lunch date with a DW. Could that be Daniel Williams? Why not just say Daniel Williams? Parker told us they knew each other, but is it possible she found out more than she let on? As I rewind through the previous few months of her life, I come across a sticky note, 'must talk to Lily about the krill photophores,' followed by two exclamation points, tucked away as if to hide its presence. What did she want to tell me? Was this written earlier or right before her death? I should do a deeper dive into her notebook. But Parker's got it. Oh, Sara. I failed you.

I leave her office with more questions than answers. With time before tonight's dinner date, I decide retail therapy might help take my mind off Sara. A store not too far away carries my favorite brand of shoes. I've already seen them online. Clunky heels may be in, but I still love sleek stilettos with a sharp pointed toe. Shoes are the boost I need right now.

With successful shopping behind me, I return to the hotel, place my phone on the nightstand, and sit on the edge of the bed. The maid's left some fresh towels, and I push them aside. Why didn't she put them in the bathroom and save me the trip? I delicately unpack the shoebox and turn one of the lavender suede and etched patent leather shoes in my hand, admiring its beauty before putting it carefully back in the open box on the floor. I will wear them tonight.

Big breaths. My body falls onto the bed, and with arms spread wide like angel wings, I take another deep breath and close my eyes. A vision of Sara appears behind my lids, and guilt creeps in despite the new shoes. Free-floating. Drifting. My senses—dulled to the world around me.

I see Rose in the jungle. In the tent.

"Don't touch the basket, Rose. Those yellow frogs are poisonous."

"Mommy says don't touch the basket." She giggles.

She brushes my hand. Her small fingers tickle the hairs on my arm. A strange feeling like delicate tiny footsteps. Real or imagined? I shudder. My other hand tries to quell the sensation when I feel a sharp pinch at my wrist.

Eyes flash open. Reflexively, I scream. Pain.

I gasp. "Rose. Are you all right?"

But I'm in the hotel room, not the jungle.

Then I see it. The size of a silver dollar.

A black hairy spider scurries across the bed and circles back toward me. I leap up.

Nausea from fright takes hold of my stomach, and my breaths become shallow.

Where is it, where is it?

My heart races out of control, and I cry out again.

My hand throbs, and I notice two fang marks over a small blood vessel on my wrist.

A spider bite! Given the size, I'm guessing it's a funnel web spider.

Where is it? Where is the goddamn thing?

A tingling sensation surrounds my mouth, and the nausea gets worse.

Where's my damn phone? Leigh, I need to contact Leigh.

I dial his number, but the room begins to spin, and I fall onto the bed.

I hear Leigh's voice.

"Lily Robinson, I have just left my room. I am on my way. Lily Robinson?"

"*Atrax*." It's all I manage to say.

I'm awake now and recognize I'm in a medical facility. I see Leigh nod, turn, and call for the doctor.

A young man wearing scrubs smiles at me. "Well, g'day. Glad you're back with us." He checks the cardiac monitor, as do I, and sees I have a regular rate and rhythm. Blood pressure looks good, too. However, my hand is sore and very red.

The doctor sticks a thermometer in my mouth and continues talking. "Ya got a nasty bite from a funnel web spider." He holds up a specimen cup with a squashed dead spider and shakes it. "Usually, the bites occur when the spider is disturbed in its natural habitat. You're my first patient who has ever been bitten while in their hotel room. Time to warn housekeeping." He gives a slight chuckle and checks the IV. "I'm going to keep you overnight for observation. We've administered the antivenom FWSAV, so you should make a complete recovery." He checks his notes and leaves.

Leigh has been standing quietly, waiting to speak.

"Thank you, John Chi. You've saved my life for the third time. I don't know what to say."

"Ah, Lily Robinson. You only needed one word. *Atrax*. The rest was straightforward."

Atrax robustus—the Sydney funnel web spider. Formidable terrestrial species that build silk-lined tubular burrow retreats. The entrance to their tunnel or funnel is lined with silk trip lines, which alert the spider when prey is present. The spider that bit me was large, and a male funnel web spider can be almost as big as two inches. They're also generally more toxic than females. Their toxin, delta-atracotoxin, is another one that inhibits nerve conduction. Eventually, the victim's blood pressure bottoms out, the brain swells, and they stop breathing.

"Yes, *Atrax* was the only word I could manage to speak. I guess somewhere in the back of my mind, I knew if you heard it, you would realize the danger."

He leans in toward the bed and whispers over me. "We both understand this was not an accident. It is the same person who enjoys taking risks with live animals. Perhaps it has become their game." He straightens for a moment, then leans in again. "You are irritating someone, Lily Robinson, just as your friend Sara Wilder did."

Trembles travel my spine. Spiders are one of my vulnerabilities. Having a huge one jump out at me was beyond terrifying. Yet, I've encountered them clinically—examined the tissue damage from a bite or identified their lifeless remains in a specimen cup—with little emotional effect. Years ago, some researchers were bitten by *Loxosceles reclusa*, the brown recluse, running rampant in their laboratory. Though not native to New England, several spiders were brought back from South America for study in Cambridge. But once they got loose, they became a growing problem. Another patient came to the ear, nose, and throat specialist for hearing problems. The ENT unexpectedly found a spider in her ear, removed it, and sent it to the laboratory for identification. As the toxicologist, it was my job to determine whether it was a poisonous spider. It wasn't.

I take a few deep breaths and touch John's hand. "Sorry, we can't have that dinner tonight. I even bought a nice pair of shoes for the occasion."

"The lavender stilettos?" He brushes out a wrinkle in those tan slacks.

It occurs to me I don't have any shoes on, but maybe my heels are in the plastic bag labeled 'patient's belongings.' "Yes, those are the ones. Where are they?"

John Chi closes his eyes for a moment. "They were the only weapon I found, and I used the heel to impale the spider. You may find it needs cleaning." His words are flat. His face blank.

Not the new shoes. We both hear the blood pressure monitor's alarm. I take another deep breath to calm down.

Now that I'm in a private room, I call JP. I tell him the whole story, and he is deeply concerned.

"*Ma chérie,* Parker was right. We left you with the killer."

A large breath escapes my lungs. "I'm with Parker on this one. My gut tells me Holly Miller's somehow involved in all this. She's avoided me each time I've tried to connect with her."

"You believe she is capable of murder?"

"Possibly. Sara likely learned something more and was about to tell me when we planned to meet. Whatever she knew got her killed." The monitors to the side of my hospital bed show an increase in my heart rate and breathing. I take another deep breath.

"The three climate scientists. They must have discovered something more than changes in the ocean's temperature and swathes of bleached coral." JP pauses. "*Et,* as for you, my Lily, was it your persistent questions that prompted an attempt on your life?" His voice drops.

Ouch, I find the sting in JP's words, and if I could see him, he would be fixed on my eyes. "Yes."

"What did they know, and who else knows the end game? I expect there will be additional targets."

"Whatever it is, JP, krill are involved. I found a reminder note in Sara's calendar to speak with me about krill photophores. Did Parker find out anything more in her notebook?"

"He is taking his time going through the book. Chad is working on the location of the krill pen, given the coordinates we found earlier."

"I also found a reference to a lunch date Sara had with a DW. I'm assuming it was Daniel Williams. They must have talked about krill. Even Harmon said Williams asked him about that. But Holly Miller, who's supposed to be the krill expert, acted like the krill Sara found in the whale were no big deal. She's the key, I'm sure of it."

"I will ensure that if a Holly Miller comes to Belgium, we know it. Passports will be checked. So far, nothing. *Mais*, if she was the one who gave you the spider as a gift, she would still be in Australia."

"She could have left today. I'll call the aquarium tomorrow and see if she's there, and I can speak with her."

"Be careful, my Lily. What role, if any, she plays in all this is unclear. *Et*, I am having second thoughts about you on this mission." He pauses, and his voice sounds stiff and formal when he starts speaking again. "Perhaps you should consider returning to Boston. I do not want to see you hurt again."

I feel my blood pressure shoot up. The monitor pings. "No. JP, if nothing else, I owe it to Sara to catch the killer. Parker was right. We need to nail the monster who's killing world-class scientists." My head begins to throb, and I need to sleep. "Good night, my love. I will see you in Brussels."

I'm released the following morning and again go to the aquarium, determined to meet with Holly Miller.

The director greets me. "Dr. Robinson, nice to see you again, even if the circumstances are not the best."

"Yes, I still can't believe Sara is gone. I'm back to see if Holly Miller is available."

"I just saw her go toward her laboratory. I'm sure she would like to see you since you were a friend of Dr. Wilder."

Finally. I head in the direction of Holly's lab and stop when I get to the door. Through the small glass window, an attractive woman with blond hair wearing a white coat is sitting at the lab bench. She appears to be thumbing through a lab notebook. I knock, and her head pops up abruptly. I push the door open slightly.

"Can I help you?" Holly Miller's tone is not cordial but not unpleasant either.

"Yes, I'm Dr. Lily Robinson, a friend of Sara Wilder. Are you Dr. Miller?"

Her expression moves from neutral to one of surprise. "I am. What can I do for you?"

"May I come in?"

I swing the door wide open and walk toward her to the lab bench. She closes the notebook and points to a stool for me to sit on while she occupies the adjacent one.

I look into her eyes. There's no softness there, and I'm struck by her violet irises. Is that her true eye color or colored contact lenses? "Dr. Miller, Holly, I was upset to learn of Sara Wilder's accident. She and I have known each other for a long time, although we didn't do well at keeping in touch." I pause to see how she responds.

"Absolutely tragic. Sara was well-loved by the staff, a first-rate veterinarian, and everyone knows that her animals loved her too." Her voice is almost robotic.

Somehow, I didn't expect Holly to say that. "I understand you and Sara frequently had lunch together. I guess you were friends, too."

"Yes, very much so. We frequently talked about aquarium animals, aquarium politics, and research. The typical office chit-chat." She shifts in her seat as if sitting on pins.

Her answer seems inauthentic, given what Sara had told me. "Were you aware if Sara was worried about anything? Her work, her personal life."

"No, nothing other than her penguins. She did fuss over her penguins. Sammy's the one who probably did her in." She lets out an unexpected laugh. "He can be a wicked little pissah."

What a strange comment. Does everyone know Sara was in the penguin exhibit to give Sammy his medication? "Yes, I did see some pictures of penguins on Sara's bulletin board."

Holly's eyes narrow like I've done something I shouldn't have.

"You were in Sara's office?" Her tone hardens.

I nod. "I wanted to feel her presence, if you get what I mean."

She forces a smile. "Unless there's anything else, I need to get back to work. I have an experiment cooking." She stands, which is my cue to leave.

"Of course. I'm sorry to have disturbed you. Just one more thing. Sara mentioned that you were an expert on krill. Have you any idea why there would be a krill enclosure in the Southern Ocean?"

Holly's body stiffens, and she sits back down. "What is your interest in krill, Dr. Robinson? Sara said you were a pathologist on holiday with some colleagues."

"I am. We saw the enclosure while looking for whales during the flight to Antarctica. I guess I was just curious."

"I have no idea what's up there. I doubt it's a krill enclosure. However, krill are an important source of pharmaceuticals, so they garner a lot of interest."

I'm sure Holly is lying. I can feel it. But I can't do anything about it now. My gut says something's not right here. I look around the lab again, and I don't see tanks of poisonous species. It's mostly lab equipment used for cloning. I hope Chad was able to find out more about her background.

I force a smile. "Thank you for seeing me. I'm glad Sara had some friends here at the aquarium." Yet, I doubt Holly was one of them.

"Not a problem. We'll miss Sara. Are you headed back to the States?" Her shoulders relax.

"Maybe one more stop before I get back to Boston."

"Boston. Across the Charles River from the universities in Cambridge." Her eyes grow big. No blinks.

And whatever image Holly's holding onto is trapped in the deep interiors of her mind.

* * *

I'm back at the hotel to finally have that dinner with Leigh. Dinners and poison. In my life, they are connected. The first time I planned a "poison dinner," I wanted to get the shoes right. Sophie had laughed. What she cared about was eliminating a traitor at an academic function and hoping it would pass for a natural death.

I had worn a sleek black sheath and black satin sandals—ones fashioned with delicate crystal buckles. I still have those shoes. Within my handbag was a vial containing a potent toxin that I would use later in the evening. Sophie had the caterers prepare the meal to my specifications. We had mussels steamed with leeks, celery, onion, garlic, and parsley, followed by a watercress and endive salad and the entrée of wild salmon grilled with tarragon and rosemary. I was ready by the time the dessert came out.

The chocolate mousse was airy—flavor melted on my tongue. The traitor ordered an herbal tea. I had that, too, in place of my regular cup of coffee. JP had moved to the other side of the room, and when he nodded, the waiter dropped the tray. Dishes and cups crashed to the floor, and all heads turned but mine. I took the small vial of poison from my purse and dumped the contents into the traitor's tea. A very concentrated solution. No chance for hope.

The deed done, I folded my napkin and waited. Minutes after consuming his tea, the professor complained of tingling and burning of his lips, tongue, and mouth. We asked the waiter to bring him a glass of cool water to quench the heat. The traitor drooled and clutched his head and stomach in distress. I took his pulse. It was slowed, and he began to have difficulty breathing. Call 911, the other guests cried out. I concurred. When the traitor fell to the floor, vomiting and seizing, I knew it would end soon. It made me sick to my stomach, and I gagged, seeing the struggle before me, holding back my instinct to care.

By the time the ambulance came, the traitor was dead. I excused myself and walked to the ladies' room on rubbery legs and with pain in my belly. Palms flat on the edges of the sink kept me from falling. A frightened woman stared back at me in the mirror—my watery eyes flecked with remorse. I took a deep breath, bit my lower lip, and instinctively reapplied my eyeliner and lipstick. I left to inhale the cool night air and met JP at a predesignated place.

"Dr. Robinson, you handled that well," he said, touching my shoulder.

I started to heave into the bushes lining the Charles River and then stopped. This man was serious and acted as if congratulating me for having won a prize. Then I switched to anger, realizing just how much I'd been used.

"You goddam son of a bitch," I screamed. "You didn't need me; you could have done this yourself."

My fists pounded his chest, the tears streaming down my cheeks. JP grabbed my wrists and held them until they hurt.

"*Arrêtes*, stop."

His voice became quiet, and there was hesitation in his body language. Hold me or let me be. Then he took my hand and led me to a bench overlooking the dark water.

"*Oui*, you are right, Dr. Robinson. I could have gotten the poison and done this myself. But you will become our biggest asset. An unexpected resource in more ways than one. *Et*, you have the perfect cover. The respected academic and doctor who no one would ever suspect. Pixie Dust was right."

"Pixie Dust? Who the hell is Pixie Dust?" In the darkness, I searched his eyes for answers.

"Ah, the woman with the bright pink streak in her hair. That is what we call her." He handed me a tissue to wipe my eyes and my nose.

"Sophie? Sophie Martin?"

"From now on, she will only be Pixie Dust. *C'est compris*?"

"Yes." I had calmed down.

"Perhaps your poison was, *eh*, a little over the top. Vomiting, seizing, I thought you planned to mimic his heart condition."

I felt criticized. But the dark-haired man was right. It wasn't subtle. My cheeks burned, and I wanted to punch this Frenchman again. I only had myself to blame. I could have said no. Yet, I went along with this crazy plan. "Probably, but that's why mussels were on the menu too. The professor was the one to have eaten a bad mussel. The ones contaminated with saxitoxin."

"Just him? Why not me?"

"Bad luck?"

He stared at me, making me feel uncomfortable. "But I didn't use saxitoxin. I used aconitine. A plant poison, I was going for a heart poison. You're right. I probably didn't handle it correctly." I found my fists in tight balls, ready to strike.

"Next time will be better. *Oui*?" He sat so calmly.

"Next time? There is no next time. And give me a damn break. This may be what you do, but it's not what I do."

I stood up in a huff. JP remained on the bench, unrattled, as if he had just had dinner with old friends. My gut was in knots. "Don't call me. Don't ever call me again," I yelled.

"What was the name of the poison you used?" he asked as I stomped away from him.

"Aconitine. From monkshood. The queen of all poisons."

"*Oui*, the queen of all poisons."

I killed a man that night. And I have killed many since. Did I make the right choice? I turn my lavender shoe in my hand, searching for answers.

I'm ready to meet Leigh. I did my best to clean the heel but found spider juice hard to remove. A pity. These shoes were so beautiful. Dr. Leigh is waiting in front of the restaurant. The dullness and dark shadowing around his eyes concern me.

"So, Lily Robinson. You are feeling much better today and well enough to have dinner?"

I reach out and touch his hand. "I'm feeling much better, thank you."

We've chosen an outdoor table that's off in the corner. The view of the Harbour Bridge is spectacular. While the air smells like salt, it's not the same ocean air I inhale at my cottage. Leigh and I scrutinize the menu for ten minutes before we decide. I'm having Tandoori roasted salmon with spinach and chickpea masala for the main course, and Leigh orders swordfish with green bean, tomato, and potato puree. I wanted to share a starter of crab cakes, but then I remembered he's allergic to crab.

"You've come all this way, John Chi, just to bring me some TTX even though you know I would be traveling with some of my own poisons."

"True, Lily Robinson, but it is more about seeing you than the poisons. I left hastily when we were in Washington. I never had a chance to visit you when you were in the hospital."

"You were chasing down some bigger problems."

Leigh's eyes glaze over for a moment. "Yes, the Poison Tsar."

His old nemesis. He frowns, so I change the topic to the new derivative toxins he's been working on. Once we've exhausted that subject, we return to discuss the Climate Council. I hope the terrorists behind the recent deaths are not connected to the Poison Tsar.

"John Chi, I worry about the future of the earth and our children. Mother Earth is not happy with us. Unfortunately, there's a prevailing short-sighted view of what climate change means to certain people."

"It is all about greed, Lily Robinson." He shifts. "And power."

His brown eyes stare hard into mine, and I move in my seat. Then, an interruption by the waiter as our meals are served.

He picks up his fork and asks, "What have you learned about this Holly Miller?"

"JP called me this morning. There is something strange. Holly Miller only began her existence about twenty years ago. Not much of a record of her before that." I take a bite of salmon. It's tasty.

"A name by marriage, perhaps?"

"Possibly. She has an Australian passport, according to Chad. Her birthplace is listed as Cairns, Australia."

"Cairns. Interesting. A gateway to the Great Barrier Reef. This Holly Miller is an accomplished scuba diver?"

"That's what Sara Wilder said. But I'm waffling on her involvement. One minute I'm sure it's her; the next minute, no. She has no known connection to poisons other than she works at the aquarium, where there are stored vials of toxins. And toxicology is not her field of expertise."

"You miss the point again. This is someone who recognizes which animals in Australia are poisonous. Perhaps she has a unique collection of animals hidden somewhere. I would expect most Australians could tell you about a funnel web spider, a blue-ringed octopus, or poisonous sea snakes. The person who killed these individuals uses natural resources to get the job done."

I sigh. "I suppose you're right. But you found palytoxin in the Patels and Harmon. It's possible they were exposed naturally and drowned, but I don't believe that." My fingers tighten around the handle of the knife. "I'm leaving on the next flight for Brussels to join JP. I'm sure we'll find out the answers there."

After dinner, John Chi walks me back to the hotel and I consider what he said. I'm not sure what to think about Holly Miller. Perhaps there was a moment of surprise on her face when we met at the aquarium—but I'm unsure. And one thing puzzles me. I'd known Sara for a long time, and her accent and expressions differed from Holly's. Holly's Australian accent is not as pronounced, and I find it strange for someone who's lived their entire life in Australia. And wicked little pissah? Now, where have I heard that before?

CHAPTER 17

SYDNEY, AUSTRALIA

Holly Miller entered her bedroom, pulled a metal cookie tin from the upper shelf in her closet, and sat on the bed. She opened the lid and took out a stack of photographs. Most of the photos were from an old album her mother had before it had all fallen to pieces. Like the album, her mother was gone, and these memories were all Holly had left. Remnants of another life, hidden away in a box. Holly rubbed the worn photo of a little girl sitting on her father's lap. How excited she was that day. What a great scientist he had been. Someone Holly wanted to emulate, but he was taken from her much too soon.

She stared at the photo. Her pink party dress, tiara, and rainbow sneakers with flashing lights showed she was an outlier even back then. All the other kids that day were in play clothes—jeans, plain sneakers, and no crowns on their heads. Holly was like her father. His unruly hair, untied shoelaces, and wild imagination. Years later, Holly realized her mother had been pregnant with her before she and her father had married. It didn't matter. He left his first wife and son and moved in with her mother in a small house in the Boston neighborhood of Dorchester. Life seemed idyllic to Holly then.

Before his son died, her father had doted on Holly, teaching her how to read and write before kindergarten. Nightly bedtime stories were a treat, but Holly especially loved the walks along the Charles River, where they would stroll hand in hand while she listened to his stories or plans for inventions, even if she didn't understand anything he said. Sometimes, he'd take her to visit his son, her much older half-brother, whom he said was clever and brilliant and had an exciting future ahead of him. Holly listened to them talk, usually with a twinge of jealousy but mostly with pride that she was related to these two men.

The walks took the place of the road races her father had run in his youth—Holly had seen the pictures—a number pinned to his jersey, a big smile on his face. Her mother told her that her father had given up running because of his heart condition. Still, he remained active. Until his much-loved son died in some war in the Middle East. After his son's death, her father had moped in his bedroom, wringing his hands and cursing under his breath, or stayed in his laboratory well into the night only to come home stumbling up the stairs. Holly watched him fade over time, the sadness digging deep fissures in his face and heart. His grant money dwindled as he struggled to find new ways to fund his research. It had been an unhappy time. Her mother started to drink, and Holly found herself in a household with walls crashing in.

She traced her finger over her father's face in the photograph. Her mother had shared truly little about her father's death. Holly only knew he had agreed to go to a dinner to welcome a new colleague and meet with a representative from a foundation eager to provide money for novel technological projects. If he hadn't died that night in Cambridge, Holly's life would be different. They would have stayed in Boston as a family. She could have made her father proud of her, even happy though his son was dead. She knew she could do it. She was just as clever as any son.

One of her father's inventions would have made them rich—he always said so—and Holly would have been able to go to MIT, which was her dream. Instead, her mother sank into despair, where she could barely keep her small family together. In a last-ditch effort, she contacted a cousin who worked for a passport office in Queensland and arranged for a new start in Australia. He was not opposed to creating false documents for a sum. They took his name, Miller, obtained Australian passports, and began a new life in Cairns, leaving the painful past behind.

Holly got off the bed, put the photos back in the box, up on the shelf, and shut the closet door. She circled back to the living room and padded down the basement stairs. Florescent lights illuminated a huge glass aquarium filled with brightly colored fish, some corals, and anemones. Cone snails dotted the sand below. Delicate jellyfish floated as if caught by a breeze, and a sea snake bumped the glass. She climbed up the ladder and opened the lid to throw in some food. How lovely these creatures were all swimming toward the surface. She watched for a few moments before stepping back down the ladder. The terrestrial tank was much smaller. She tapped the glass and watched a few spiders scurry before dropping in a dozen millipedes. They didn't stand a chance. Satisfied her creatures were cared for, Holly returned to her bedroom.

It only took one simple event to change an entire future. Even so, Holly was sure that her father would have been proud of the scientist she'd become. She packed her suitcase and grabbed her American passport. Time to go to Brussels.

CHAPTER 18

BRUSSELS, BELGIUM

The plane landed at Luchthaven Zaventem with a screech of the wheels and a force thrusting them deep into their seats. Just southwest of the airport, the European hub of Brussels loomed with its residual regal flare and roots going back to the ninth century. A city where multiple languages are spoken, it serves as the capital of Belgium and is considered the capital of Europe, given the presence of the European Union.

JP and Parker booked into a comfortable hotel on Place Jourdan. The facade appeared more modern than the historic buildings in the city, with a dark mansard roof covering a tiled sandstone exterior. The lobby greeted them with billowing ceilings and brightly covered balconies sweeping in semicircles out from the elevators. JP felt almost at home speaking French to all the staff while getting Parker ensconced in his room. Once settled, they made their way on Rue Vautier, past the Museum des Science Naturelles, to the Climate Council to see Hans Lundberg.

Chad had relayed additional information about the Climate Council and arranged for JP and Parker to meet Professor Lundberg. The gray stone building with the small iron filigree balcony bordered a cobblestone sidewalk and housed the Council. Once inside, they were shown to the office of the Chair, where Hans Lundberg greeted them with a firm handshake. JP and Parker were directed to sit in the generous armchairs anchored before his desk.

"Thank you, gentlemen, for paying me a visit," Lundberg said, his white hair perfectly framing his gray eyes.

JP nodded and spoke first. "*Mais oui*. We are concerned for the safety of the Council members and for you as the Chair."

Parker bobbed in agreement while his eyes darted around the office, scanning the tall bookcases and oversized windows filled with light. "Have you any cause for concern about your well-being? We were sorry to learn about the deaths of Drs. Williams, Patel and Harmon."

Lundberg's eyes opened wide, and his jaw dropped as he took a deep breath. "Did I hear you correctly? Did you say Dr. Harmon is also deceased?"

JP's face twisted, and the creases in his cheeks deepened. Had Chad failed to follow up with the proper authorities to ensure the information had reached Lundberg? Maybe it wasn't his direct responsibility, but JP and Parker should have been told that Lundberg had not received the news about Harmon. "*Pardon*. My sincere apologies. We were under the impression that you were aware of Dr. Harmon's death."

Parker sat up straight and leaned in toward the mahogany desk. "I'm sorry. Unfortunately, Dr. Harmon was home alone, and his body wasn't discovered for a few days. It looked like he collapsed at his pool."

"I was not aware he was suffering from any medical issues. Was this an accident?" Lundberg shifted in his seat as if sitting on a pin cushion. He didn't wait for an answer.

JP and Parker looked at each other, lips in a line, not even breaking into anxious smiles. The air seemed unexpectedly stifling, and they watched Lundberg rise from behind his desk and move toward the bookcases. He rolled the ladder to the farthest corner and climbed until even with the top row. He grabbed a black file folder organizer box and carefully descended the ladder. Parker met him halfway and took the box from Lundberg's hand so the older man could use both hands on the side rails.

"You do not know if it was an accident. Do you?" Lundberg took the box from Parker and set it on his desk. "I have some papers from Williams and Harmon that each sent me. They had been communicating with one another and were worried about their findings." He pulled out some photographs from the holder. "As you both are aware, each scientist was working on some aspect of how climate change affects the oceans. Williams focused on the bleaching of coral reefs and the importance of the enormous biodiversity contained within these hydrospheres. The disappearance of reefs would mean a loss of critical marine food webs and essential spawning grounds for fish and other marine organisms. Harmon knew that just a few degrees of variation in the ocean's temperature could change weather patterns around the planet. But beyond that, these men were classmates—friends—and unearthed some surprising information." Lundberg sifted through striking photos of dead coral—bleak and desolate—until he came across several pictures of whales feeding underwater. He stopped, a photograph in his hand, and pushed it toward JP.

JP leaned in and took the blurry photograph so he and Parker could review it together. "What is this?"

"These photographs were taken in the Southern Ocean during a whaling expedition that Daniel Williams attended. Cameras were sent overboard to capture diving whales. But they also found something else. Williams emailed the pictures to Harmon and then sent them to me."

Parker squinted his eye and moved in closer to view the dots that filled the image. The underwater photograph showed small shrimp-like organisms behind a fine net. Although he realized what it was, he held back. "It looks like a bunch of dots to me."

"Yes, it does. But to the trained eye, we can see these are unusually large krill found in an apparent enclosure." Lundberg traced around the outline of the container and stopped at what looked to be a breach in the structure. "Williams recognized these crustaceans were extraordinary and consulted with Harmon, who knew something about photophores."

JP stroked his chin. The photographic proof of all their speculation lay on the desk before them. Had Daniel Williams shared these photographs with Sara Wilder, spurring her to search the Southern Ocean? He looked back to Lundberg. "Why would climate scientists be interested in krill? Do environmental changes impact their bioluminescence, or…?"

Lundberg tapped the photograph. "You tell me. The discovery is not about climate science, but climate scientists were involved in the discovery."

JP and Parker exchanged looks of recognition. Lily Robinson's hunch that krill and the cookie-cutter shark were at the center of the deaths could be correct.

JP scrutinized the photographs again. "Professor, I assume you hid these images," JP pointed to the top of the bookcase, "because you were unsure of their implications."

"Precisely. Williams had become fearful. I believe he thought he had discovered something that might get him killed."

JP brushed his hand over his graying hair. "What reason would he have had to think that?"

"Gentlemen, Williams was not a man to shy away from environmental controversy. Coral reefs were his passion, and he spoke out boldly to make others aware of the implications of climate change. But there is always the fanatic who does not believe in science or facts, for example, those who subscribe to the flat-Earth theory."

Parker snickered. "I've heard there were still flat earthers around."

The Professor nodded and collected the photographs. "You see, Williams was very much aware of climate change deniers and those who believed in conspiracy theories. These were individuals who heckled him throughout his career. He told stories from his early days—of summers in Woods Hole, Massachusetts, with other oceanographers and colleagues in Cambridge. Cambridge, Massachusetts. Greedy industrialists made threats, hoping to keep their industry alive despite their effects on the oceans. But Williams never backed down."

Parker spoke up. "Did Williams share any of these threats with his colleagues? Sara Wilder, for example." Parker struggled to understand Sara's death.

"I don't know any Sara Wilder. However, I recognize some scientists were wary of their discoveries getting into the wrong hands. Harmon was one of them." The Professor stuck the envelope with the photographs into the file folder. "Williams was used to looking over his shoulder. Harmon, not so much." Professor Lundberg settled in his chair and stared at JP and Parker as if to ask, 'Now what?'

JP looked at his fingers before folding them into one another. He cleared his throat. "Professor, do you believe that whatever Williams discovered led to his death and that of his colleagues?"

"Williams could not explain why these krill were where he found them and wondered if he stumbled onto something untoward. He was spooked and asked me to secure the photographs."

JP shifted in his seat. "You are saying Williams thought he could be killed for his discovery."

"I believe so, Monsieur Marchand. And now that you tell me Dr.

Harmon has died, I believe Williams may have been right. Radical alterations in science can produce paranoia and personal attacks if changes disrupt the status quo."

JP ran his fingers down his cheek to his chin. Lundberg's sense of the situation seemed well-founded.

"*C'est vrai*. Could Williams have shared this information with anyone other than you and Dr. Harmon?"

"Unknown." Lundberg tapped his desk.

Parker spoke up. "What about any companies using krill in their work? Are there any that Williams could have contacted?"

"One comes to mind. Please, do not mention my name. You will understand why. NovoGeneOne is such a research facility located just north of here in Bruges. Bruges is a picturesque medieval city, surprisingly modern, and NovoGeneOne is located close to the coast, allowing it to launch ships at the port near Zeebrugge into the North Sea."

The tie-in. Mais oui. *NovoGeneOne and Ilse Knight*. JP grabbed his right hand with his left and rubbed his fingers, feeling down to the bones. "*Je comprends*. Ilse Knight. *Oui*?"

"Yes, Monsieur Marchand. Ilse Knight, the former Climate Council Chair, politician, and CEO of a technology corporation. I do not pretend to know what goes on there, and I do not want to know any details. However, I understand, at the very least, it is a company interested in farming bioceuticals from the ocean." Lundberg's eyes darted around the room as if he were concerned he was being observed.

Parker straightened in his chair. "Are you suggesting Ilse Knight has something to do with the deaths of these men?"

"I am suggesting no such thing. I am merely saying there may be research at NovoGeneOne that involves krill. The company, as I said, is not far from here and perhaps a visit would be in order. However, I will deny we ever had this conversation. It is enough that I have to deal with Ilse Knight via the Climate Council."

"The problem there?"

"She was not well-liked by the Council members. They found her unyielding and stubborn in her views. Yet, she was influential in getting nations to join, but some later resented that it was only on her terms. Global politics is an art." He tapped his desk with his finger again, this time with more force. "We cannot stop one country from burning down the Amazon Forest, for example, but we, as a group, can try and influence, and then generate guidelines and goals everyone can live with."

Parker nodded. "Thank you, Professor. I want to reiterate what we asked earlier. Are you concerned about your safety?"

JP added, "We could arrange for you to have protection until the meeting." JP thought about Lily's plea.

"I have reconsidered since our earlier conversation. Now that you tell me three climate scientists were presumably murdered, some protection is warranted. I could be next." A frown crossed his face, and his eyes looked past them. "However, I do not want my wife frightened, so if you gentlemen can make arrangements that are not overtly conspicuous, I would appreciate it." Lundberg stood up in anticipation of his visitors' departure.

"I will see to it. Thank you for your candor." JP leaned over and shook Lundberg's hand.

"One last thing, Monsieur. I mentioned that Williams spent time at Woods Hole. It was a close-knit community of marine scientists. This is where Williams first met Ilse Knight when she was building her career in physical oceanography. Perhaps he shared with her his findings."

Parker's jaw dropped.

JP looked directly into Lundberg's eyes. "This has been most helpful, Professor."

JP and Parker waited until they were in the car before speaking.

"So, what are your thoughts, boss?"

"I think Dr. Robinson was right, and we need to look at what is going on at NovoGeneOne."

"No, I mean about Daniel Williams knowing Ilse Knight more than twenty years ago."

"Like most scientific fields, many players know one another or have at least heard of one another."

"I wonder what the stories from Woods Hole or Cambridge could tell us." Parker touched his brow.

JP paused. He weighed his words before continuing. A memory stirred in his brain. "I suspect Daniel Williams believed scientists were targets then, as well as now." JP frowned and drew his eyebrows together. He wondered what Lily would say. "When is Robinson expected here?"

Parker recognized the sudden subject change and didn't press. "She should be here tomorrow."

"*Oui*. *Et*, we will go to Bruges as soon as she does. Time is running out."

JP and Parker returned to the hotel and later reconvened in Parker's room.

"JP, I've gone over Sara's notebook." He laid open the notebook on the table.

JP took a seat and pulled the notebook toward him. "*Et*, your findings?"

"In addition to the coordinates of the krill pen, she had some notes here about a meeting with Daniel Williams a short time before his death. They shared an interest in whales. It seems like she already knew about the enclosure from Williams. She just needed the coordinates." Parker turned to the page where Sara had made some notes. "He must have told her about his findings, and now we know from Lundberg that Williams sent him the photographs of the krill enclosure, too."

JP shook his head. "A secret worth killing for?"

Parker inhaled sharply, his fists in a ball, his jaw clenched.

JP flinched at his own words, seeing the distress in Parker. Sara's death was unexpected. Lily had taken it hard as well. "Could they have discovered a remarkable drug from these krill, or are we missing something?"

"When Robinson gets here, we go to NovoGeneOne, unless you want to go now." Parker's eyes were wide and pleading.

Stiffness plagued JP's shoulders. "The jet lag is catching up to me. Let us pick this up when she arrives." JP stood and returned to his room.

CHAPTER 19

BRUSSELS, BELGIUM

I'm eager to speak with JP after having talked with Leigh. And I have mixed feelings about leaving Australia and Holly Miller. But JP contacted me last night and confirmed that Holly Miller was still in Sydney—she's not in Brussels, even if she is my number-one suspect.

JP waits for me at our Brussels hotel. I know there will be connecting rooms in anticipation of my arrival. He's got the bigger room with a small table for dining and meeting, while I have a room with two queen beds. His blunted smile greets me as I unlock the door and step in.

We fall into each other's arms. "God, so good to see you." I squeeze tight, and he lets it happen.

"My Lily, you look no worse after being bitten by a spider." He scrutinizes my hand and wrist, looking for fang marks.

"Yes, thank god it wasn't a radioactive spider, or who knows what could have happened." I give a little laugh, but the quizzical look on JP's face tells me he doesn't get the joke. My fingers sweep his cheek. "I'm exhausted from the trip. Would you mind if I took a little nap?"

"*Mais oui.*"

He moves a strand of hair behind my ear and kisses me. His lips feel soft, and I find my shoulders drop, releasing the strain of travel. I strip off my skirt and blouse and let them fall into a heap, seeing that JP has already shed his clothes. We climb into bed, and I curl up on his chest and stroke his chin.

"JP, we always manage to tumble into bed when we see each other."

"*Ma chérie*, better to live in the moment than live to regret." He kisses my eyelids.

"What are you saying? We may not have a future?" My hand brushes his chest.

"In this business, nothing is certain. *Oui*?"

I close my eyes and swallow hard. I can't ever imagine my life without this man. Not now, not after all that we've been through. He gently rolls me onto my back, takes my hand, and kisses the palm, then the wrist where the bandage covers the latest assault. His kisses travel to my belly, and he stops at the surgical scar—one more reminder of our ever-present danger. He pauses, scoops me into his arms, and hugs me tight. I can hardly breathe.

I push away ever so slightly to catch my breath. "JP, is everything all right?" I can feel the tension in his body—his broad back tight and stiff. If he could only tell me what troubles him behind those blue-green eyes.

His grip eases, and he cups my face with large, beautiful hands. "*Ma chérie*, my Lily. *Je t'aime*." He says my name in two syllables, pronouncing the second with much more emphasis than usual.

"I love you too," I tell him, feeling there is something more he wants to say. "Are you sure you're all right?"

"*Mais oui*. You are safe and in my arms." He strokes my hair and kisses my breasts, better able to use his hands and lips to speak his mind.

The heft of his body is like a weighted blanket—heavy and secure. My throat tightens, and I feel his arousal, and pounding heart through his chest. Our ragged breaths free my mind, and we ride together until the excitement explodes. Afterward, I stay in his arms until I fall asleep, leaving the world's problems far behind. For now.

Later, we settle back into JP's room, with tea and some biscuits. Parker's joined us and eager for me to catch up.

JP shows us a satellite view of a building complex. "Now that you are here, Robinson, we will go to NovoGeneOne."

Parker nods. "Finally. I've been waiting for this." The frown on his face betrays him.

JP continues. "We need to have greater access than just the office area."

The complex has multiple buildings, probably containing offices, research laboratories, and possibly manufacturing. "What's this?" I ask, pointing to the large half dome looking structure.

"An airplane hangar. See what appears to be a small runway from this aerial photograph," JP says, tracing his finger along a grassy strip behind the structure.

"I see it now. Maybe the company has a corporate jet. It wouldn't be unusual for a tech firm to have its own plane," I say.

"Yeah, definitely a hangar." Parker brushes his fingers through his hair.

"*Oui. Mais*, we do not know for sure what is in there."

"NovoGeneOne probably has tight security. No way they're gonna let us in that tin can. So, under what premise would we meet with Ilse Knight?" Parker asks.

"Possibilities. We are assigned to look out for the security of Council members; we are business investors; we are scientists. If we stick with security, Parker and I will meet with Knight. And perhaps, Robinson, you could lose your way on the grounds, so to speak."

My eyes open wide. "I can't believe that's going to work."

JP stares me down. "You will improvise. As you usually do."

I let out a big huff and stand up. "Improvisation is not a plan, JP, and you know it." I push the chair hard into the table. Even after the sex, I feel tightly wound.

Parker gets up and comes over to me. "All right, calm down, doc. We've skated before, and you know it. I think we're all still a little shaken about Sara. I know I am. And don't give me bullshit about the hardened operative piece. Yeah, we've all killed. I get it. And shit, we all know plenty of good guys who've been knocked off. This just feels personal."

It does feel personal.

JP rises too, and places a hand on my shoulder. "Robinson, we are exploring ideas. Let us discuss options."

"Sorry. Parker's right. I think losing Sara made me feel vulnerable once again." I sit down, take a deep breath, and push all my feelings to the depths. I engage my clinical mind like that fine focus I use on my microscope to bring what's important into view.

I've already done a little upfront reading. "Here's the scoop on NovoGeneOne from the link Chad sent me. Its research focuses on developing innovative therapeutics through harvesting natural ocean resources. Ilse Knight is listed as its CEO, and the board of directors consists of venture capitalists, scientists, and a former military man. They list some of their current medicines in development, such as ones to treat high blood pressure, liquid tumors, and progressive neurological diseases. All good stuff. I can only imagine that Ilse Knight's interest in a company like this stems from her oceanography background. Its investor site says they have research vessels that patrol the deep sea for medicinal sources. There's nothing here that seems out of the ordinary."

JP nods, a big smile lighting up his face. "*Merci*, Dr. Robinson. Excellent work." He turns to Parker. "First, we will go to Bruges to assess the security measures at the NovoGeneOne compound *et* the surrounding grounds. That will help us determine a more precise plan."

"Sounds good to me. I'm ready anytime you are, boss," Parker says.

The clinical connection kicks in. "Wait, I have an idea. This is a research and manufacturing facility."

Parker turns to meet my eyes. "What's up, doc?"

I give him that look that says, ha ha. "What if we said we are at the facility for an unannounced inspection?"

"An inspection? Don't you have to tell them in advance you're coming? I kinda liked the idea of us being part of Council security."

"Not necessarily. In the States, if someone makes a complaint at a workplace, an oversight organization can arrive unannounced to investigate."

"So, we would have to create a complaint that would normally be investigated by what?" Parker asks.

"They must have the equivalent of OSHA here. Do you know, JP?"

"OSHA?" Parker asks.

"Occupational Safety and Health Administration. In the States, it assures safe and healthful working conditions. JP, do they have that in Belgium?"

"They do. It is similar. An OSH system for the country. It could work."

"Maybe a worker is concerned about the inappropriate use of biological agents. Do you think Chad could pull off getting us some official-looking IDs?"

JP laughs. "Has Chad ever let us down. I am sure he can come up with something."

Parker agrees to stay behind and work with Chad to obtain the necessary documents while JP and I go north to check out Bruges and the NovoGeneOne location.

It's just under an hour and a half to Bruges. We get on E40 and head north toward Ghent. JP is driving, and I'm in the passenger seat, lost in the blur out the window.

We enter the city of Bruges, or Brugge as it is known in Flemish. Canals, reminiscent of Venice, weave throughout the Gothic architecture, and chocolate shops are everywhere. The sound from the bell tower rings in the distance. Our destination for NovoGeneOne is north of Bruges, but JP parks the car so we can take in a little of the city before going to the facility.

There's so much to see and do. I only wish we were visiting as tourists and not looking for the assassin picking off Council members one by one. The walk along one of the canals is breathtaking, with views of the Old Palace, the former residence of the Burgundian aristocracy. We wind along the cobblestones to a small bridge overlooking a canal and heritage architecture—stone houses surrounded by broadleaf trees. JP stops and pulls me into him. His kiss is gentle, and the tension in my body slips to my feet.

"Sometimes, *ma chérie*, I wonder what it would be like if we both lived in France."

I blink. My stomach bounces like a chair on a Ferris wheel that stops unexpectedly. What has gotten into JP? Such a fiercely independent man would never settle down with anyone. Even me.

"What are you saying?" I can hear the shake in my voice. So can he.

JP strokes my hair. "What I do for a living is all I have ever known."

"You've told me many times you couldn't imagine ever living a risk-free life."

"When we were in Central Asia last year, I also told you I loved you, *mais*, could never possess you."

My legs feel wobbly. I nod. "Of course, I remember. No woman can be possessed just as I could never possess you."

"*C'est vrai.*"

"You said you were wed to this existence until you could no longer carry on. I think those were your exact words. Why are you bringing this up now, JP?" I bite my lower lip and stare into those blue-green eyes.

"After you almost died during our last mission, I felt responsible in many ways. *Oui*, it was Pixie Dust who brought you to our team, and you have performed admirably. *Mais*, you have rediscovered your daughter, and I have a cousin who knows nothing of me." He stops and puts both hands on my shoulders.

"Are you telling me you would give this all up and return to Reims?"

"That is my birthplace, and I have an affinity for my home country."

"But what about me? I live and work in Boston."

"*Je comprends*. It has always been your choice, my Lily."

Oh god. Why drop this all on me now? Is JP telling me he wants out of the business, and I can join him in France if I want to? "JP, I can't talk about this now. I need to concentrate on what we are about to do."

"*Mais oui*. I suppose I was moved by this beautiful place."

For a time, we behave like tourists, walking hand in hand around Burg Square. A charming chocolate shop off a cobblestone path entices us as we look through the multipaned windows filled with chocolate craftsmanship. We enter and sample probably the finest chocolate in the world. Would the Swiss argue? Later, we satisfy our craving for coffee and a Liège waffle. Despite a short line at the takeout window, we are patient. Soon, a thick, sweet waffle piled with strawberries and fresh whipped cream sits in a small paper container. Two forks are all we need.

A small dollop of cream floats on the edge of JP's cheek, and I take my thumb and wipe it off. He grabs my hand and takes my finger into his mouth. My chest heaves as my breathing deepens, and I feel I've missed a signal to this overt sexual gesture. His stare bores into me, and I sigh. What is going on with JP? When we are alone, he is affectionate. But in public? Is it a ruse so we look like tourists and not assassins? My heart beats wildly as the possibilities run through my mind.

Back on track, we leave our medieval refuge and drive toward the North Sea until we reach the NovoGeneOne facility, well-hidden beyond the main roads. JP manages to circumnavigate the compound for our first look. A sprawling three-story brick building with a bay of windows that run along the entire first floor stands at the end of the drive. There's ample room for parking, but JP turns the car around and heads back out.

"Where are we going?"

"I wanted to see the main entrance, and now we go to where we saw the hangar." JP drives round to the other side of the compound and pulls the car over just outside the fence near the airplane hangar. It is surrounded by a chain-link fence—nothing too imposing. In fact, the security seems less than robust, so I wonder if that means there's nothing to hide or if everything is hidden in plain sight.

JP takes out a pair of field glasses. "There is a windsock over to the right. This facility definitely stores an airplane or two."

"I'm not sure why we are making such a big deal about this. So what if they have a corporate jet. We've already agreed that's no big deal."

"Lily, you were the one extolling the virtues of the cookie-cutter shark—with its photophores making it nearly invisible to those viewing from below. You suggested the possibility of engineering a technical skin that could allow stealth aircraft to escape detection. What if NovoGeneOne has done that?"

"A cloaking device."

"*Oui*. Science fiction meets reality."

"If that were the case, then this technology could revolutionize the world. There are stealth planes already, but this would be a huge step ahead." That phrase, the one about technology that could change the world, sticks in my mind. I've heard it before.

"We need to get into that hangar tomorrow."

Once we are back at the hotel, we meet with Parker to discuss our options and see if Chad has obtained some documents allowing us to enter on the grounds of inspection.

Parker, a smile on his face, lets us into his room. "Glad you two tourists are back." He raises an eyebrow at JP as I hand him a small box of chocolates. "I've got good news. Chad was able to pull some strings, and we're going to be an inspection team tomorrow."

"That's great," I say.

"Since JP speaks fluent French, he will be the team leader, and you and I, doc, will follow directions from the boss." Parker pats JP on the shoulder.

"Oh, a nonscientist for the lead. We will all inspect the laboratory, but at some point, one of you will need to get into that hangar." I smile broadly.

JP shares his thoughts about the cloaking skin with Parker.

"Shit, so you think the doc is right?" He turns to me. "You were obsessed with that cookie-cutter shark."

JP rubs his chin. "America has led the field on low-observable aviation. There is the B-2 Spirit, and we have word that the U.S. Airforce's Next Generation Air Dominance program seeks a replacement for the F-22 Raptor."

Parker jumps in. "China and Russia are working on their own versions, for example, the Xian-H20, and the Tupolev PAK DA, respectively."

"What makes these current planes stealthy?" I ask.

"These aircraft are planned to escape radar detection by virtue of their design and technology. For one, they reduce the reflection or emission of radar, infrared, and other signals. It is fairly complicated, and I do not intend to be the expert. *Mais*, you will also notice that they adhere to a basic shape, which helps limit radar cross-section." JP points to an image of a stealth aircraft shaped like a triangle on his phone.

"I see. So, if they can take that virtual wing-shaped plane and coat it with reflective photophores embedded in shark-like skin, it could also be visibly undetectable. Basically, a Klingon ship."

"Star Trek again?" Parker asks.

"Yes, Parker." I turn to JP. "If what you say is true, it would confirm what we suspected. These scientists were not murdered because of their work on climate change."

"*Oui*. I believe that in the course of Daniel Williams's and Graham Harmon's work, they uncovered evidence of this program's existence. It is only a theory, *mais*, could explain why this has been so volatile."

My lower lip trembles, thinking about the implication. "Who would have sanctioned such a project?"

A frown takes hold of Parker's face. "Any global power." He taps the picture several times.

"What are you saying?" I ask.

"Doc, don't be so naïve. Chad has his ear to the ground. There's always background chatter about new threats. This could be it, and I wouldn't be surprised if the United States is interested."

JP clears his throat. "Once we establish its existence, we can discuss next steps."

Why do I feel a wave of anxiety cover me? I've been there before—my muscle memory of fear. "I hope Chad and OSH have come up with a viable complaint because if it's true what you say, I don't think for one minute these people would hesitate to kill us."

"Chad took your lead, doc. The anonymous complaint has to do with ineffective biomonitoring." Parker hands me his phone, where he's pulled up what Chad has sent along.

"Great. We'll assess if there are any ill health effects on their staff exposed to chemicals harvested from ocean organisms." I pause to think. "For starters, we can ask what biomarkers they use and whether they are measured in blood or urine."

"Let us work out the details tonight so we will be organized for tomorrow. Parker, how are we picking up identification badges?"

"Chad arranged for us to collect them in Ghent, so we'll stop on our way."

I leave my fear behind and switch to my clinical focus. "I'm going back to my room to familiarize myself with the OSH standards required for our visit."

"*Bon*, Robinson. I will remain with Parker. We should meet for dinner tonight. Although it is already late." He checks his fancy watch. "One cannot come to Brussels without eating *frites*."

"That sounds good. Steak *au poivre avec champignons et frites*. I remember we served those arms dealers a modified version of that dish."

JP laughs. "In that little bistro in Paris. *Oui*?"

"Nasty deaths, as I recall."

Parker's head shoots up. "What are you two going on about? And what are we having with the steak?"

"Oh, that was an early mission JP and I took in France, eliminating some arms dealers. We fed them toxic mushrooms, *Amanita phalloides*, with their peppered steak."

"*Oui*, the Death Cap."

"Christ, sometimes you two are just a shit load of fun." Parker shakes his head.

JP and I laugh, and I excuse myself to go back to my room. If NovoGeneOne is building stealth aircraft, I assume the killer must be from that company. I was probably wrong about Holly Miller. Maybe Williams knew about her cloning work and was only trying to get background information. Her evasiveness may have more to do with her quirky personality than with killing Climate Council members.

Despite my earlier nap, I look forward to putting my feet up and calling Kelley. My watch says it's late in Boston, but Kelley should still be up.

"Hi Kelley, I thought I would check in with you quickly. How is the consultation service?"

"Hey, Dr. Robinson. Funny you should ask. We've gotten slammed."

"More fentanyl?"

"Not just fentanyl. It's xylazine. Even when we bring them around with naloxone, the patients struggle with the toxic effects of xylazine."

"Oh god, tranq—an effective animal tranquilizer. It's making its way across the U.S." Xylazine causes low blood pressure and slows the heart rate in addition to drowsiness. Add that to fentanyl, and you have a potent central nervous system cocktail.

"One more thing. Xylazine is causing necrotic wounds at the injection site. Reminds me of those necrotic fingers, toes, and ears we saw with levamisole-contaminated cocaine. We're seeing all kinds of infections and dead tissue. The Infectious Disease team is all over this one."

"Are we ever going to solve this opioid crisis? It only seems to be getting worse."

"Unfortunately, you're right. On a more positive note, Rose is doing well and enjoying her clinical rotations."

My ears perk up. "That's so good to hear, Kelley. I'm glad she hasn't been turned off to medicine after everything she experienced last year. Has she indicated any subspecialty preferences?" I keep my fingers crossed because I would love to have her join Kelley and me in the field of pathology.

"You know Rose. She loves everything. I like to tell medical students that you can love all the disciplines and subspecialties, but then you have to pick one you will live with the rest of your life."

"Or almost the rest of your life."

"You know what I mean, Dr. Robinson. She'll settle and then let us know. You have been a major influence in her life so far."

I recall the irony of her telling me how she was excited by my presentation at student night when she was in high school. I didn't even realize she was alive then. Funny how life's twists and turns lead to paths unknown.

"So, tell me, Kelley, how is the relationship?"

"Solid. I think we both enjoy sharing science, and Rose is intuitive and sensitive at the same time."

"Are you talking about what makes her a good doctor?"

"Well, yes. But it's more than that. Surgical pathology, in particular, can take away the human interaction aspect of medicine. True, we occasionally see patients on our toxicology consultation service, but for the most part, we're lab rats. We deal with facts and numbers, bits of tissue or body parts, without an introduction to the person. Rose brings medicine into focus. She has a true sense of what it means to be a healer.

I admire that."

"That is commendable. I'll give her a call when I return. We can have lunch together."

"She would like that."

I hang up with Kelley and think about seeing Rose again. I'm comfortable being her mentor for now, but what would it be like to share the whole truth with her?

I'm prepared for a late-night dinner at a restaurant with JP and Parker. My blue flower print dress hugs my body, and I slip into a sleek pair of black stilettos. JP and Parker are waiting for me in the lobby.

"Nice dress," Parker says.

JP raises his eyebrows.

"Thank you, Parker." I give JP a smile.

We head to a restaurant on Rue Eugène Cattoir in Ixelles, not too far from the hotel. Subdued lighting and brick-lined walls with high arches create an untroubled atmosphere. We're shown to a quiet table in the cellar—perfect for discreet conversation.

Parker puts down the menu. He wiggles the knot of his blue-striped tie, presumably to reduce the pressure at his neck. "I'm getting that big steak and French fries."

JP nods. "I will have the same." He turns to me. "Robinson?"

"Make that three, except I only want a petite filet." Even Shakespeare recognized there was too much of a good thing.

JP gives the waiter our order and then reviews the wine list before picking out something flavorful to pair with our meal.

Our glasses, filled with a nice Cabernet, and *petit pain* in a basket covered with a crisp white linen cloth, arrive at the table. I butter a roll before the salad serving.

"Cheers," I say to the others, picking up my glass and waiting to clink with theirs. "I've heard the custom of toasting began as a way to detect poisoning. Bumping full cups caused a splash of drink into each other's goblets. Poison one, poison both."

Parker laughs. "You can be sure I haven't poisoned your glass, doc."

"Are you letting us know that we need to be careful?" JP swirls his wine in his glass and sniffs the bouquet before drinking.

"Just making a little small talk."

"It's a lot better than your usual lectures." Parker grins.

"You two have been very out of character on this trip. I don't get it. I'm waiting for one of you to tell me there have been no deaths, and it was all a dream."

"Unfortunately, it is not a dream. Tomorrow, we will go to NovoGeneOne and gather as much information as possible. I think during the inspection, Robinson, you should start wandering. Preferably near the hangar."

"Why me again?"

"You are the least menacing to anyone who would stop you. A woman lost on the grounds, one who could easily be overpowered, does not appear threatening."

"Ha. Little do they know." Parker winks.

"Well, I'll try not to get myself shot." I roll my eyes. But JP has a point. I could play the innocent, although leaving the main facility and getting lost by the airplane hangar seems a stretch.

The meal is delicious, and we enjoy non-work-related conversation before heading back to the hotel. Our car is waiting, and once we are all in, JP takes us for a drive around the city, so we can appreciate the night lights. I feel relaxed, until…

The car slows.

"I think we are being followed," JP says in a low tone.

I can see his eyes in the rearview mirror.

Parker slowly turns his head to get a better view. I duck so he can see past me.

"You're right, JP. There's a black sedan tailing us. How do you want to play this?"

JP nods.

He slows the car and pulls into the left lane as we approach the traffic light. We idle to see if the vehicle passes or holds its place behind us. It keeps its distance. The light turns yellow, and JP waits until it's almost red before doing a dizzying U-turn at the intersection.

"Hold on." The engine roars.

"Shit!" My head knocks against the back seat.

"Whoa, ol' man. Make us fly."

I see the black sedan across the divider still heading in the opposite direction. The person behind the wheel stares at us before he drives through the red light, tires screeching. Most of his face hides in the shadows, but he's wearing a cap, and I am sure it is a man. There are no pretensions now.

We head south on R21—the Boulevard Géneral Jacques.

The tailing car makes progress.

I lean forward and yell into JP's ear. "Go faster. He's gaining on us." My pulse races.

The black sedan pulls beside us and rams into our car. We veer from our lane onto the sidewalk.

Parker's body slams against the door. "Shit, JP. Where is my fucking gun when I need it?"

"What the hell? We were out to dinner. Not in pursuit of one of our terrorists." The next ram pushes the car hard to the side.

JP sends the gas pedal to the floor, and his right elbow darts into the air as he turns the steering wheel. Nausea creeps up to the back of my throat as I bounce from side to side. I see the woods ahead—the *bois*. We run the red light. Our car ditches the main road as we turn onto a smaller road within the *Bois de la Cambre*. Woods outline the way, and the trees are a blur. The car that's been following us has dropped behind.

Was their intention to intimidate but not kill? JP slows the car and circles the lake. The meal in my stomach churns, and I open my purse for an antacid.

JP stops at the side of the road. There's a small island in the center of the lake with a Swiss-looking chalet, only accessible by boat.

"Is everyone all right? Robinson?"

I take a deep breath, hands grabbing JP's seat in front of me. "What the hell was that?"

JP wipes his brow. "That," he pauses, "is someone aware of our presence."

I catch my breath before speaking. "Do you really think we can pull off this phony inspection tomorrow?"

"*Oui*. NovoGeneOne and the Climate Council may overlap, but they are not the same."

The muscles in my arms twitch, and I release my grip on the seatback in front of me. My body collapses. Darkness surrounds us. Not a moving car. No birds singing. A laugh echoes across the water. The chalet.

Parker laughs. "It looks like they were expecting us."

The sign near the dock catches my eye. "What?"

"*Le Chalet Robinson*," Parker says.

JP laughs, too. A renewed lightness in his voice. "Another time, *oui*."

CHAPTER 20

BRUGES, BELGIUM

By the next morning, JP has already gotten another car, and we're on our way to Ghent to pick up our IDs for the inspection. Chad has a man stationed there who helps our allies obtain spurious documents as needed. He'll take our pictures in our current disguises—me in my blond wig and brown contacts, JP in a dark-haired wig and mustache, and Parker looking distinguished with a beard. Intent on our mission, we have no time to explore Ghent—the churches steeped in medieval architecture or the béguinages where women once lived together in a safe community.

The guard at the front desk of NovoGeneOne raises his eyebrows when JP shows him the letter from OSH. I flash my ID along with Parker, and the guard makes a call to the Director of Quality Assurance. Minutes later, Karin Kaechele struts out of the elevator wearing a smart dark suit, white blouse, and stylish kitten heels. She approaches us—shoulders back, head straight, and chin high. She extends her hand first to JP, then Parker, and finally to me.

"Welcome to NovoGeneOne. I understand you are here to investigate a complaint." She uses English, although it's clear to me that she has a distinct Flemish accent.

"Thank you, Ms. Kaechele. Do you have a conference room for us to discuss the issues?" JP uses English, as well, his French accent distinct. Since the French and the Flemish have grappled with this dual culture, I hope there will be no tension. "I would like to introduce Dr. Laurent," he says, pointing to me, "and Mr. Jeremy Jones," he says, pointing to Parker. JP, of course, is using his alias, Dr. David Lavigne.

Once we reach the conference room, JP lays out the complaint—an anonymous employee reported that there are little or no biomarkers being measured to detect any deleterious effects of exposure to the natural products the staff works with.

Damn, if JP doesn't nail that perfectly. "We are particularly interested in the biomonitoring of blood, urine, and hair. The latter is important if heavy metals are obtained or used in manufacturing your products."

Karin Kaechele's expression reveals little. "I see. We are closest to a pharmaceutical company in that we hope to create novel therapeutics for common and uncommon medical conditions. We take the safety of our employees very seriously. Frankly, I am quite surprised there is a complaint." She shakes her brown hair off her shoulders with the aid of her hand and purses her lips.

"We are specifically interested in the cloning laboratory. I assume you're using 6-dimethylaminopurine and cycloheximide."

"We are." Her eyelid twitches.

"*Et*, are you also mining any products from the seafloor?"

Karin Kaechele wrinkles her nose, her head tilted to one side. "What about seafloor mining?"

JP clears his throat. "Are you also engaged in mining the seafloor?"

"We are well aware of mining for heavy metals in the seabed. Copper, magnesium, to name a few, but none of that takes place in this facility. We have partners in other countries, such as Australia, performing those functions."

I perk up at the mention of Australia. "Do you have any personnel that are shared between sites?" I hope she will say yes, but we'll see.

"We have employees that work at one site or the other, but they all ultimately report here." Her eyelid twitches again.

I turn to JP and give him a blank stare. He gets it. "Before we begin reviewing the policies and procedures, I wonder if we can tour the facility. It would be helpful to see the layout, and later, we would like to speak to a few employees."

JP nods. "*Oui*, that would be helpful, Ms. Kaechele."

She turns up her nose at us. "Of course, please follow me."

JP, Parker, and I are led out of the conference room and asked to don white Tyvek suits and booties. We are given N95 respirator masks required in some manufacturing laboratories to prevent contamination. The first lab is a fairly standard research laboratory with small bench-top equipment, a tabletop centrifuge, pipetting stands and pipettes, test tube shakers, and vortex mixers on high-grade phenolic countertops. Rows of lab stools neatly tuck between lab drawers and counters—some occupied, and others not. There are standard tissue wipes for laboratory use and plastic film for covering beakers, flasks, and test tubes. Some of the staff stop what they are doing and stare at us.

We are taken to several similar laboratories, and I drop back, alerting everyone that I would like to use the lavatory and will catch up with the group back in the conference room. Ms. Kaechele gives me directions and offers to have me escorted. I decline. JP nods and continues the tour with Parker. I remove my booties, slip out the closest door, and head to the airplane hangar.

I stop at the side door of the hangar to catch my breath. My heart pounds against my chest. A bitter taste reaches my mouth. My breaths get shallow.

If I'm gone too long, there might be an incident.

I'm in luck. The side door is unlocked, and I slip inside. My eyes adjust. I get my bearings. There's a small airplane. Conscious of what JP and Parker told me, I study the outline. The plane is not in the shape of a triangle—a wing. The company's name is printed on the tail, with some numbers. Expansive front windows sit above the nose, and twelve smaller windows line the fuselage. It's a corporate jet—nothing special. I use my phone to snap a few shots as I sidle up to the plane.

I want to touch the frame. It seems like typical metal, but I want to be sure.

"Hey, what are you doing there?" A shout echoes across the hangar. A man wearing a white jumpsuit strides across the vast expanse.

I inhale sharply. The man speaks English, and I'm unsure if I should answer. I wave like I'm supposed to be here. My heart races, and sticky sweat collects under my jumpsuit. I slide around to where I entered and pull on the door.

It sticks.

"Stop. What are you doing?" His hand waves in the air, and I wave back, hoping he won't follow.

I pull harder until it finally gives.

The cool air chills my wet body. I look back. I'm not being followed.

The main building in the distance appears farther now than before. I get back to the facility without incident. My booties are where I left them.

"Dr. Laurent," Karin says when I enter the conference room. "Did you get lost on your way, or on your way back, from the WC? I should have given you an escort." Her tone is sharp, and she looks down her nose at me.

She's guessed I took a stroll across the grounds, but I smile politely. Does she assume I was looking for further violations or something else? I bury my nose in the hard copies of NovoGeneOne's policies and procedures—no centralized computer manuals for me. Much of the information is in English.

After a couple of hours plowing through the documents, I ask to visit a lab to talk to some technicians at the bench. One young man sitting by himself, a microtiter plate in front of him, appears vulnerable. I introduce myself and ask if he speaks English.

I see him eye my ID and nod.

"Hello, Doctor. How can I help you?"

Karin is with JP while he interviews another tech, and Parker walks around the lab looking at equipment.

I smile. "I'd like to ask you a few questions."

He sits up straight and waits.

"How long have you been working here?"

A supervisor swoops in. We're interrupted.

She looks me in the eye. "I am happy to help you with your questions."

I take a step back. "I was just asking this young man how long he's worked here."

He sticks his head between the supervisor and me. "About five years. I came soon after I graduated from school."

The supervisor takes a breath, and I ignore her, directing my question to the bench tech.

"Have you any concerns about your safety in handling any of the compounds?"

"Not really. I wear my disposable PPE."

He's wearing a protective coverall like the rest of us.

"I can see that. Do you do any cloning in this laboratory?"

He's quiet for a moment, thinking or hesitating, I'm not sure. He looks at his supervisor.

"I do."

I nod. "Is this the only laboratory that does cloning?"

The supervisor answers. "We clone certain cells and compounds in the main facility, but we also have techs who work off-site."

"By off-site, you mean where?" I'm surprised she is so forthcoming. But why wouldn't she be? It's an inspection, and being difficult with the inspectors never helps.

"Sydney. We occasionally get information via email that originates in Australia."

My ears perk up, and I'm quite anxious to finish this line of questioning before Karin comes over and stops it. "I see. You wouldn't happen to have any of those emails for me to see."

The tech shifts his eyes to his desk and then to the computer screen.

The supervisor glares at me. "We cannot reveal company emails. But if you would like more information, ask Ms. Kaechele about what we receive from Sydney."

Karin Kaechele shoots a glance my way, and I take that as my cue to walk away from this tech and his supervisor.

I catch up with Parker, who is chatting with another tech. "I think I have everything I need."

Parker nods, and we join JP and Karin.

"Ms. Kaechele, we've spoken with a few techs, and if Dr. Lavigne is satisfied, I would like to return to the conference room."

JP nods.

We are first taken to an area where we can discard our PPE. I check my hair in the mirror. My blond wig looks stylish, and sometimes I wonder what it would be like to really be blond.

Once we are in the conference room, Karin leaves, and we give each other discerning glances. I write an official note saying we have not uncovered anything untoward and believe the complaint was unfounded. We save any discussion of our findings on NovoGeneOne's activity outside of what is expected when we return to the car.

JP has the wording down perfectly. "Ms. Kaechele, here is a preliminary note regarding our findings," he says, handing her a form with handwritten notes. "It appears that the laboratory is compliant with the biomonitoring standards for those who work with dangerous chemicals. In addition, your staff told members of my team they felt safe working here. The PPE that you provide is adequate for their protection."

I nod, and we collect our papers and leave the facility. When I turn to look back, Karin is watching through the glass doors, no doubt to make sure we reach our car.

Parker closes my door before getting into the passenger seat, and we are off.

JP begins. "Robinson, were you able to get what we were after?"

"Of course."

Once we are back at the hotel, we retreat to our rooms to freshen up before gathering to discuss more of our findings. I pull off the blond wig and shake my long, dark locks. The heavy makeup comes off easily, and the brown contacts land in the waste bin.

Parker's suite has fresh coffee and pastries, and I sit with a thump in the chair, eager to eat and talk. JP and Parker have clean-shaven faces, having disposed of their fake facial hair, and I like the way they look. This is how I picture them when we are not together.

I grab a warm almond croissant and take a bite, followed by a sip of hot coffee. "JP, you were wrong about the airplane hangar. What I saw was a corporate jet. Plain and simple. I snapped a few pictures."

JP takes my phone and skims through the photographs. "This does appear to be what it is—a NovoGeneOne jet. *Mais*, I am sure there has to be another plane or at least some drones. Another facility must be in proximity of the complex we visited today."

"We only focused on NovoGeneOne. We should broaden our search for airfields to the surrounding area," Parker says.

I scratch my head, still a little itchy from the wig. "Are there any old military bases around? They might make a good place to hide a plane."

JP pulls up a map of the area on his phone and clicks on all the possibilities. "There is an airfield north of Ghent. Since it is close to NovoGeneOne, it is a possibility."

Parker does a quick internet search on his phone. "That one was a former military base. And this operation stinks of the military. I agree with JP. We should check it out."

JP nods. "*Mais*, if this plane or its prototype exists, was it commissioned for the military?"

"Makes sense. Military types want toys they can play with on the world stage. Who's got the biggest, baddest dick. This plane would be a game changer." Parker pauses and then stares at me. "Doc, didn't you tell us there was a military guy on NovoGeneOne's board?"

"I did. Chad is looking deeper into the board members. So, we were probably right about the connection between NovoGeneOne and the deaths of the climate scientists. It wasn't so much about the climate as about what they stumbled on."

Parker agrees. "Doc, you said NovoGeneOne uses scientists in Australia for some cloning work. Maybe contracted. I overheard two techs talking about data from a Dr. Watson, but I couldn't figure out if that Watson works in Bruges or Sydney."

"Hmm. Dr. Watson. A common enough name. Like James Watson, who, along with Francis Crick and Rosalind Franklin, discovered the

DNA double helix."

"You think this is a relative?" Parker asks.

I laugh. "No, Parker. Sometimes I can't believe you're serious. I'm merely thinking out loud. Making an association between the two names. I don't think we met any Dr. Watsons in Sydney, but then we only visited the aquarium and the ME's office."

Parker frowns. "JP, there was no Watson listed among the Climate Council members, was there?"

"I do not recall."

I make a face. "Damn. I wish Sara was around so I could ask her if she knew any Watsons in Sydney."

JP brings us back to NovoGeneOne. "While we are contemplating Watsons, from what I observed of NovoGeneOne's policies and procedures, work is done in silos, and each section is unaware of how other sections operate."

"So, this could explain how some cloning work could be done in Sydney, and the person there might not be aware of the bigger picture." Parker takes a big bite of a chocolate something and washes it down with coffee.

I nod. "Agree, Parker."

"We should return to the facility and speak with Ilse Knight," JP says. "The visit today only established the contents of the hangar, not NovoGeneOne's involvement."

"If there is one," I add.

JP scratches the top of his head. "We will return under the pretext of Climate Council business and see."

"That's doable," Parker says. "Karin Kaechele said she thought Dr. Knight would be back tomorrow morning. The inspection wasn't announced, so she wouldn't have known to be onsite."

I nod. "That's true. Leadership might be engaged elsewhere for any unannounced inspection, so laboratories ensure backup—people who understand the process and can provide the information." JP contemplates his hands. What is he thinking?

"JP, when should we go to see Ilse Knight?"

The creases in his cheeks deepen, and the furrows around his eyes intensify. "There is still twenty-four-hour protection for Dr. Lundberg, *oui*?"

"Sure as shit, boss."

"JP, you're worried that Lundberg is the next target."

"I am concerned that he possesses some sensitive information and could be targeted. In addition to Harmon and Lundberg, someone knew what Williams saw and photographed and wanted to protect that information from leaking. They also assumed Williams shared the information with his fellow climatologists. This Climate Council conference is just a distraction. *Mais*, the killer, may attempt to finish the job knowing Lundberg is the connection."

"Or Ilse Knight."

Parker stands. "And time is running out. I'll check with Chad to see if we can track down Watson."

JP commands. "We need to find that plane. It is Ghent tomorrow and the abandoned airfield. Now, I would like Robinson to come with me."

"What's this about, JP?"

A subtle smile crosses his face. "I want to see the Atomium."

So, with business done for now, we drive to the Atomium, where the banquet dinner on the last night of the Council meeting will be held. Constructed for the 1958 World's Fair held in Brussels, the exhibit represented a future positive relationship with the atom after mankind had harvested the devastating power of the atom bomb used in WWII. The monument, built to look like a basic iron crystal magnified 165 billion times, underwent renovation in the 2000s to fortify the construction from the Expo58 original, which was considered only a temporary exhibit then. Time only increased its popularity, and when the flimsy aluminum was replaced with steel, it expanded its ground-floor exhibit and created a concrete esplanade at the entrance. The structure looms 335ft, or 102 meters tall, and houses permanent cultural exhibits in the lower spheres. Two levels house archived documents, photographs, and videos of the history of the Atomium.

I gasp as we pull up to the metal Goliath. "It wasn't that long ago that we had dinner in the Panoramic Restaurant. I recall an exhilarating ride in the elevator to the top." I poke JP in the arm, hoping he remembers our evening. They were heady days—full of excitement and bravado.

"*Mais oui*. We left the NATO lunch, spent the afternoon touring the city, and then had a romantic evening together. We have had many missions together, my Lily. Some more memorable than others."

He grabs my hand and squeezes it, forcing a purr from my lips. Although the exhibit is closed for the day, I look forward to the Climate Council banquet. May there be no drama—only champagne and a panoramic view of the city.

CHAPTER 21

URSEL, BELGIUM

Hours before the sun comes up, we are on the road to Ghent. Night is still with us, but JP wants to approach the abandoned airbase under cover of darkness.

"Chad sent some information last night. Parker, please read the email."

"Sure thing, boss. Chad gave us the intel on the NovoGeneOne board members. One guy does catch my attention. He's a retired Admiral from the U.S., and, get this, he's retired to Australia."

"You think he could be behind all this?" I ask.

"He's the only person on the board with connections to the military. It doesn't mean he could be the only board member involved, but it's a start."

I nod and wonder if Parker will get motion sickness from reading in the car.

"The guy's never been married. He's also an avid scuba diver and boating enthusiast. Kind of fits right in with the crowd we've been investigating," Parker says.

"Is there any connection with Holly Miller?" I can't shake the feeling that she's involved somehow.

"Chad doesn't say, but the Admiral's on the donor list for gifts to the aquarium."

"Wow. I'm going to assume they're connected. That would put Holly right in the middle of all this." I make a mental note to review everything I know about Holly.

JP concentrates on driving while Parker and I discuss various NovoGeneOne board members. He slows the car as we approach Ursel, a city north of Ghent.

"This is the abandoned air base built in the 1930s and used after the German invasion in 1940. It became known as Airfield B67 after four squadrons of the RAF landed there. They were flying the Typhoon fighter bomber and targeted the German troops on the Dutch island of Walcheren, which controlled the entrance to the harbors at Anver, otherwise known as Antwerp in Dutch," JP says as the car slows.

"No one uses it now that we know of?" I press my nose to the car window to get a better view.

"The airfield was destroyed after the war and bought by some private investors. Much of the land was used for agriculture, *mais*, as you can see, they rebuilt the runway, and there is a large airplane hangar in the distance."

Even in the dark, the curved metal housing looks imposing and larger than the hangar I saw on the NovoGeneOne grounds. "How do you expect we will get in there."

JP starts up the engine and pulls the car around under a set of trees. "You wait here. I am going over the fence, or through it." He pulls out some wire cutters from a bag under the front seat.

"Boss, you need coverage. Let me go with you."

"We only have about two hours before the sun rises. Parker, give me ten minutes. Robinson, keep watch and text us if you see anything or anyone. Follow the plan."

I wrinkle up my nose and let out a huff. But I get it. Those two will get themselves killed, while I have to drive the car back to Brussels myself.

"Okay, JP. Good luck, you two."

JP heads out first, and I see him cut through the chain link and sneak toward the hangar. We assume there are video cameras on the grounds, so JP and Parker are dressed in dark clothing and wear balaclava masks to hide their faces.

My fingers curl into my palms while I wait. I check my personal phone for any messages. Kelley lets me know that, per the medical examiner, drug overdoses in Boston continue to skyrocket. Most of it is due to fentanyl. There seems to be no stopping precursor drugs from leaving China for Mexico, where the cartels can manufacture fentanyl with ease. That potent opioid is finding its way into all the illicit drugs—heroin, cocaine, methamphetamine, and even fake oxycodone pills.

My watch signals it's been thirty minutes. The sun should be up soon. I close my eyes for a moment.

I jump. An unexpected rap on the car window. Damn. The hairs on my arms stand at attention. My hand instinctively goes to my eyes as the flashlight shines brightly on my face. A man dressed in military gear motions for me to step out of the car. He's speaking Flemish, so I don't understand his exact words. Before I open the car door, I send a pre-arranged signal to JP and Parker to alert them. I slip the phone down the front of my slacks.

With my prettiest smile, I exit the car. "I'm sorry, I got lost on my way back from Bruges. Do you speak English?"

He scrutinizes me and motions with his rifle for me to move away from the car. He opens the back door and pokes around. Then, opens the trunk. It's a rental, so there is nothing there. JP took the wire cutters with him.

My heart's pounding.

"Excuse me. I was trying to retrace my steps to Ghent." I flash an even bigger smile and try fluttering my eyelashes.

His face remains blank. "Get your car," he says, not quite getting all the words out in English. I'm not sure he understood what I was saying, but I won't argue.

Vroom—the engine starts, and I slowly pull away. Another smile, another wave. I drive about a mile before stopping, text JP and Parker, noting my location, and wait.

An hour later, I see them walking along the road, outlined by the rising sun. I retreat to the back of the car, and JP and Parker assume their usual places.

"Thank god. I had a military guy in my face."

"*Mais,* you handled it," JP says as if it happens all the time.

A bit of steam creeps under my blouse. I ignore it. "So, what did you find out?"

JP swings onto the road, and we head back to Brussels.

"The hangar houses a winged aircraft. It is unfinished. Perhaps a prototype. There were also substantial drones of a similar design. The larger plane is set up to be a stealth bomber. I briefly ran my hand over the frame like you suggested. A possible biological skin fused to the metal. There are a few pictures on my phone."

Parker, who did not go inside the hangar, takes the phone and scans the photos. "There's a cockpit in that big fucker, so that's not a drone. I'll forward the pics to Chad, and he can get some of our military guys to look at it." He hands me the phone.

"Simulated shark skin. Is that what you felt, JP? Scientists have created a way to clone shark skin embedded with photophores. They did it. The science here is remarkable."

"Remarkable, maybe, but this plane and the drones are a threat.

Chad said there were rumors about a novel weapon delivery system," JP says.

"Do you think Ilse Knight is behind this? I mean, I think if this Admiral is on her board, she might know something." I take a few deep breaths to gather my thoughts.

JP steps on the gas once we hit the E40. "Let us find out."

Now back at the hotel, the morning light pours through the window and highlights JP's and my go-to breakfast of coffee and croissants. Parker chose to go back to his room and will meet with us later.

I pick the chocolate pastry. "I'm curious about Ilse Knight. She's such an accomplished woman—scientist, politician, CEO—hard to believe she would be mixed up in all this."

JP pours another cup of coffee, the first having gone down quickly. "As you said yesterday, we do not know her involvement." He pauses, and his fingers linger on the handle of the coffee cup. The creases around his eyes multiply as he captures my full attention. "Stopping an assassin set on derailing the climate conference is our mission. What worries me more is that we found an aircraft that could possess extraordinary military capabilities. Perhaps, as Lundberg said, it is not as much about climate change as it is about what the climate scientists discovered."

"And Lundberg, unknowingly, may have tipped off Ilse Knight about the discoveries. If her company *is* involved, Lundberg could be the next target."

JP nods and takes a sip of his coffee. He closes his eyes for a moment, then asks, "What if the technology is for sale?"

"What are you saying?"

"This technology could be used as a novel weapon. *Et* very desirable to any military in the world. For all we know, this project was commissioned."

"God, JP. Then the assassin wanted to stop Williams and Harmon from making the connection between the krill and shark photophores and this technology."

"I think they already suspected that, and that is what they planned to reveal at the Climate Council conference."

"But if the technology used in this plane was developed by private industry, no one has the right to stop it. Right?"

"*C'est vrai. Mais*, it does not mean it cannot be sabotaged so it will not fall into the wrong hands. We have done this before."

JP is right. He and I stopped a Chinese missile scientist from sharing his technological designs with North Korea, and at the start of our partnership, we eliminated a Cambridge professor for his revolutionary encryption technology. The good of the many.

"But JP, they'll just build another one."

"There are international laws about the use of chemical and nuclear weapons. This plane could fall into the same category if exposed."

"What if it's for a NATO contract?"

JP shakes his head. "There are many possibilities. Did you not tell me that in your Star Trek universe, cloaking ships were banned by the Federation? Those ships were mainly used as offensive weapons—a surprise attack on the enemy. Offensive technology could be banned if it came to light."

I laugh. "I'm so impressed you paid attention to my musings about Star Trek."

"I heard every word." He flashes a toothy smile and winks. Is there a lightness taking over him? Does he see his future differently than at the start of our mission?

"So, it doesn't matter which side of the world wants this ship."

"In my opinion, *no. Mais*, Chad should have some information for us later today." JP stands, wanders to the window, and stares at the street below.

We have traveled to many places together and have seen so much over the years. Yet, my lover's craggy facial lines have deepened with worry, his hair grayer. Our missions in Asia and the shootings in Washington at the Air and Space Museum have taken their toll. I've never seen JP so reflective as he's been lately.

I amble up behind him, wrap my arms around his waist, and rest my face on his back. "Hey, what's up with you? You have been so strange on this trip. I mean, since we got to Brussels."

He turns around and pulls me in tight. "My Lily, *ma chérie,* you are beautiful in the morning light." He strokes my hair. "Come to bed with me."

My eyes widen. "Now? We're in the middle of a discussion about a serious topic."

"The perfect time for a distraction."

We sit on the bed, and his kisses sweep my lips, then my neck. His hands are gentle, and I feel his fingers on my breast. His breaths warm my ear and my heart. My head finds the pillow, and JP unbuttons my blouse while speaking to me in French. Some words I understand, and others I do not. In return, I unbutton his shirt and kiss his chest.

"Jean Paul, what's wrong?" I feel his stormy brooding surround me.

He rolls back onto the bed and pulls me to his chest. I can hear his heart beating—fast, steady—and in step with mine.

"Lily, when this assignment is over, I will return to France. I would like to spend time with my cousin Adrienne at the vineyards, my boyhood home in Reims."

I bolt upright. "You've made up your mind."

"It is time."

"And your job with Chad? What about that?" My heart starts racing. I take a few deep breaths.

"I was wrong when I said I would do this until I die. I want something different."

"What about me, JP? Are you saying you want someone different than me? Is there someone else?"

He sniffs. And smiles. "You have called us soulmates. I believe we are. There is no one but you. Come live with me in France. We could find happiness without danger."

A huge breath escapes my chest. I have seen this man change in a way I never thought possible. I could have a real life if we lived in Reims. Adrienne and Rose would learn who I am. How JP and I are connected. Can we do this? Can I do this?

"My job at the hospital?"

"My Lily, you are talented and resourceful. You can lecture using virtual conferences and spend time in Boston as you wish. I understand this is a big ask."

A big ask? No shit, James Bond. My mind is spinning. I open my mouth to speak, and he puts his finger on my lips, then his lips. My back arcs.

His hands are warm on my skin, his tongue wet. We melt into one another, hot wax dripping into hot wax. Our bodies drift across the horizon, beyond the visual, and disappear from view. We are one now, and I know what my decision will be. I find myself free-floating.

We arrive at NovoGeneOne around midday. Sunrays reflect off the large, tinted windows and hit my eyes as I step out of the car. I shift my hand to my face, forming a protective shield.

JP greets the receptionist, someone different than the person at the desk when we had the unannounced inspection. After a few minutes, Ilse Knight's assistant asks us to follow as we make our way to Dr. Knight's office.

The waiting room outside has two comfortable chairs for JP and me, and since Ilse Knight wasn't expecting us, her administrative assistant went off to locate her. That makes me think of my assistant, Lisa. I'm sure she is taking good care of Dr. Kelley.

After ten minutes, the assistant returns and informs us that Dr. Knight will be here shortly. JP and I nod, and she hands us each a coffee. I never had a chance to finish mine this morning.

Voices fill the hall, and the assistant stands up and nods.

"Dr. Knight, these are your visitors on behalf of the Climate Council."

JP and I introduce ourselves.

Ilse Knight smiles. "Please, won't you come into my office?" She opens her arm and points the way.

The office is modern. A sleek white table for her desk, reminiscent of my own, and comfortable looking chairs of metal and mesh. Only one or two files on the desk. No clutter of huge piles of papers. There are two bookcases containing volumes on oceanography and marine law, and some photographs on the wall.

"I see my assistant brought you some coffee. I favor tea myself." She plugs in her electric tea kettle and fills a mesh tea ball with loose tea before placing it in her cup. "Now, I understand you are here regarding the Climate Council. You do recognize I am no longer the Chair." She shakes her head, and her gray hair sways. "Lundberg said I might expect you."

"*Oui,* madame. *Mais,* we have concerns for your safety and Dr. Lundberg's. Several Council members have died under suspicious circumstances, and we are seeking information."

Knight examines her hands. They are bare with brown spots and crepiness. Thin, more fragile skin comes with advanced years, and although her face appears more youthful—fewer wrinkles—her hands betray her.

"Yes, I am aware of the deaths of Drs. Williams, Harmon, and Patel. Most distressing. I knew them all. They were admirable researchers and well known in the field of marine science."

A whistle of steam blows from the kettle, and Ilse pours the boiling liquid over the tea ball in her cup. Holding the chain, she dips the ball up and down, obtaining just the right strength for her drink.

"Are you aware of anyone who would want to harm Council members? Have you had any threats on your own life?" JP asks.

"I have focused my energy on my company since I left the Council. I'm sure you are aware that we harvest biologicals from the ocean with the hope of discovering new and exciting drug therapies."

I lean forward in my chair. "I'm curious. Do any of your projects use cloning techniques?"

"To the extent that I do not reveal any trade secrets." Ilse pours the tea into her teacup, her eyes following the steam. "Water covers seventy-five percent of the earth's surface. The pharmacology of marine organisms has yet to be fully explored. They come in the form of plants and animals, and we screen these organisms for anti-inflammatory, anti-fungal, and antibacterial activity. They may contain anticancer, neuroprotective, or analgesic properties. Once we identify the important molecules, we can use our gene technology to create a potential drug for study."

"Other than drug discovery, do you use your technology for any other kind of research?"

"I'm not sure I understand." She sips her tea, which has now cooled.

"I mean, is it possible the technology you have developed here could be used for other purposes?"

"Of course. The technology we use is widely available. We may have modified certain techniques to improve them for our desired outcomes, but for the most part, we follow standard laboratory practices."

I shake my head. "Perhaps these three scientists discovered something related to your company's work."

Ilse squirms in her chair. "I can't imagine why you would think that."

"We believe certain cloning technology you may have developed could have been used for other purposes."

Ilse raises her eyebrows. "I pride myself on knowing the intricacies of my company. However, I admit I am unfamiliar with every employee and their projects. If you want specific information, I can have one of my people talk to you."

"Thank you for that. It would help us greatly with our investigation. One more thing, I'm curious if you have an ocean research vessel."

She narrows her eyes. "We do. Our research vessel is currently off the coast of Australia. The marine life there is rich for potential discoveries."

"Has your ship ever sailed in the Southern Ocean?"

Ilse licks her lips. "Most likely. The oceans, Dr. Robinson, as I'm sure you know, are continuous. Each part of the planet has its share bathing its coasts—some warm, some cold—environments with creatures that have adapted to different temperatures and salinity."

"Has your company done any research on Antarctic krill?"

"You are curious." She brushes the front of her black suit jacket while collecting her thoughts. "I'm certain we have looked at a variety of sea creatures, given our line of work." A frown crosses her face. "Now, if you have no more questions, I need to return to my business." She sips her tea.

Tension fills the room. Ilse's eyes meet mine, and I feel a chill run up my spine. Two women sizing each other up. Ilse's mobile phone rings, and our moment is broken.

"Will you excuse me, please?" She steps outside to take the call.

JP puts his hand on my thigh. "What are you doing?"

"I'm not sure. Maybe I said too much. Then again, Ilse wouldn't tell us if she did use the novel technology to create a stealth weapon." Pushing back my chair, I stand. "I wouldn't."

My uneasiness causes me to pace the office, checking the books in the bookcase for specific titles, and the pictures on the wall. I'm captivated by one photo showing a marine research vessel named James Cook, knowing he was an early British explorer. The assembly of people on the deck appears to be more than research scientists and crew because there are children in the picture. I can see a duffle bag to the right of the crowd with the words Woods Hole printed in distinct white letters. This picture must have been taken in Massachusetts. There are other familiar features on the dock that remind me of my time there.

Was this a family day for an outing at sea? I scrutinize the photo more carefully, looking for clues. Another man wears a sweatshirt with Woods Hole printed on the upper right corner, and a woman wears a ball cap with the same logo. Two people catch my eye. There's a younger Ilse, a smile on her face and her brown hair in a bob. Next to her is a boy who looks around ten years old, and next to him is a man with wild dark hair. I move in for a closer look, my nose almost touching the glass. I assume this is Ilse and her husband and child. I can barely make out the wedding ring on her finger, with her arm wrapped around the boy. She wears no wedding ring today. The husband's face is familiar, but I'm having trouble placing it. I pride myself in remembering faces—features and eye color. And then it hits me.

My heart beats wildly, and I let out a gasp.

"Lily, what is it? The color is drained from your face," he says with urgency.

"This photograph. It shows a young Ilse with whom I presume was her husband and child. I recognize the husband. JP, I know this man." My voice is sharp and shaky. I sit down next to JP before Ilse returns. I grab his hand.

"The man in the photograph is the man I assassinated all those years ago in Cambridge. I'm sure of it." I press down hard on my knee to stop the incessant bobbing.

"Are you sure?" I can hear JP draw in a deep breath.

"You know I'm sure."

CHAPTER 22

GHENT, BELGIUM

The autobody shop said removing the dents in his car would take two weeks. He nodded and told the shop owner there were some shit ass drivers on the road these days. Sideswiped. They never even stopped. The Admiral left with his rental. The climate scientists had been easily eliminated, but the original plan hadn't anticipated these other interlopers. He returned to his apartment and made some decisions about Holly.

The Admiral had been stationed in Australia during a stint with the Navy and fell in love with the country. Enamored with the environment, Sydney became his destination when he retired. Married only to his command, there were no wife and family to restrict his freedom. Never lonely, the Admiral had no trouble finding lovers along the way. As a younger man, he had a thick head of sandy hair and filled out his six-foot frame with good bones and hard muscle. Women found him handsome with his angular face, strong chin, and bushy eyebrows that feathered over deep-set blue eyes.

The Admiral and Ilse Knight had crossed paths years ago when he worked for the National Oceanic and Atmospheric Administration

Corps (NOAA Corps), mapping the seafloor. There had been some flirting back then, but Ilse was married, so he kept his fly zipped. Until that one time on the boat. Ready for a dive, the Admiral and Ilse put their regulators in their mouths, held their masks with their palms, and jumped over the side, making a splash. The others were already in the water. After about thirty minutes, Ilse moved her hand in a slicing motion across her throat. The cloud of bubbles grew larger and came faster until there were none. The Admiral watched Ilse's eyes grow wide under her mask. Then he nodded and shared his regulator until they reached the surface. Ilse gasped when she broke over the waves. She coughed as a splash of water entered her mouth. They swam to the ladder and removed their fins.

Her voice was breathy. "What the hell happened there? I checked my gear before I went into the water." Her white knuckles gripped the ladder railings as she lost her footing.

He took her arm and eased her up. "Don't know. But sometimes there are failures." Yet the Admiral did know. He had drained the tank of some air while Ilse wasn't looking.

After stripping off their wetsuits, Ilse returned to the cabin to change. Banking on her vulnerability, he came up behind her and soothed her trembling body.

The breath trapped in her chest escaped with a sigh. She turned and looked at him. "Thank you for being my buddy. I couldn't have made it to the surface without you." She'd become a prisoner of those deep blue eyes.

"You're safe now." He stroked her damp hair, and she let him kiss her. And he stepped out of his wet shorts and made love to her.

They kept in touch over the years, and when Ilse asked him to be on the board of her start-up NovoGeneOne, he accepted with pleasure. Ilse Knight knew a great many influential people through her various careers—science, politics, business—and the Admiral took advantage of those connections. As a NovoGeneOne board member, he became privy to information on drug discovery and the innovative technology used to fine-tune the breakthroughs. He funneled NovoGeneOne's IP to other countries and made money doing it. Yet, his one big regret was his failure to accumulate great wealth during his lifetime. There was always more. His mind buzzed with the possibilities.

The Admiral enjoyed spending time at the MWDU aquarium in Sydney and frequently attended their seminars. One evening, he heard Dr. Holly Miller speak about her work. He approached her after the talk to learn more about her field of expertise.

A smile reached to the very edges of his cheeks. "What a fascinating seminar on the speciation of krill. Who knew whale food could be so exciting." He touched her arm as if with a feather and saw her head turn and look at his hand.

"I'm glad you liked it. Are you a fellow scientist?" Her eyes were violet, and bore into his.

"I'd like to learn more about your work. You." He searched her eyes.

He waited for the reaction. Her lips parted, her shoulders dropped. Hooked like a fish.

Holly started talking.

As he listened, the idea percolated through his mind—Holly Miller would be the key to developing the perfect military weapon. But how could he get this scientist to help him with his plan? Time would give him the answer.

The Admiral set up several meetings with Holly to learn more about her work, and soon, meetings turned into lunches and dinners. He found Holly attractive and intelligent, but mostly independent, untethered by convention. He thought her behavior was more about provocation—crazy eye contacts or sneakers with blinding colors, her bravado "pets"—as a way to distance herself. But mostly, he found her needing someone to hold on to. A sea fan without its anchor. He became the bedrock.

In the months that followed, he and Holly dived the Great Barrier Reef many times and sailed his forty-foot sloop in the beautiful waters off the coast of Australia and New Zealand. His exploitative personal radar had detected rare skills in Holly Miller during their first encounters that would guarantee success in a project already underway. Cultivation of a close relationship—trust, as he understood it—was paramount.

Holly had been guarded initially. Reluctant to share the beginnings of her life, the Admiral viewed her as greenwood and whittled away each time they met. He heard about her mother's affair with an older scientist, the life-altering events that followed, and recognized a little girl's anxiety as Holly's voice changed when speaking of her father. How secure she had felt in her father's lap and how he doted on her, declared her a prodigy, and looked forward to the day she would join him in his laboratory. The Admiral mirrored those feelings and extolled her genius each time she told him of her discoveries.

But Holly's father's death tormented her. Ate away at her like a worm inside an apple. She had been the apple of his eye. So, given the span between their ages, the Admiral played the father figure that Holly missed and craved. He knew he had found the perfect mark.

About six months into the relationship, Holly became the Admiral's lover. He hadn't pushed it, although he wanted to. Holly's desire for protection in the arms of an older man fueled their physical bond. It also satisfied his need for a woman. They never openly acknowledged their relationship. When they were together in public, they refrained from any displays of affection. Each kept their own home in Sydney, and the Admiral also had a small pied-à-terre in Ghent.

His current project, funded by Global Tectonics (GT), was housed in an airplane hangar near Ursel. The location had been arranged through the Admiral's military connections, the same connections that introduced him to GT. At the time, Global Tectonics was rumored to be Russian affiliated. But as the oligarchs distanced themselves from the state, they focused on the business of making money without a political agenda. Businessmen first with no allegiance to anyone. GT's acquisition of the mining rights to rare earth minerals meant the production of advanced communication systems and future aviation technology was in their grasp. They desired to create winged aircraft—full planes and drones—with stealth capabilities based on organic properties. They expected a bidding war among Russia, China, the Middle East, and North Korea. What they didn't anticipate was the terrorist factions and guns for hire to also show interest. The Admiral's share in the deal would allow him to live in luxury for the rest of his life.

He tidied up his apartment and reviewed the notes on his desk about the upcoming meeting at the hangar. Only a bit longer, and the money would be in the bank. Maybe he'd sail around the world. The Admiral poured himself a scotch and sat on the couch. What to do with Holly? She'd served her purpose. The carrot worked. He never needed the stick. He swirled the drink in his glass, tipped back his head, and let the scotch slide down his throat. The short burn cleared his mind.

CHAPTER 23

BRUSSELS, BELGIUM

Goosebumps cover me almost the entire drive from Bruges to Brussels. The world is a blur as I stare out the window and allow my mind to run free. Ilse Knight was the collateral damage I never knew. Now, in the safety of our hotel room, we discuss the revelation further.

"JP, this is madness. What have we stumbled onto?" I throw myself onto the bed, shaking my head. "I assassinated her husband. Didn't I?"

The ruby forming the snake's head of my grandmother's ring gleams while the gold tail embedded with diamonds wraps around my finger with a serpent's grip. Instinctively, I twist it and search JP's face.

He strokes my hair and nods. I can tell, looking into those blue-green eyes, that trouble has found its way into his heart. He grabs me by the shoulders and pulls me towards him.

"*Oui*. Let us assume that Ilse Knight was the wife of the scientist you took out in Cambridge." JP pauses, "His name, Lily?"

A noisy breath leaves my chest. My throat tightens. "Ian Watson." I twist the ring a few more times.

"*Oui*, Ian Watson, who was about to betray his country."

"I can still see the dossier Pixie Dust left me. This man had been treated for a fainting spell after running a 5K road race in Cambridge when he was younger. During his workup at one of the Boston teaching hospitals, it was discovered he had Long QT Syndrome—a defect in the ion channels that allow small molecules such as sodium, potassium, and calcium to move in and out of heart muscle cells. It's the movement of these ions that produces the electrical activity in the heart, causing the heart to beat."

"Forget his medical condition." His voice is sharp. "Let me get Chad to track down the information from that time. Pixie Dust ran the team then, not Chad."

"Of course, I remember that." Now my words come out with a bite. This is not JP's fault.

JP calls Chad to see what he can find about the mission regarding the death of Ian Watson. I push off my heels and pace around the room. Acid swirls in my stomach, and I wonder if this is getting personal.

Does Ilse Knight suspect I had anything to do with her husband's death? Is she out for revenge? But why kill the scientists if it's only me she wants? I remember Ian Watson had been on medication for his disorder for most of his adult life, with maybe one additional syncopal episode. I initially felt calm when I sat next to him at the dinner. We were able to converse about science, although his field was far from mine. It was hard to believe he had sold out his country. To me, he appeared only as an eccentric, with wild gray hair and stormy dark eyes.

JP is still holding while Chad finds out more about Ilse Knight. We only inquired about her scientific background previously, not her personal life. It's time to reapply my lipstick, and I return to my room.

"Lily, are you all right?"

I hear JP's gentle rap on the door. "I am."

I pull him inside and scan his face. Frown lines greet me, and the thump in my chest grows louder.

"What? What did you find out?"

JP clears his throat. "Ian Watson was married to Ilse Watson née Knight. They divorced sometime after he got another woman pregnant, whom he later married. When we met him in Cambridge, he was already married to his second wife."

"Please don't tell me they had a little girl." I'm jumping out on a limb here. My imagination runs wild, and my antacids beckon me.

"*Oui*. Holly."

I gasp; my feet feel anchored to the floor. "So, it's possible that Dr. Holly Miller is also Dr. Holly Watson. Is she working with Ilse Knight? Is all this about retribution, climate change, or evil weapons?"

"Either all of the above or only one of the above."

"It's not an exam question, JP." I pop two antacids in my mouth.

"Ah, Lily, we do not have all the answers." He sounds dismissive to me. I'm thinking of my personal safety.

I bring the conversation back to Ilse and Holly. "What's their endgame? Do they realize we were the ones who murdered Ian Watson?"

"I do not believe so. As you are fond of saying, 'true, true, and unrelated.' I was there under an assumed name representing a foundation, and you attended the dinner at the behest of an academic colleague. There is nothing that ties us to Ian Watson's death."

"Maybe not you. But if you remember, I was window dressing with poison. I was there under my real name." Regret shifts through my thoughts.

"*C'est vrai. Mais*, you were among other academic colleagues. A bona fide doctor at the event."

Despite the antacids, the bitter taste creeps to the back of my throat. "Holly's mother may have known who her husband spent his last night with. Or someone might know."

"My Lily, we had not thought about that night until you reminded me when we were up at your cottage before we left on this assignment."

JP is right. I'd been reminiscing about meeting Pixie Dust. Then, knowing I was going to South Africa, memories of my relationship with Charles and our daughter Rose got stirred into the pot. It's bubbling like a witch's brew.

"If you believe Holly knew your role in her father's death, she could have confronted you at the medical school years ago."

When I met Holly for the first time at the aquarium, there was no aha moment. JP is right that her suspicions of me had more to do with my relationship with Sara. But the attack?

"So, you're saying it's just a coincidence that we met this Holly Watson twenty-something years later? If that's true, why did she come after me, if it was her who put the spider in my hotel room?"

"First, we are not certain it was Holly. *Mais*, if it was, the attack could have been because Sara took you into her confidence, and perhaps Holly guessed it. *Et,* you do ask *beaucoup de questions*."

I do ask lots of questions. That's how I operate. "Okay, here's another question. Do we assume Ilse and Holly are in communication? Are they aware of their connection through Ian Watson?"

"That is complicated. How much would Holly have known of her father's former wife as a child? It appears Ilse assumed her maiden name after the divorce. If Holly's mother had not shared details, her little girl would have been none the wiser. *Et*, if they changed their last name and created a new life in Australia, Ilse is unlikely to be aware of Holly's true identity. Holly's work for NovoGeneOne could have been done through an intermediary. She may not be wrapped up in NovoGeneOne's world at all."

"So, if they're not working together and aren't even aware of each other's existence, Holly may not have made the connection between Ilse Knight and her father. Are we back to Holly Watson murdering these scientists because they uncovered a piece in the puzzle about stealth technology?"

"*Oui*. Chad is to contact me later with more details about the disposition of the plane. I suspect they will want it destroyed. *Mais*, we have no idea who is aware of its existence."

"I'm sure it's all the usual suspects." I'm thinking of our friends in Russia, who have plagued me from the start.

"As for the banquet. We are scheduled to attend and will sit at the head table with Dr. Lundberg. I expect Ilse Knight will be there too."

"That's going to be uncomfortable."

"She is not aware of what you do for us, Lily. Trust me on this." His hands rub my arms in an effort to soothe me. It's not working.

I think JP knows more than he is willing to say. What if Holly Miller, aka Holly Watson, has come to Belgium? Would there be any chance she could show up at the banquet unexpectedly? There's a knock on the door.

It's Parker. His eyebrows narrow when he sees my face.

"Hey, what's going on?" He takes a seat and gives us his full attention.

JP fills Parker in on our discovery. I add a few details about my first mission with the Agency.

"Shit. Pixie Dust was before my time, but she was legendary for snuffing out the bad guys." Parker pushes a lock of hair away from his eyes. "So, you think Holly Miller is Holly Watson?" He nods, letting out a hmm.

"I do," I tell him. "Have you discovered anything else?"

"Funny you should ask. I just finished going through Williams's papers. Tucked away between pages on his coral work, I found a handwritten note, likely in anticipation of his meeting with Harmon. Seems like he had already experienced some personal threats about his climate research. But, get this, he expressed concerns that the military could be involved with krill and planned to say something at the Climate Council conference." Parker stops and casts his eyes on his shoes. "I don't think Sara was aware of any of this."

"Of course she wasn't." I wish I had handled my time with Sara differently.

"Next steps?" Parker turns and looks at JP. "Boss, I went to Ghent and picked up those items we discussed." He nods.

I look at JP. "What are you two talking about? What are you keeping from me?"

"Robinson, we are not keeping secrets, merely working all the angles. Chad wanted us to have some explosives on hand when we return to the hangar."

My heart's pounding. "Return to the hangar? And what? Blow it up?"

"Perhaps. Now that we have uncovered this new weapon technology, there are concerns about it falling into the wrong hands."

"If you're going back to the hangar, I assume we're all going."

"Possibly. I told you I am waiting for more instructions from Chad. *Et*, you have some syringes loaded with lethal toxins? He smiles. "*Mais*, a gun may be better in these circumstances. You do not have to get as close." He winks.

I see the smirk on JP's face. "I don't find this funny."

"Doc, what JP is saying is that your talents are best used when we need to be subtle. Like all the dinners where you poisoned the bad guys, and we, meaning the U.S., don't want anyone to figure it's us. But in this case, if we blow up the plane, you can believe, sure as shit, the world is going to know what we did. I'm not sure how it's gonna go down, but when it does, it's gonna be hard."

"And Holly Miller?"

"Chad is checking to see if Holly Miller or Holly Watson, under another passport, is in Brussels. If she is, this is where I suggest you have toxins at the ready."

CHAPTER 24

GHENT, BELGIUM

Holly's relationship with the Admiral filled the void of her father's death. Perhaps their age difference reminded her of the man who abandoned her as a child, but whatever it was, she continued to obsess over the hows and whys of her father's demise. When the Admiral asked her to help in a research project, in exchange, she later asked him to learn more about the circumstances surrounding her father's death. Holly's mother never spoke of it. And as a little girl, she found herself only confused about the events of that evening. Why didn't he come home that night?

After Holly and her mother moved to Australia, her mother's alcoholism only got worse. Holly found herself spending more time with the Millers. Once her mother passed, the Millers were the only family Holly had left, and they, too, were unaware of the context of her father's end. So, Holly's demand of the Admiral was her best hope. He had connections. However, his delay in providing any information only frustrated her, so she continued to push him hard to learn more.

Holly arrived in Ghent and settled in the Admiral's apartment a few days before the Council banquet. She entered using her key, dumped her bag, and found the bottle of scotch in the cupboard. Another long flight. She poured a drink and sat down. The apartment was only sixty square meters, a little less than 700 square feet, and simply furnished with a living room that blended into the kitchen. A tall metal table stood parallel to the single countertop, with two battleship gray bar-height stools tucked neatly under the bench top. The ceiling loomed a good thirteen feet tall, with three pendant lights suspended above the counter. A gray curved sofa and a steamer trunk serving as a coffee table occupied the middle of the room. To the left of a glass door that opened onto a narrow balcony facing the street, a wooden desk and chair filled the space. A small bedroom and bath were off to the right. Only one photograph, a stone bridge gracefully suspended over a canal, hung above the couch, and the bedroom had a single picture of sea anemones on a coral reef. The Admiral used the apartment when he had business in Belgium, spending most of his time at his larger home in Sydney.

Holly had only been to the pied-à-terre a few times before, having spent more time at the Admiral's home in Australia. She was most comfortable there; its gauzy white furniture, blue and green pops of color, and outdoor living space complete with a barbeque grill. That house on the coast became a springboard for them to dive and sail. This was a city house. Holly stood up and circled the apartment a few times, peering out the door to the balcony. She checked her watch. Pushed the gray curtain aside. Looked out the window. No sign of him. Then, her phone pinged a text message.

Can't get to the apartment. Unexpected business. Make yourself at home. Meet you later as planned.

Holly shook her head and released a sigh. She circled the living room again and stopped at the desk. Bills and correspondence sat in a stack, and she thumbed through, looking for a diversion. There, she found a letter dated several months back from an administrator of the university department where her father had worked. Holly felt her heart pounding, and she sat and read the letter through.

Her hand shook.

The hairs on her arms bristled.

The letter acknowledged the Admiral's inquiry regarding the participants at the dinner Dr. Watson attended. Poor, poor man, she said. Present were a new colleague who had just joined the department, a representative from a foundation—whose name she couldn't remember, neither the foundation nor the representative—looking to sponsor new projects, and a few local scientists and physicians. The assistant couldn't remember any specific names of the attendees and was sorry she couldn't be more helpful. Holly's jaw clenched.

She popped off the chair, then rounded back, and hunted through the rest of the papers on the desk. She found a second letter buried at the bottom, dated after the assistant's letter. No signature or letterhead identified the source. The missive acknowledged some omissions, indicating these were the only names they could find. Holly ran down the list. One stood out. Dr. Lily Robinson.

Why hadn't the Admiral shared this with her months ago? And why now, as the project was nearly complete with a clandestine sale imminent? Holly had provided everything he had asked for. The photophores she had created were neatly incorporated into the simulated biological skin to make an even more radar-absorbent aircraft that could fly undetected. He acknowledged that this plane would have powerful capabilities as a military weapon and be the latest in stealth bombers. It would become a platform for gathering intelligence and conducting surveillance and reconnaissance. The Holy Grail. The ultimate military plane. And with an airframe of titanium combined with the rare earth metal ziyantium, it made for a light aircraft rendering it fuel efficient.

It would be too much to believe there was more than one Lily

Robinson, and indeed hard to accept more than one in Boston. Is it possible that Lily Robinson knew more about what happened that night? Robinson had asked too many questions about Sara and about the krill. Holly found it difficult to accept that there wasn't a conspiracy against her and her father.

Holly took out her phone, photographed the letter, and stuck it back into the pile. No more listening to rules and plans; she had her own agenda. She was no longer taking orders from the Admiral. He could go fuck himself. His betrayal stung. She would track him down and get answers.

Holly went into the bedroom and pulled open the closet door. A duffle bag sat filled with diving gear left after a trip doing a wreck dive in the North Sea. Their dry suits hung in the corner, and Holly rooted around her fins, booties, and gloves until she came to a smaller bag within. She unzipped the bag and found her diving knife in its sheath. It wasn't her favorite, but a spare she had used for the excursions in the north. Holly tossed it aside, opened the Admiral's dive bag, and pulled out his two-edged dive knife made of titanium. Exactly what she wanted. No more poisonous marine creatures.

CHAPTER 25

URSEL, BELGIUM

As with most secrets, some escape the jar they are kept in. Thanks to JP, the existence of a prototype stealth aircraft had been confirmed by visual inspection. Chad later learned from a U.S. asset in Russia that Global Tectonics was behind the project, and their lead man was the Admiral who served on the board of NovoGeneOne.

Chad Jones had been chasing Global Tectonics since the team was in Central Asia, unraveling the plot that resulted in the deaths of a U.S. senator and the leader of a small Central Asian country. Russia, entangled with GT at the time, sought control of the rare earth mineral deposits in the adjacent country. Military defense applications, including aviation, electronics, and communications, required these precious elements, and GT wanted market dominance. The Russian government divided the spoils amongst the oligarchs, who focused on developing stealth aircraft technology.

Chad picked up his phone and, with JP, put their plan together. They learned a meeting between the Admiral and GT was to take place at the Ursel Airbase. Whether others would show up was unknown. Chad agreed to send the team to the airfield to establish the identities of the interested parties and gather any intelligence on the aircraft if possible.

"We've been following GT's scent for a while now. This could be our lucky day." Chad sounded excited about the possibilities.

"There are guards around the airbase, but Parker and I got in through the perimeter fence. We believe only a few security personnel are present to give the impression the airbase is primarily abandoned," JP said.

"Hell, this time, make sure you are appropriately armed. There won't be much chance of Robinson getting close enough for poison."

JP laughed. "She will remain with the car, and keep watch."

"Good luck with that."

Darkness settled over the city, and JP, Parker, and Lily Robinson left the hotel room and headed to Ursel. JP drove, and Parker rode shotgun with Lily in the back seat. No words were exchanged, as they had worked out the logistics hours before. They embraced the silence and listened to the gentle hum of the tires on the highway.

JP pulled the car over to the side of the road about a half mile from the hangar. Parker and JP exited, and left Robinson behind as planned. They walked along the road until they reached the opening in the fence created during the previous visit. Their dark clothing hid them while they waited on a small promontory that gave an unobstructed view of the hangar.

"You think this meeting is going to happen, boss?" Parker said.

"*Oui*. Chad heard through our Russian asset that Global Tectonics would be here."

"Are they the buyers or the sellers?"

"Most likely, they funded the project and are viewing their investment. *Mais*, the technology is most valuable because it can be used in other applications."

"Why don't we want that technology? It could be a game changer." Parker asked.

JP laughed. "A game changer? Chemical weapons were game changers. Nuclear weapons were game changers. The United States may desire this aircraft technology, but they also recognize its existence is more than problematic. Other technologies and weapons of mass destruction have been outlawed, and there is a desire to keep nuclear arms at bay. This technology will probably go the same way."

Cool air settled around them as they waited for any indication that the meeting would go forward. The silence was broken by a car slowly moving along the entry road. A large black SUV pulled up to the front of the hangar. Car beams bounced off the metal structure and were left in place as a man exited the vehicle. JP focused his night vision binoculars and identified the Admiral. While the view was less than perfect, he made out a tall man wearing dark pants and a leather jacket. Ample gray hair spilled from underneath his ball cap, which had the word NAVY in gold letters emblazoned across the front. A pin with four stars was secured near the brim. The Admiral returned to the vehicle and turned off the lights once he had unlocked the side door to the hangar. Within minutes, another car pulled up, and a man wearing a dark suit exited. JP could not distinguish his features. The car beams were turned off. But he looked younger than the Admiral and had a thick head of dark hair. The Admiral grabbed the man's hand and shook it vigorously using both his hands. They disappeared inside the hangar, and JP and Parker made their move.

They scrambled down the embankment.

A crack of light came from the side door to the hangar. JP stopped and listened for voices. There were none. He pulled open the door, and he and Parker entered. The vastness of the space was overpowering. Steel rafters with beams spanning the ceiling allowed suspended lights to project onto the cavernous room beneath. Catwalks adjacent to the plane, yet above the ground floor, allowed workers and buyers to access the aircraft from all angles. JP and Parker crept up the metal stairs to the second level to get a better view.

The aircraft's triangular shape barely reflected the light from above. Its gritty, dull surface of biomechanical skin would allow it to disappear in plain sight—that and the embedded photophores. Filling the floor below were huge metal containers housing tools and supplies. JP and Parker crept along the catwalk and hid within the metal canopy.

They watched. And listened.

The Admiral and his guest toured the facility on the first floor below.

JP noticed a second-story office on the other side of the plane.

"Parker, wait here. Cover me."

He inched his way around the scaffolding until he reached the office. The shades were drawn, and the door unlocked. JP held his breath and entered the room. He stopped and listened again. Distant voices came from below. He scanned the room and though the light was dim, made out the shapes of several desks and filing cabinets. Another door cut into the back wall. His hand reached for the door handle, and his pulse raced. He swiftly swung into the second room into pitch darkness. One click on his phone brought the flashlight up, and JP saw a drawing table in the center of the room. The detailed design of the aircraft sat in plain sight. He took pictures of the notes on the plane's structural, control, and performance aspects and the final design. Damp under his gloves, JP's fingers clicked quickly while the muted camera shutter worked in burst mode.

His phone vibrated. Parker. JP turned off the flashlight and hid in a small storage closet.

The voices were muffled, but the footfalls on the stairs were distinct.

The door opened to the back room, and JP could see the light seep in under the closet door.

The man with the dark hair walked to the drawing table. "You build from these plans?" His Russian accent was heavy.

"Yes, our working set." The Admiral fanned through the pages showing the drawings. "So, how many buyers have we got?"

"We only need one. If everyone has new toy, it dilutes threat. Aircraft is up for auction on black market. Highest bidder. We keep technology."

"Makes sense. Let me get you a brochure I've prepared." The Admiral turned and walked to the storage room. He turned the handle.

JP took out his gun. His back pressed against the wall. He steadied his breathing.

"No need. Send digitally. No paper."

"Your call."

The voices grew more distant, and the sound of doors closing drew JP out of the storage room. Parker pinged.

In the clear.

JP crept back along the scaffolding, finally returning to Parker.

Parker reached out and touched JP's shoulder. "Fuck, boss. I had my silencer on and ready for fire."

JP nodded. "Let us finish and get the hell out."

"We got what we wanted?"

"*Oui*, and more. The plans were out in the open. Perhaps in anticipation of this visit."

"It is Global Tectonics. Isn't it?"

JP nodded. "Cover me. Time to set the explosives."

The explosives Parker had collected in Ghent were in JP's backpack. Chad's instructions were explicit. Rather than allow the aircraft to fall into the wrong hands, they were to blow it up. The explosion, they hoped, would appear accidental, perhaps from a design flaw, and discourage any future buyers. JP crouched along the periphery and climbed down the scaffolding. He silently made his way to the cockpit, weaving in and out of the storage barrels. He climbed up the crew entry ladder. Several windowpanes looked out from the cockpit toward the hangar door, and below were multiple screens that monitored oxygen-supportive equipment and various aircraft functions.

JP placed a small explosive device underneath one of the pilot seats. Another was placed at the rear of the seats. Whether this was the prototype, or the final plane didn't matter, it would be gone. He crept down the entry ladder and saw the two men approaching. He slid behind some prominent containers and waited. Parker was perched above with his gun drawn.

The Admiral and the Russian stopped.

"Well, what do you think?" the Admiral asked.

"I will report Global Tectonics money well invested. In weapon, not just aircraft. Any nation who owns plane, will have world dominance in air." He nodded, a toothy grin displaying slightly uneven teeth with a small chip on the right central incisor. "Any loose ends?" His Russian accent was undeniable.

"Maybe one or two. I will take care of it."

"Do. I have potential buyer who will outbid everyone else." The man in the suit reached into his pocket and pulled out a pack of cigarettes.

The Admiral waved his hand. "No. No smoking in here."

The Russian put the cigarettes back in his pocket. JP took pictures of the two men talking and bumped the metal container as he changed his angle.

The Russian turned sharply. "Did you hear that?"

"There's no one here but us." His eyes darted around the space.

"No, someone is here."

JP held his breath and pulled his gun out from under his jacket.

The man in the suit walked toward the containers and stopped. He turned his head slowly and scanned the enormous hangar, realizing it would be difficult to look behind every box, every container, every scaffold.

Parker saw the man in the suit looking for the origin of the noise. He readied his gun, took aim, and waited.

"There's no one here," the Admiral said. "How about a quick peek in the cockpit before you go?"

The Russian and the Admiral climbed the entry ladder and disappeared inside the cockpit.

JP scurried back to the entry point where Parker was waiting.

"Let's get out of here, boss."

They ran in the dark back to the promontory and waited. JP patted the detonator in his pocket.

"Let them return to their cars, and then I will blow up the plane. I want to find out more about the man in the suit. The Russian."

A car drove along the entry road and pulled behind the two large SUVs. A woman got out and slammed the door. JP thought it could be Holly Miller from the photos he had been shown. But it was dark. If it was, then they had their connection.

The two men heard the activity outside the hangar and left the building, only to find Holly at the door.

"I thought I might find you here, you piece of shit." She shouted in his face, her fists in a ball. She charged at the Admiral, oblivious to the man in the suit.

He grabbed her wrists and twisted her arm around her back until she cried out in pain.

Parker and JP continued their vigil, confident they would learn more.

"Not now," the Admiral said between gritted teeth. He dragged her to her car and pushed her inside. "Wait here. I have business to finish."

The Admiral returned to the man in the suit. He ran his fingers through his hair and managed a smile.

The Russian pointed to Holly in the car. "What fuck is that?" He pulled a gun from inside his jacket.

The Admiral pushed down his arm. "One of the loose ends. I'll take care of it, but I need her for one more job."

"No loose ends." He tucked the gun away.

JP and Parker looked at each other. They were too far away to hear what was said. Yet they had established a connection among Holly, the Admiral, and likely Global Tectonics. The Admiral probably functioned as the intermediary between Holly Miller and NovoGeneOne. She had provided vital research on the cloning piece.

The man in the suit returned to his vehicle and pulled from the parking area to the access road. Tires screeched as his car picked up speed and barreled toward the highway.

The Admiral got into Holly's car and faced her.

"Don't you ever pull a stunt like that again." His shout filled Holly's ears, and her head moved away.

"Me? You're the lying bastard. I provided you with key research for this project. And you betrayed me." She punched him in the shoulder before he grabbed her arm.

He slapped her face. "Stop it. What's got into you?"

Her head reeled, and Holly sat still, holding her cheek. "I went to your apartment, and among other things, I found a map to this old airbase. I figured out this is where you were hiding the aircraft."

The Admiral leaned back in the seat and took a breath. "I don't understand why you're here."

Holly grabbed his chin and turned his face toward her. "I made a simple request in exchange for my help. I asked you to find out who attended the dinner the night my father died. You've been sitting on the information for months. Why, you goddam bastard? Why?" Her hand dropped. Holly's eyes filled with tears, and her voice shook.

The Admiral paused before speaking. Holly would have to die. But not now. He needed her to eliminate Lundberg first—save him the trouble—and he had just the plan to get her to cooperate. "Holly, if you read the letter, you already know there isn't a complete record of the people who attended that night. Some were colleagues of your father and a representative from a defunct foundation."

The Admiral decided at that moment to implicate someone he had little knowledge of but had heard about from several sources. With a few lies, that person could become a convenient reason for Holly to attend the dinner. "Holly, there is one person who might have more information about that night."

Holly stopped and looked directly at the Admiral. Her contacts, brown with swirls of yellow, seemed to spin. "Who?" But she already knew the answer.

"Dr. Lily Robinson. You told me she was a friend of Sara Wilders. She was at the dinner the night your father died."

Holly rolled her hands into tight balls. "What more do you know about her? The nosy bitch. Too many questions about krill and the enclosure in the Southern Ocean. Sara went on and on about her. I thought the funnel web spider would frighten her, but she only came around with more questions." Her knuckles, blanched, banged her thighs.

The Admiral considered the question carefully. Why was Lily Robinson in Brussels after having visited her friend in Sydney? It seemed too much of a coincidence. He had been so focused on the sale of the aircraft and its technology that he had overlooked the obvious.

"Holly, what if I told you that Lily Robinson is in Brussels and will be at the Climate Council banquet and will sit at a table with Hans Lundberg." The Admiral had heard these plans from Ilse Knight, who also planned to attend the banquet. This would be the perfect opportunity for Holly to confront Robinson and poison Lundberg.

Holly's eyes opened wide, and the brown iris swirls moved like a pinwheel. It would be a chance to do more than scare Lily Robinson.

The Admiral saw Holly tumbling the idea in her mind and polishing it. He pushed forth. "You should talk to her there. Get some answers."

"How can I do that? I'm not on the guest list." Some of the steam had left Holly. Her blood pressure dropped, and her shoulders did, too.

The Admiral paused, then spoke, capturing the moment. "Catering always needs help. I could get you in. You'll show up as one of the servers. Perhaps drop some poison into Lundberg's drink while you're there." His eyes examined his large knuckles as he moved his hand around the back of Holly's neck.

She threw her head to the side to escape his grasp. "You bastard. Haven't I done enough for you already?"

"Let them think it was all about climate while we collect our money, and you get your answers to your father's death." He patted her head. "So, now get your shit together, and let's move forward."

Holly bit her tongue. She didn't need the Admiral's help, but he gave her an idea. "I'll find a way to get to the banquet. I need answers."

"And Lundberg?"

"We'll see." Her upper lip curled, and she sniffed. Holly turned on the ignition and listened to the hum of the engine. "Get out."

The Admiral exited the car and walked back to his own. Had he done enough to push Holly in the direction of Lily Robinson?

JP and Parker watched the cars drive down the road, leaving the hangar in darkness.

"Wish I could have been a fly inside that car. What the hell was that all about?"

"If nothing else, we have made the connection between the Admiral and Holly Miller. So, are you ready?"

"I am."

Parker and JP moved farther away from the building, and JP took out the detonator and pressed the button.

The explosion in the hangar shot pieces of metal and bio-manufactured skin throughout the facility. Cabinets filled with hardware tore open, and nuts, bolts, and screws rained shrapnel with each tiny crash making a clink as it hit the floor. The scaffolding surrounding the aircraft dropped in a tangled mess over the broken plane, now in pieces—a puzzle too difficult to reassemble. This would be a major setback for the organization. But once the U.S. Government saw the plans, and understood the potential danger to the world, restrictions would be put in place. That was the hope.

CHAPTER 26

BRUSSELS, BELGIUM

The sky above Ursel looks like it's on fire after the explosion. JP and Parker are back in the car, and we're ready to escape to Brussels.

"Thank god, you're both all right." I lean forward, hands on Parker's seat, eager to hear what occurred. "So, what happened?"

We hear the sirens blare.

"The plans for the aircraft were spread out like a picnic on the banks of the Seine," JP says as he pulls out onto the main road.

"And Holly Miller is definitely acquainted with the Admiral." Parker laughs and nods towards JP.

"Oh." I fall back into my seat, and Parker fills in the details.

By the time we return to the hotel, it's the wee hours of the night. I try to sleep, knowing that the banquet will be later this evening and more lives may be at risk. JP worries Hans Lundberg is the next target, and the killer is running out of time before Lundberg gives his address and reveals what he knows to a broad audience. Lundberg might not know everything Williams planned to say, but he might know enough to make big trouble for Global Tectonics. Everyone else who may have suspected a military twist is dead. And although we have no hard proof, I bet either the Admiral or Holly Miller murdered the scientists, and Sara, too. As for Ilse Knight, I expect to see her at the event, but I'm not sure of the extent of her involvement.

JP and Parker did the right thing blowing up that plane, but I can't help but think that a technology this unique will be exploited by others working in the same field. A discovery so exciting, someone somewhere will argue that it can be used for good. Possibly, but the greed, selfishness, lack of charity, and political posturing in today's world troubles me.

* * *

I'm wearing a sleeveless floral lilac-colored gown with a plunging neckline and scoop back. There is an embroidered mesh overlay with crystals and a beaded accent belt. It's exquisite. I'm pairing the dress with the shoes I bought in Sydney—the lavender ones, spider free. They are not exactly the right shoes for the dress; a delicate sandal would be better, but this is what I have, and it will have to do.

JP raps on the adjoining door. He enters, and wow. How magnificent he is in his tuxedo. I move in close and straighten his bowtie.

"My Lily. You look beautiful. So elegant."

His lips meet mine, and I feel the warmth of his body next to me, surrounded by loving arms.

"And you, my superspy, look dashing. A touch of James Bond with a dash of Vincent Cassel."

"I see," he says, holding me closer, "I am both a man of fiction and a movie actor. I will take it as a compliment." He laughs. "Let us get Parker."

We meet Parker in the lobby. He's also dressed in a tuxedo and looks very handsome.

"That's a good look for you, Parker."

"Doc, you look amazing, and the shoes. Only you can pull off stilettos with poison."

"These are just shoes, Parker." I tilt my head, giving him a sideways glance.

The banquet will be held in one of the lower spheres of the Atomium. We take the red stairs framed with turquoise blue railing instead of the elevator or escalator to the Ilya Prigogine side sphere. Round tables are set with fine china, and purplish light bathes the room, creating a cozy atmosphere even in the presence of soaring ceilings. I read the lighting was designed by Ingo Maurer. JP and Parker scan the room and meet with some local Agency staff from Ghent that Chad has asked to attend. While the view of Brussels is gorgeous, I want to see it from the highest vantage point—the Panorama.

I grab JP's arm, and we take the elevator to the top of the Atomium, where the doors open to 360° views of Brussels. The Panorama gives us a stunning view of the city and its surroundings. Although the light is fading, we see the King Baudouin Stadium and Mini-Europe, a park filled with more than three hundred miniatures of the wonders of Europe—like the Grand Place, the leaning Tower of Pisa, Big Ben, and, of course, the Eiffel Tower. We are the only two here, and my body is overcome with a warmth, a tingling, from a place deep inside. I look at the man I'm with, his craggy face, his seductive blue-green eyes, and feel the kind of once-in-a-lifetime love.

"Jean Paul, you are indeed my soulmate. Whatever you want to do, I will be there for you. I want to be with you."

He tucks an errant strand of hair behind my ear. "My Lily, you know I feel the same." He takes out a small box neatly wrapped and hands it to me. "This is for you."

The only gift JP has given me in all the time I've known him is the platinum bracelet. The bracelet allows him to find me anywhere in the world. We agreed years ago that a ring, a sign of commitment, would be too dangerous. Does this box hold a ring? Is it a sign of change in our lives?

"This is unexpected." My fingers tremble as I unwrap the gift and open the box. It's not a ring, but two beautiful open-heart pendants, the smaller one with a red diamond highlighting its sensual curves.

"We said no rings. *Mais*, consider this a commitment of my love for you."

"Two hearts?"

"*Oui*. Our two hearts. They fit with one another. The red diamond is from the Moreau family. I had these hearts made for us." He strokes my hair and kisses my forehead. "I wanted to give this to you when we got to Paris, where we first made love, *mais*, I thought, why not now."

"JP," I pause, "we'll always have Paris. I love you." My knees feel weak.

"*Je t'aime, ma chérie*."

Our embrace seems to last minutes, although it is only moments. It's not the Eiffel Tower that perhaps JP would have preferred as a venue, but it's such a romantic gesture, high above a thriving city, from a man who keeps much of his feelings to himself. I hand him the necklace so he can help me put it on. It's perfect for the dress and fills in the neckline.

We return to the Ilya Prigogine sphere, where the dinner is being held, and people are filling the space. Parker paces the room, looking at the tables, checking out the place cards, and chatting with guests. His eye never strays too far from Lundberg. While the evening brings unexpected romance, I feel an uneasiness in my stomach, knowing that yesterday's explosion at the Ursel airplane hangar has left the team on edge and the assassin dismantling the Climate Council is still at large. Chad has men looking for both the Admiral, and Holly Miller—our prime suspects. We remain vigilant and hope the banquet goes off as planned.

We settle at the tables, and Lundberg congratulates the scientists for presenting their findings with courage and accuracy. "I would like to recognize the work of Daniel Williams, Graham Harmon, and Omala Patel. Their efforts on the effects of climate change on the ocean have opened the eyes of the world to what it would mean if life in the sea died."

Ilse Knight raises her glass. "To our colleagues."

Voices join, "To our colleagues," and some of the tension dissipates now that we have paid tribute to the dead.

The meal in honor of the meeting consists of responsibly harvested salmon and fresh vegetables—namely Brussels sprouts. Belgium white wine, some from Chardonnay grapes, and Flemish sparkling wines from Auxerrois grapes. I choose the sparkling wine, although nothing could replace the champagne from Reims in France. Parker is still sitting on the edge of his seat, his eyes following various people around the room as if they could be suspects. He has not let up for one minute.

Professor Lundberg appears tired, his face drawn, and his eyes fixed on his dessert plate before turning to me. "Dr. Robinson, so nice of you to attend with your colleagues. I must say, it is reassuring to have Monsieurs Marchand and Parker here tonight."

His own safety must weigh heavily, knowing the person responsible for the deaths of his fellow Council members hasn't been caught. We've managed to keep him safe, for now, but going forward? There are great risks in leading this Council. And he knows it.

"Yes, they are good at their job." I manage a small smile.

Lundberg nods. "Have you been to Brussels previously?"

"I have. And I've even visited the Atomium before."

"Yes, such an interesting history. I pushed to get this venue for the banquet."

He tells me he is happy tomorrow will be the last day of the conference. Weariness has found its way into all of us.

Ilse Knight is at the adjacent table. Earlier, she and I nodded upon seeing each other. Is she aware of Holly Watson Miller, the daughter of her now deceased ex-husband? The death of Ilse's husband and Holly's father still haunts me. But I'm convinced that we saved countless lives by ridding the world of Ian Watson. It's so complicated.

I'm feeling mellow. No sign of the Admiral or Holly Miller. We wait for word from Chad on their capture. Warmth fills my body as we engage in our small talk. I'm ready to return to Boston and look forward to my last night in Brussels with JP. He's given me a lot to think about. Will he truly return to Reims, his boyhood roots, and become part of the family wine enterprise? I can't imagine him settling down, but who knows. This trip feels full circle for me.

"*Excusez-moi*," JP says as he rises from his seat. "I am going to the bar to get a bottle of champagne for later and stretch my legs." He winks at me.

I catch his smile, aware he is relaxed as the evening has been quiet, and dessert and coffee will soon be served. My mind jumps from one thought to another, like hopping on stones across a stream. It's been lovely to dine in public even though we are on assignment. Maybe I should move to France and start anew. Yet, I want to be close to Rose, and I'm unsure if she will remain in the U.S., but my guess is yes if she ends up marrying Kelley. But she has roots in France, too. She was raised by JP's cousin Adrienne. I understand why I should give up this risky existence for a simpler life. I have given much of my life for my country, but perhaps now it is time for my country to give back to me.

Hans Lundberg leaves the table to speak with Ilse Knight. Parker watches them intently. From my perspective, it seems they are enjoying the evening. She's wearing a red sheath dress with a matching long coat, and he is wearing a tuxedo like the other men. They speak for several minutes before he returns to our table.

"And how is Ilse Knight?" I ask.

"She wanted to applaud me for the Council's recommendation to support an end to fossil fuels. She also acknowledged the work of Williams, Harmon, and Patel." He checks his watch, and I see his eyelids are heavy.

JP returns to the table with a bottle of champagne. He whispers in my ear. "For our last night in Brussels. It will be just like it was in Paris."

I smile and notice Parker is watching us. He realizes what's going on.

"Excuse me," Lundberg says. "I'm going to use the restroom before I leave. It is getting late."

JP shifts his attention. "Let me accompany you."

The two men leave the Ilya Prigogine sphere. It is two flights of red stairs down to the toilets, passing a landing on the floor with the caterers. I check the time, thinking about returning to the hotel, having that last sip of champagne, and making love with my soulmate. Lost in my thoughts, drifting in my own space, time passes. And then…

Lundberg appears at the table. There's no JP.

My heart beats a little faster. "I see you left Monsieur Marchand."

"He was right behind me," Lundberg says. "He will be along in a moment."

A breath escapes me, and I stand up, having decided to refresh my lipstick before leaving for the evening.

Parker catches my eye and indicates "stop" with the palm of his hand.

"Wait here, doc."

He gets up and moves across the room, weaving in among the tables like a ball in a pinball machine. He disappears down the red stairs, his steps ringing out as they press hard on the metal treads.

My impatience grows.

A shout echoes from the stairwell. It's Parker's voice.

Prickles fan throughout my being. Delicate body hairs rise.

My heart races, pumping blood to every cell in my body, feeding them energy, propelling me forward at full speed. Across the room I fly directly to the stairs. My stilettos click on every step until I reach the landing. I see Parker, his pale face, his bloodied hand holding a gun.

"Doc, he needs medical attention." Not waiting, his blur flies down the red stairs leading to the floors below.

I choke on my breaths. There's a growing commotion around me.

"Get out of my way. I'm a doctor!" Waves of nausea wash over me. "Someone call an ambulance!" I shout.

I know the man splayed on the cold gray floor.

My wail fills not just one sphere, but the entire atmosphere. His body, motionless, lies on the floor like a discarded sack of clothes. His gun at his side.

"JP!" I scream. My fingers struggle to find his pulse, my knees slipping in the sticky red wet as I probe his neck for signs of life. His heart slows, and his pulse erratic.

Impending doom.

My kiss dwells on his forehead, and warmth radiates from my body to his.

I hold him tight.

"JP, don't let go. I'm here now. Please, don't let go."

Tears drip from my chin.

I put pressure on his wound. And rock him back and forth gently in my arms. We need an ambulance. No, we need a miracle.

JP coughs, and blood splatters on my face. Warm and red, I feel darkness about to cover him like a shroud.

His eyes flutter. His bloodied hand reaches for my necklace. He pulls my face to him. "*Ma chérie, je t'aime*. I never said it enough. You made my life worthwhile. This business ruins a man, ruins a soul. Get out, my Lily, get out."

"Stay with me Jean Paul. Don't leave me. Please, don't leave me." A desperate plea. I beg. I choke on my words.

His eyes close, and the blood pools around us until we become an island in its midst.

In the distance, the sound of sirens grows louder, and I feel someone's hand on my back. I lean into JP, holding him ever more tightly, my body bathed in his blood, my lips on his.

"Let him go, Lily." Parker pulls me from the body of my lover.

I cannot see through the tears. My hands cannot wipe them fast enough, and I bite down hard on my lower lip until I wince in pain. I know he is gone—the love of my life. I beg my clinical mind to blunt any more emotions. I need to function, but how can I when the man I have loved for most of my life has left me.

"Parker, who was it?"

"It sounds like Holly Miller from the description the kitchen staff gave me. She must have been working with the caterers. We'll get her. The guys are out looking now. By the time I got down the stairs, she was gone. Chad's been alerted. He'll muster enough fucking forces to bring this place down. He's on the next plane."

We wait for medical help, but I recognize it's too late. I dissociate from my body and watch the events unfold from above. I'm not dead, but I feel like I am. I must get myself together.

Parker and I insist JP is taken to the hospital even though I know he is gone. Parker's back on the phone with Chad but stays with me, holding my hand now and again. When medics arrive, they give JP oxygen and jam an IV in his collapsed vein. It's all for show.

A handsome yet lifeless body lays on a gurney, waiting to be transferred to the emergency department. For diplomatic reasons, JP will "die" in the hospital. My lilac-colored gown is covered in blood—like the picture of a former first lady's pink Chanel suit stained with her husband's blood. A stark reminder of reality.

The trip is short. Sirens blare.

Once in a private bay, the hospital nurse brings me some scrubs, and I change, still clinging to my red-stained lavender stilettos. I wait for the next part of my journey with JP. The medical examiner is notified and sends someone to pick up the body.

The medical examiner meets with Parker and me, and we agree to a limited autopsy at her facility to document the wounds. She states that these results will be useful in court when the killer is identified. Yet, Parker and I share a bond. We both vow there will be no killer apprehended and no trial. Holly Watson Miller will be dead. We agree to document the wounds.

We watch the body wheeled into the autopsy suite. The room is cold and vast, and several tables are covered in white shrouds, which hide the bodies underneath.

The medical examiner's voice is soft. "Dr. Robinson, did you want to attend this autopsy?"

Parker holds onto me, squeezing my arm. Tears cling to my lower eyelids, and I bite my lip again to divert pain from one area to another. "No. I'll wait out here."

So many times JP waited for me while I donned scrubs and coveralls when investigating an unexpected death. I know what will happen in there. I don't want a forever image of my soulmate with a neatly stitched Y-incision marring his beautiful body. This is someone I loved deeply. I knew every inch of his person—perfect, from the crease that traversed his cheek, the gentle etches surrounding his eyes, to the scar from the bullet that grazed him. I will remember him from the days of his dark hair, from before the gray, and the sparkle in those blue-green eyes.

I double over, clutching my sides, and sob.

Parker holds me, and I hear him sniffle. Yes, we are not so hardened that we can't cry for someone we love.

Sometime later, the medical examiner returns and describes sharp force trauma—a four-and-a-half-inch blade that ran deep into JP's side, severing major blood vessels. The cause of death was exsanguination from the stab wound.

It's what we thought. They agree to hold his body here until we can fly home. Together. I'll have JP cremated, and he and I can spend one last weekend at the cottage before I scatter his ashes to the wind.

"Here are some of his personal effects," she says, handing me his Luminox watch and silver cuff links. She keeps his clothes for evidence.

I cradle them in my palm, thinking of how he'd pull his cuffs over the watch throughout the day. A little quirk. Something I'd notice and wish I could see right now. Tears start flowing again, and Parker rubs my shoulder.

I grit my teeth and turn to him. "JP will be safe here. But before I bring my love home, we must find the bitch that took him from me."

CHAPTER 27

BRUSSELS, BELGIUM

After Holly left the Admiral at the airplane hangar in Ursel, she sensed he planned to kill her. His demeanor had changed once the project neared completion. He had wooed her, taken advantage of her knowledge, her expertise, and her need for fatherly love. But she was done with him. She had plans of her own.

The next morning, the news reported the explosion at an abandoned airbase near Ursel in the middle of the night. Holly recognized the location. Though she hadn't gone inside the hangar and never saw the plane, she assumed the whole project had been blown into bits of bioluminescent hail. The news only recounted an explosion and fire, nothing about the structure's contents. Holly laughed.

She planned to slip into the Council dinner as one of the wait staff. She liked the Admiral's suggestion. Just show up, ready to do the job, and look like she belonged there. The website for the catering service had several pictures of kitchen and wait staff, as well as set-ups from various events, including ones held at the Atomium previously. Although the Admiral was a board member of NovoGeneOne, he was not part of the Climate Council and had no invitation to the event. She would meet him after the banquet—after she took out Hans Lundberg. Maybe Lily Robinson, too. Her call. First, she wanted answers from Dr. Robinson. What did she know about her father's death?

Holly had donned her catering uniform—a black skirt and blouse, finished with a crisp white apron. She tied her hair into a tight bun and secured it with a floral print scarf. The knife, its four-and-a-half-inch blade tucked neatly in its sheath, fit snugly in her apron's deep pocket. Yes, she would meet the Admiral as planned. He would get his answers, too.

At the Atomium, she easily slipped into the event. Although security was tight, the titanium blade was undetected as she stepped through the metal detector. Only one person from the catering staff questioned her, and Holly replied that she was a last-minute substitution.

She kept her distance from the dining tables and worked in the kitchen for the caterers on the floor below the Ilya Prigogine. With her eyes on the door and the red stairs, she watched and waited for Lily Robinson. In between—appetizers, entrees, and desserts—were placed on trays ready for the banquet. Surely Lily Robinson would come down the stairs to use the toilet at some point. Hans Lundberg, too. It was only a matter of time.

But time ran late, and Holly's impatience grew. Where was Robinson? The knot inside her begged to unravel during the planned confrontation. Depending on Lily Robinson's answers, she would decide whether or not to kill her. Holly unsheathed her knife and touched the blade. Cold. A chill traveled up her spine and radiated out to her limbs.

Her fists balled and shoved into her pockets, she stomped out the door, and onto the landing below the red stairs. And then it happened.

Holly caught a glimpse of an older man heading up the red stairs on his way to Ilya Prigogine. Hans Lundberg? Her heart raced, and her eyes grew wide.

She didn't see the man coming up from the floor below.

JP recognized Holly Miller from photographs and Lily Robinson's description. The woman he saw with the Admiral outside the hangar stood before him. He prepared for resistance, and readied to take her in. Slowly, he removed his gun from underneath his black jacket.

Holly raised her head. She felt his blue-green eyes fixated on her violet irises. She hesitated and inhaled a breath that didn't escape.

"You are Holly Watson," JP said. "Let us step off to the side so we do not make a scene." JP moved his body toward Holly's, his eyes never leaving her stare, and backed her up against the wall. A momentary glance up the red stairs confirmed Lundberg was nowhere in sight.

Holly's lips curled like a cornered animal. "Who the hell are you?"

"That is unimportant. I want to know who you are working with and your involvement in the deaths of several climatologists. *Et*, Sara Wilder."

Holly's eyes flared. "I don't give a shit what you want to know."

"What is your mission here tonight? Are more Climate Council members to die?"

"What do you care?" She moved her hand toward her apron pocket. "Now I have a question for you. You know me as Holly Watson. No one has called me that in twenty years. Did you know my father?"

"I did not know your father. My understanding is that he died unexpectedly."

Alarm bells rang in Holly's brain. How would he know that? What is his connection? "If you know he died unexpectedly, you must know Lily Robinson." Her lip curled.

Holly's eyes grew wide, and her chest heaved.

JP's instinct took over. He knew Holly would look to Lily for answers and likely kill her. He swallowed hard, his mouth dry. A deep breath shifted in his chest. He had wanted a subdued capture. But not now. "It is time to go." He moved in closer.

It happened so fast and so unexpectedly that JP was caught off guard. Holly snatched the dive knife from her apron and plunged it into his abdomen. His gun dropped to the floor, and as he followed, he grabbed Holly's arm, pulling her down with him.

She kicked him in the side, smirked at his flinch, and seized the metal stair railing to pull herself out from under him. With a roll, she sprang to her feet.

JP pushed himself up and went for his gun. His arm shook, and he fell back to his knees.

Holly darted down the stairs, never looking back. Distant footfalls and shouts only made her run faster. She sprinted in the dark.

The Admiral's car was parked at the designated location. She saw his silhouette in the streetlight and yanked open the driver's side door.

The Admiral was startled. "What the fuck, Holly." He stepped out of the car.

"I'm tired of all the lies, the manipulation, the bullshit." Her teeth were clenched.

The Admiral watched the unraveling. Now or never. His gun was in his breast pocket. Although the aircraft prototype had been sabotaged, the technology was safe. Holly had served her purpose. He took her into his arms, pretending to dry her tears. A sharp pain in his side caused him to pitch forward. He gasped.

Holly held him until his weight became too much, then let him fall to the ground. "You exploited my bitterness, my despair. Men who want to rule the world," she said with venom, "with their greed and hunger for domination. If my father had lived, he could have saved me from all of you."

"Your father was one of them." His head dropped to the pavement, eyes open, blank.

CHAPTER 28

BRUSSELS, BELGIUM

The hotel feels empty now. There is no knock at the adjoining door, nor will there ever be again. JP is gone, and I push into his room to find the remnants of the man I love. The closet holds a few of his jackets, one navy blue, the other gray. Three bright white shirts appear luminous, and the material, soft to the touch. I can see him pulling the cuffs over his watch and out from under his sports coat.

Chad will be here tomorrow and likely take the contents of JP's briefcase. I open it and find various papers on the aircraft technology we have chased these last few weeks. I find a curious note about the Admiral and put it aside. JP was good at his job. There's a false pocket in the back of his case that contains a small tracking device. So, this is how he located me via the bracelet he gave me in Paris all those years ago. My fingertips brush the platinum bangle on my wrist. Tears fall from my eyes. Hollowness consumes me, and the sobs rip open protected places in my being. I cannot stop the flow.

Jean Paul, an introspective man who shared little yet felt deeply. Instinctively, I reach for the necklace. With my eyes shut, the sterling feels cool to the touch, and the curves of the hearts smooth. We've come full circle, JP.

A huge sigh, trapped in my body, escapes, and I flop on the bed. I smell the last of him on the pillow, his hair, sun-dried after an ocean swim, the muskiness of his masculinity. And I weep. I weep until I have used all the tears my body can make. I weep for a man I wanted to spend the rest of my life with. Now, I feel lost and vulnerable. In the quiet of this space, this place where I felt JP's arms wrapped around me, I let it all go. I pretend he moves the hair behind my ears and wipes my tears. His voice whispers *ma chérie,* and he says my name with two syllables—Lil-ly.

I hear a faint knock from my room. I leave JP's and take a white shirt he'd recently worn along with the piece of paper back to my room. I want to have him near me, know that scent that feeds my soul.

"Just a minute," I say.

I wipe my tears and peek through the peephole. It's Parker.

"Doc, I realize it's late, but I wanted to see how you're doing." His voice is soft, and I hear his words and look around him to see if JP will follow him through the door.

"I'm… I'm okay, I guess. I haven't been able to sleep anyway." My voice trembles, tears streaming down my cheeks.

Parker sweeps me into his arms. "Doc, Lily, I feel it too. You don't have to say, but I wasn't blind when it came to you and JP. He never said, and you never said, but the undeniable chemistry between the two of you…" His voice trails off. "And I've lost the best partner I ever had. What a fucking shit assignment." We both fall to the edge of the bed.

Parker's eyes are filled with tears. We hold one another without speaking as if we were holding a moment of silence.

After a while, Parker stands. "Doc, Chad will be here tomorrow. We can deal with JP's things then; if you're up to it. Or I'll take care of it."

"No, I want to."

"It's up to you. There's something else you should know. The Admiral was found stabbed down the way from the Atomium. I assume it was Holly. We're looking for her at every stop, the airport, trains, buses, whatever."

"You'll get her, Parker. Won't you?"

"Fuck we will, doc. But you've got to be careful. She could be after you. Got your poison booties with you or something?"

I laugh. "I always carry some poison. I'll be careful."

"Careful doesn't cut it. I think chasing Markovic was easier. When you're dealing with a terrorist, it's about the agenda, what are the political gains, the global moves. I think Holly is a crazy person on a revenge binge."

"Why do you say that? Williams and Harmon couldn't have been personal."

"I bet Holly had a thing with the Admiral. He used her in more ways than one. He probably promised her something for her help. And Sara's death was personal. No love lost there."

"And JP? What could she possibly have against JP? She couldn't have known he was an operative."

"I think JP recognized her. She was at that event waiting for Hans Lundberg, Ilse Knight..." He pauses, "or you." He studies his shoes.

Is it possible Holly Watson learned about her father? I can't believe so. I need to know.

"Listen, Parker. I have something to take care of tomorrow morning. I'll meet with you and Chad later in the afternoon."

"What could you possibly have to do tomorrow?"

"I have some loose ends to tie up."

He frowns. "Don't do something crazy, doc. Listen, it's late. We should both get a few hours of sleep anyway." He rubs my shoulder and closes the door behind him.

After Parker leaves, I return to JP's room and take his pillow. I want to sleep with it tonight. To smell him next to me. With the covers wrapped around me, I hold the pillow close—and pretend.

I startle awake in the wee hours. JP. My hand searches the bed in the dark. Where are you? You can't be gone. I hear his voice, see his blue-green eyes, and cry myself back to sleep.

The sun rises early, and so do I. My emotions are buried for the moment, and my unyielding clinical mind takes hold. Ghent is in my sights, and I have my GPS programmed with the address JP managed to track down. That's what the note in his briefcase said. Once on the E40, it's a straight shot. JP and I drove this route many times over the last few days. JP. JP, I need you now.

I finally reach the apartment complex in Ghent and take a deep breath. JP discovered that the Admiral had a small place in Ghent. I'm betting Holly is holding out there with plans to jump on one of the vessels and go to sea from the Port of Zeebrugge. I think that will be her escape route. It would be my plan.

I park the car around the corner from an older building on the canal. The buildings are narrow and huddled together shoulder to shoulder along the water. I easily enter the vestibule. Now, inside the building, I plan to knock on the Admiral's front door and take my chances. I've done it before. Steely resolve. The worst that can happen if Holly is there—she will try to kill me. She's taken the love of my life, so I have nothing to lose. Rose will only miss her mentor. She will not know the loss of a mother. Adrienne will continue to love her, guide her, and cherish her.

After walking up three flights, I catch my breath, knock at the door, and stand to the side. "It's Lily Robinson." I hope to catch her off guard.

There are sounds coming from inside the apartment. "Who's there?"

"Lily Robinson."

"Are you alone?" Her tone is tense.

The door opens slightly, and I make my move.

I shove Holly backward through the door, and she loses her balance and grabs onto me. I begin to fall into her but catch myself while she is still on the ground.

"What are you doing here?" she spits.

"I heard you were looking for me. So here I am." I take a breath, thrust my shoulders back, and keep a hand in my purse.

Holly slowly rises and dusts off her pants. "How did you know where to find me?"

"It wasn't hard once I realized you were the Admiral's lover."

Holly glances down as if found out in an embarrassing moment.

"We were lovers. So what," she hisses.

It's confirmed. Parker was right.

"I actually don't care if you were lovers. But I do care about a few things. Why kill Drs. Williams, Harmon, and Patel?"

"I never killed the Patels. That was the Admiral's doing. He had access to the dive shop and poisoned their air tanks."

I knew it.

"And Williams and Harmon?"

"That was me. But the Admiral called the shots."

Heat creeps into my cheeks. "And Sara?"

"She was a nosy bitch who got in my way. Like you."

I see Holly's eyes dart around the room—looking for some weapon she can use.

"And why the poison animals, Holly. Why go through all that trouble?"

"That made it fun, Dr. Robinson. I would have thought you would appreciate it, given your area of expertise. You know I looked you up after Sara went on about you. God, she was annoying."

My heart sinks thinking Sara had suffered in the cold, a blow to her head. "Sara was my friend."

"Sara was everyone's friend. That was Sara. Miss Goody Two Shoes."

"And the reason for killing the man at the Atomium?" I bite my lower lip so hard I can taste the blood. I cannot cry.

"He recognized me and assumed I was there to get to Hans Lundberg—and you. It's not like we had a long discussion."

"Was this all about the Climate Council business or something more?"

"It was never about the Climate Council. But certain members discovered information about the cloning of the photophores and the recent technology that the Admiral said would be a turning point in military applications."

"That's what I assumed. You realize you have to give yourself up." Am I really going to let that happen?

"I will do that after you answer something for me."

I don't trust Holly. But I know what she might ask.

"I learned you attended the dinner in Cambridge the night my father died."

So, she knows I was there. I will never betray my country or my team. The lies are about to pour from my mouth. "I'm sorry, I don't understand. What night are you talking about, and who is your father?"

"Ian Watson. A brilliant man whose life ended far too soon. It's true he had a bad heart, but he was murdered. Wasn't he?" There's a burn in her kaleidoscope eyes. "You see, my life and my mother's became hell after he died."

God, how I hate collateral damage. "Holly, that was a long time ago. I vaguely remember attending a dinner in Cambridge with some scientists. You said your father had a bad heart, and I recall something about a Cambridge scientist whose cause of death was natural causes."

"If that's what you choose to believe. But I think there was someone there, someone from the government, who wanted him out of the way. And now you're here mixed up with the Climate Council, so I assume you are that person."

"Holly, you're a scientist. Sometimes, we say things are true, true, and unrelated." She cannot expose my cover. I must protect myself, JP, and our government at all costs.

"I think my father created something so spectacular that he had to be eliminated from existence, just like you've done with the new aircraft. I believe you had a hand in that, even if you didn't physically blow up that plane."

I'm at a crossroads. Holly is no fool, and if she is allowed to live, so many more lives will be in danger. She sidesteps toward the tall glass doors that open onto the balcony over the canal.

"A little fresh air might make your neurons work better, Dr. Robinson."

She opens the door, and a breeze blows lightly through her blond tresses. There's a small metal bistro table with two metal chairs. The knife blade on the table catches the sun's reflection.

"Holly, whatever happened to your father, happened a long time ago. You said so yourself. I'm sorry your and your mother's life was hell, but you managed to become a superb scientist by all reports."

"So what!" she shouts. She grits her teeth and bores into me with those eyes. "Do you know what it's like to lose someone who adored you, who you cared about? The relationship between parent and child is sacrosanct."

I feel that last arrow. It goes deep, just between beats, and scores my heart. The blood runs fast. My Rose, my Jean Paul. My jaw clenches, and I bury any remaining emotion under years of guilt heaped on me like piles of stone.

Holly picks up the knife. The syringe is already in my hand. JP and Parker would say this is where I should use my gun, but poison will have to do.

She lunges.

I dodge.

Holly seizes my arm, the knife in her other hand. I swing around, grab her neck, and bury the end of the needle as deep as I can into her pulsing artery.

She swipes wildly with the knife, nicking my arm, but I move quickly toward the edge of the balcony.

Holly staggers forward and grips the railing but loses her balance. Her body splashes into the canal below.

It's over. It's over.

* * *

It's evening now. Chad's at the hotel going through JP's things. I offer to pack up his clothes while Chad takes anything the government wants.

"I'm so sorry, Lily." Chad rarely uses my first name. "I know you were close to JP."

"Yes, a friend and a colleague. I sometimes forget how long we've known each other, but it's close to twenty-odd years now."

I remember exactly when and how we met. I also remember the first time we made love. It was Paris. It was winter. It was glorious. We'll always have Paris.

"We've confirmed Holly's role in the deaths of the scientists, and we were also able to find out more about the Admiral's role in Global Tectonics. This case turned out to be a breakthrough for us. We're able to see all the pies and the fingers in them."

All the pies, all the spies.

"Where's Parker?"

"Wrapping up our affairs in Ghent."

"Oh." Handling Holly Watson Miller's body?

Chad strums his fingers across the table top and looks out the window. I don't envy his job. Explaining all the deaths and wrapping up the case in a bow.

"Chad, what about Ilse Knight? How involved was she?"

"She was certainly aware of her company's cloning projects, but I don't think she knew specifically about the Admiral's scheme. She's cooperating fully. We have more to learn, but at this point, I don't think she was involved with Global Tectonics."

"And how is it that Ilse and Holly were unaware of each other's past?"

"I'm sure you've guessed at that. As a little girl she was not involved with her father's ex-wife, just as his ex-wife was not interested in his new family. I don't think Holly ever made the connection between NovoGeneOne and Ilse Watson, as she was known then. It's not as if they lived in the same parts of the world."

"That does make sense. With all the name changes, and distance, I guess they didn't know of the coincidences of their relationship."

Chad nods. "By the way, we've leaked the information about the stealth bomber's frontier-breaking technology. I believe there will be discussions worldwide on how to handle discoveries such as this." He closes JP's briefcase.

"Will there be a treaty with the Klingons?" I smile.

"I'm sorry, what?"

"Never mind." JP and Parker would get it.

"So, Dr. Robinson, when does your plane leave?"

"Tonight. I'm taking JP home with me."

"Yes, I understand he named you as the executor of his will. You will inherit all of his worldly possessions. You realize he was a very secretive man. Kept his private life private."

He did. "I'm having the body cremated, as were his wishes. I suppose you'll want to hold some kind of service in D.C."

"Yes, we'll do that. Something small. His coworkers. I don't think he has any Marchand family."

Oh, but he does. Moreau. And I plan to see them. There's a long pause, and I change the subject.

"Did Lundberg have anything to add about the Climate Council?"

"Not much. But he is concerned that climate scientists are at risk."

"Not everyone believes in science or cares. As climate change continues to evolve, there will be more challenges."

"Political representatives from around the world plan to meet to discuss technologies that would profoundly affect civilization. Some scientific breakthroughs help our survival, but some will only feed greed and discord."

"That's true. So, how do we keep the world safe while moving forward? I have no answers."

"Nor do I, Lily Robinson."

CHAPTER 29

WASHINGTON, D.C.

I wear my black pencil skirt and peplum jacket over a red silk camisole. Black suede stilettos adorn my feet, and I feel tall and sleek, and ready for the moment. My grandmother's ring, with the ruby serpent's head facing out, is on my left ring finger, and on my right wrist, the platinum bracelet. No one will ever again find me, not as JP had through all those years. The hearts pendant is the perfect caption for the image. It speaks of love and a bond between two people who never pledged to honor and obey but rather to live life to the fullest.

I'm waiting for Parker. That must be him now knocking on the door.

"Parker, thanks for coming to pick me up." He looks good. A dark blue suit with a striped tie that JP would approve of. I straighten the knot.

"Thanks, doc. Are you ready?"

"Yes." That's a lie. But I'm as ready as I will ever be.

Chad has chosen to have the memorial service in a chapel on the outskirts of the city. It's a small domed church that sits atop a hill and has vistas of tall trees. The chapel is decorated with flowers of my choosing. Cloud-like white orchids adorn the dais, and sprigs of green with white calla lilies and petite white roses stand tall on the table with the chalice. The candle burns. My heart burns with vanquished love and overwhelming sadness.

Chad remains with the minister and will help lead the service. Most of the participants are those from the D.C. office who worked behind the scenes in the Office of Climate Intervention, the pseudonym for Chad's operation. How we laughed at the irony of the name given our last mission.

People take their seats, and the minister begins with a brief introduction to life after death. It makes me wonder if I will meet JP somewhere in another world, at another time. Then Chad extolls the work of Jean Paul Marchand, never revealing JP's true surname—Moreau—and his childhood home in Reims, France. Parker remembers his courage and friendship, gathering approvals from those assembled, and I… I am too overwhelmed to speak because I cannot do so freely. I cannot tell the world how much this man meant to me.

With the formal memorial service over, the informal part begins. Some food and drink are set out on a table at the back of the chapel. Now is the celebration of JP's life. Others who have worked with him throughout the years have come to pay tribute.

"Sam, so good to see you again." Sam had been our contact in Seoul when we chased down Markovic to the shipyard in Gunsan, South Korea. We couldn't have done it without a local guide and someone who understood the culture and the language. He still works for us there, keeping an eye on North Korea and potential missile threats.

"You, too, Dr. Robinson. I was sorry to hear about JP. It had been an honor to serve with him in Seoul."

I shake Sam's hand and thank him for taking the long flight to Washington.

A familiar form ambles toward me, his black glasses neatly framed about his face. A slow, deliberate walk. I reach out with both arms and sink my head upon his shoulder.

"John Chi Leigh. You did come. Thank you."

"This is a nasty business, Lily Robinson. Maybe you should consider full-time teaching. Safer."

I laugh. Always with the lessons. "Yes, and what about you? Wouldn't it be safer for you?"

"I am just a humble chemist looking for drugs in the urine of racehorses."

"Right. And I'm only a teacher."

"No, Lily Robinson. You are more than a teacher. You made great sacrifices for your country. This was not an easy choice, and you have struggled with your conscience for years. So hard to be a healer and," he pauses, looking for the right word. "I think you know."

"I do know. Being an assassin and physician with the knowledge of poisons has allowed me to get close to those who were threats to our world."

"There is more. You were also the canary in the coal mine. Pathologists first raised the alarm about the opioid crisis. You saw the toxic drugs that took countless lives. Now, the world is aware of the drug problem. Humanity must decide between greed and life. I choose life."

"You're a funny one. Not that I ever thought you were about greed, but you have a mind that could create such terrors that I can't believe you never considered working for the other side." Well, maybe he did. Once.

He nods, and a soft murmur escapes his mouth. "We are all on the same side. Shifting sands make it difficult to stand firm, but I will hold my ground. And you should, too."

How lucky to have become his friend, knowing all those years ago, he made a choice.

"Lily Robinson, I am working on some new toxins that may free the brain from its need for pain medication. For the kind of drugs that fool the body into addiction. This could mean a start to the end of our drug epidemic."

"Physical pain, you mean. Psychological pain—the loss of a loved one—cannot be fixed with a drug."

"Of course, tincture of time. But perhaps your heart will heal better if you get your hands back in the lab and start working on cures of a less, let us say, less controversial nature."

"Is this an invitation?"

"Assuredly, but first, I am coming to see your famous poison garden. The one you always talk about."

How many times have I heard that?

"We'll always have poison." I touch his hand.

John Chi hugs me tightly, and I make a promise to myself to work in his lab. I remember those times with fondness. He walks over to Chad, who is engaged in speaking with an impeccably dressed man with fair hair and high cheekbones—Jackson Scott.

Scottie, as he's known, is standing tall and confident. Remarkable for having died. Or so we thought. He's wearing his signature three-piece suit, a waistcoat neatly framing a crisp white shirt. I remember his story all too well. As our Russian-based operative, he, unfortunately, fell in love with Alexis Popov, who was known as Bella Moreau to her mother, Adrienne Moreau, and her "sister" Rose. Her father, whom she tried desperately to escape, was the evil Grigory Markovic. Alexis/

Bella died trying to save Scottie. Adrienne and Rose never knew the ugly side of Bella's life. I hope they never will. I'm sure Bella had a premonition of her impending death and made a final visit to her mother, Adrienne, ostensibly to say goodbye and comfort her as she lay in her hospital bed. So many memories for me.

There are still people milling about, yet I feel the emptiness and loneliness in this room, knowing I will never see JP again.

A hand waves above the crowd. From the corner. A good-looking man I know, heads for me. His hair may be shorter, but he still has that fine stubble outlining a strong jaw.

"Lily, so good to see you, but so sorry it had to be under these circumstances."

Logan Pelletier takes me into his arms and holds me tight. They are the familiar arms of a man whose baby I once carried.

"God, Logan. How is it that you're here?"

"Chad. I've been doing a little work for him on the side, and he told me that JP was killed. I'm really sorry, Lily. I know you two had a special relationship."

Logan and I met while JP and I were investigating the deaths of a U.S. senator and the leader of a small nation. JP and I were on a break from our relationship. I was angry. So much regret. I had a short affair with Logan. I lost the baby.

"How are you doing, Lily? Really." His green eyes capture mine, and his smile is soft. "Don't hide behind your clinical armor."

I laugh gently. "You think you know me. Well, maybe a little. The recovery from the mission in D.C. took more out of me than I imagined. Now there's this." I wipe a tear from the corner of my eye. "I guess I'm not as tough as I once was."

"Stop. You are tough. Probably the toughest woman I know." He catches his breath before speaking again. "JP was a good man. I didn't know him well, but he did right by the world, and maybe you too."

I start to choke up. My voice gets stuck, and I feel my eyes filling with tears. "Yes" is all I can manage to say.

"Are you going back to Boston?"

"For the time being. I'm not sure what my plans will be."

"Look, Lily, if ever you want to work with me at my shop, I can always use a pathologist with your knowledge of toxins and poisons." Logan owns an independent autopsy practice where second opinions are sought.

"Thanks. I'll think about it."

"Good. That's all I can ask." He stops again and takes both my hands in his. "I plan on doing a fair bit of sailing off the coast of Maine this year. That old boat, Rogue Angel, could use a first mate like you."

I lean in and gently kiss Logan on the cheek. "I'd like that."

It's quiet now. Most of the guests have left, and Chad and Parker link up with me.

"Are you ready to go back, doc?" Parker asks.

"I am. It was nice to see some people we've worked with over the years."

"Scottie looked good. He's only doing translation work now. No longer in the field," Chad says.

"Couldn't believe Sam showed up. That was a long ride from Seoul," Parker says.

"I think JP was worth the trip. Don't you?"

CHAPTER 30

REIMS, FRANCE

Adrienne and Rose are expecting me. I discovered Rose was visiting her mother and thought it would be the perfect opportunity to set things straight. JP might have said otherwise, but he's not here now. I didn't come to this decision lightly. JP worried that if the true nature of my relationship with Rose was revealed, it would put her in harm's way. And this truth was the only significant point on which we ever disagreed. My daughter, my flesh and blood. My love will keep her safe.

The estate in Reims is just the way I remembered it. JP and I had a short holiday in France, and he took me to his boyhood home—the vineyard where he lived before his family moved to Chalandry. Rows of grape vines fill the acres, and the gothic house looms like a gray cloud perched in the sky. Rose is waiting on the steps for me as I pull my car up to the front.

She runs toward the car door, shouting. "Dr. Robinson. You're here! I can hardly believe it."

As soon as I step out of the car, her arms encircle me. "Rose, I'm so happy to see you." I hug her back, not wanting to let go.

"Come inside. Mother is waiting."

The house is grand, and Rose offers me a seat on the peach-covered sofa, lace curtains letting light through in a most delicate pattern. Adrienne walks into the room before I sit, and she is as I imagined. Her graying hair, once dark in her youth, and her soft blue-green eyes are reminiscent of her cousin Jean Paul.

She extends her hand. "Dr. Robinson, I'm very pleased to meet you. Rose has told me much about her time in Boston." Her grip is weak, and her speech deliberate. The recovery from her car accident continues, and she will need physical therapy for a long time.

"Please sit down," she says as Rose practically prances out of the room. "Rose has gone to make us some tea. I wanted to thank you for looking after her. Since my accident, it has been difficult for Rose, but between your guidance and the love of Dr. Kelley, she is thriving."

My love, too. "Yes, Rose has adjusted very well to Boston, and as for Kelley, he was my former fellow, and now that he is on staff, I only expect good things for his future."

"Dr. Robinson, I understood from Père Berger, our local priest, that you and another man visited the estate some time back."

Should I be surprised that Adrienne had heard that? When she was in a coma, Rose had to shoulder all the burdens with only the help of Père Berger. Until *I* met Rose.

"Yes, that's right."

"Dr. Robinson."

"Please call me Lily."

"Lily, I believe I know why you are here. I have always loved flowers. Perhaps you saw my garden when you drove up. Your mother named you after a flower, and I imagine you named your daughter after a flower. My priest described the woman as someone who looked like Rose and thought the man looked like a Moreau. I see it now."

I squirm in my seat, and realize that Adrienne is more than perceptive. "Adrienne, it's time we had a difficult conversation. And yes, I am also here to tell you about your cousin, the one who moved with his family to Chalandry."

Rose appears with a tray of three teacups, a steaming teapot, and a plate full of macarons. "Here you go," she says as she places the tray on the coffee table. JP and I would have preferred coffee, but this is just right.

"Rose, sit down here," Adrienne says softly, patting the seat next to her.

Rose, the dutiful daughter, takes a seat, and her smile disappears from her face. "What is it? You and Dr. Robinson seem so serious."

"Rose, you have always wondered about your beginnings. I told you only as much as I knew, because I didn't know the whole story. But I believe Dr. Robinson is able to fill in the blanks if you truly want to know the circumstances of how you came to me. Please understand, Rose, that I will always love you no matter what, and I have raised you as my own. If only Bella had not been taken from us." A frown appears on Adrienne's face, and there is sadness in her eyes.

"Mother, you're scaring me." Rose shifts toward Adrienne and takes her hand.

My heart breaks for Adrienne. She has already lost one daughter and is fearful of losing a second.

I capture Rose's beautiful green eyes and gently touch her arm. "It's up to you, Rose. Sometimes, the truth is more painful than not knowing it at all. What your mother says is true, I can fill in the background, but what you two share can never be changed in any way—like an unbreakable covalent bond—and it's a gift that you found each other all those years ago."

Tears stream down Rose's cheeks, and she buries her head in her hands. "It's true. I always wondered if it was true. Everyone said I looked just like you. Kelley went on about it, but I told him it was impossible." She sniffs, twists the gold ring with the red heart-shaped diamond, and Adrienne takes her in her arms.

"It's all right, Rose. I think you will only find love in this house."

"And my father?"

I tell Rose and Adrienne the story of Charles, his genius, his love for his unborn child, and although Rose learns she was an unplanned baby, she now knows she was loved from the very moment of conception. I tell her about our three years together in Boston, her nanny Maggie, and the fateful trip to South America. I explain that I never gave up learning the truth, but I was told my child had died, and memories of that terrible time escaped me for more than twenty years.

I ask for forgiveness from both Adrienne and Rose, for any sins I may have committed for withholding the truth and for telling the truth. Rose is sobbing now. Adrienne strokes her dark hair and holds her close.

"Thank you, Lily, for telling your part in the story. Now, it is my turn to share the awful truth."

I listen intently, my tears at full capacity, as Adrienne tells the tale of her uncle, her rape by Markovic, and the role her uncle's men had in the slaughter of my colleagues. She breaks down.

The tea has cooled, not a drop touched, and we three sit wondering how it will all end.

"There is one more thing. The man with me the day I visited your vineyard was your lost cousin. I've come to bring him home." I cannot stop the tears. I cannot bury my emotions any longer. Oh god, JP, how I miss you.

I tell them some of his story, but clearly not all. I tell them he was killed in the line of duty and that he was beloved by his colleagues. I tell them I want to spread some of his ashes, as per his wish, in the vineyards where he played as a boy with his brother. I promised I would bring him home.

CHAPTER 31

THE COTTAGE

I'm home now—emotionally drained and physically exhausted. I plan to see Rose and Adrienne as often as I can, and now that we share a bond of love, I might have the strength to say more about Alexis/Bella's fate in the future.

Spring and summer will bring foxgloves in friendly stalks of pink and purple. Flowers known to be both healing, and deadly, long before I grew them, grace the walkway. Delicate white Lily of the Valley bells will tumble from stalks of green against a backdrop of Miscanthus and Pennisetum, grasses that rise high and mighty. Years ago, my poison garden was a beautiful indulgence rather than a tool of death. I planted it after Charles died. The cottage once was his, but he left it to me, so I would always have the sea in my ears and heart. Rose will be here again.

Kelley has begged me to come back and work more hours on the hospital service. We have new residents that could use more training in forensics and toxicology. Francis Becker, the pathologist from New York City, called the other day. He had questions about a case he's working on and thought I might have some answers for him. A few years back, Becker alerted me to several unexplained deaths in Manhattan that turned out to be a mass poisoning orchestrated by the terrorist Grigory Markovic. I rode that wave with JP.

My SWEETIE coffee cup sits on the table and reminds me that the LOVER cup has been pushed to the back of the cupboard. I won't use JP's cup again.

His white shirt hangs in my closet, and I sleep in it some nights, wanting to smell the faint traces of him. What would our life have been if we had given up everything for each other?

I stopped by his flat in France, the place he left to me in his last wishes. I'd never been before and wondered what his home would be like. I was surprised. Art adorned the walls, with many French artists and sculptures of intertwined lovers. He truly was a man of mystery. No photographs were on display. I assume he didn't want to reveal any ties that could endanger anyone. But I did find two sketches that I presumed were of Pixie Dust—Sophie Martin—from when JP must have known her as a young man. I wondered if that was the woman he loved before me as I traced the delicate outline of her face and thought about our first meeting. What did she know about my daughter? There were no answers. The truth has been buried—twice now. She never said, nor did JP. Could she have foreseen that JP would forever live in my heart? *Beaucoup de* questions.

At times, I weep for him. Tears stream unexpectedly, drowning waking moments or wrenching me from deep sleep. Sometimes, through the tears, anger makes its way from its dark hole to remind me that JP left me. He left *me*. Death is so final, so brutal. And yet, I spread his remaining ashes in the sea that laps at my back door, hoping, knowing he will be here with me. Always. He is etched in my soul, my being, in a way no man could or will ever be again.

I've walked the beach many times, my collar to the wind, the water gray and cold. New England waters never have the warmth or the azure of a Caribbean Sea. I pick up a few seashells, a quahog, a razor clam, and blue mussels. That takes my mind back to saxitoxin. Saxitoxin, found in contaminated mussels, had been the smokescreen when I met Ian Watson at that fateful dinner. But it wasn't the saxitoxin at all that killed him. It was the deep blue flowers of my homegrown wolfsbane. Aconitine, the same poison I used to kill his daughter.

I've come full circle now. I lost a daughter, found a lover, found my daughter, and then lost the love of my life. My soul aches, and my heart hurts, and I feel the blow just between beats—that twenty-millisecond window of vulnerability where chaos can unravel. My future is uncertain, but one thing I know is that I'm still the Queen of all Poisons.

ACKNOWLEDGMENTS

Thank you to my colleagues from Encircle Publications for their support and to the Encircle Publications team: Eddie Vincent, publisher; Cynthia Bracket-Vincent, editor; and Deirdre Wait, book designer and cover artist.

To my first reader, Karen Krajewski—thank you for your feedback; as always, you have a "feel" for Lily's journey.

Special thanks to consultants Jim Begg, Norton Berisha, and Rachel Van Nevel from Brussels, Belgium, for their help with the Atomium, and to Professor David Deese for his input on climate change. Any mistakes in the content are mine and not theirs.

Thanks to Yim Tan Wong for her editorial review—always thoughtful and helpful—and to Anne Brewer (annebrewereditorial.com) for her help with the project. Their suggestions only made this a better book and me a better writer.

CROSSWORD CLUES

ACROSS

1 Australian spider (two words)

4 Sodium (symbol)

5 Preposition

6 Toxic _____ Gas (Novichok)

8 Toxalbumin from *R. communis*

10 Inert noble gas (symbol)

11 The Queen of All Poisons (two words)

14 Potassium (symbol)

15 Blue-ringed octopus toxin

19 Zoanthid coral toxin

21 Lily's daughter

22 A deception

23 Lily's soulmate

DOWN

1 Animal tooth

2 For____ Love

3 Caster ____ *R. communis*

5 A substance created by a plant or animal harmful to humans

7 The gem from the head of the snake in Lily's ring

9 Dr. John ___ Leigh

12 Allow

13 Short for saxitoxin

16 Rye contaminant- Salem witch trials

17 _____ Cap *Amanita phylloides*

18 A plaything

20 Short for tetrodotoxin

CROSSWORD PUZZLE

CROSSWORD ANSWERS

ACROSS

1 Funnel Web

4 Na

5 To

6 Nerve

8 Ricin

10 Xenon

11 Lily Robinson

14 K

15 Tetrodotoxin

19 Palytoxin

21 Rose

22 Hoax

23 JP

DOWN

1 Fang

2 Ever

3 Bean

5 Toxin

7 Ruby

9 Chi

12 Let

13 STX

16 Ergot

17 Death

18 Toy

20 TTX

ABOUT THE AUTHOR

BJ Magnani's fascination with toxicology led her to a career in pathology and laboratory medicine. She is the author of the Dr. Lily Robinson medical suspense thriller series *The Queen of All Poisons* (June 2019), *The Power of Poison* (March 2021), *A Message in Poison* (April 2022), and *We'll Always Have Poison* (July 2024) from Encircle Publications. *Lily Robinson and the Art of Secret Poisoning* (nVision Publishing, 2011) is the original collection of short stories featuring the brilliant yet deadly doctor.

Barbarajean (BJ) Magnani, PhD, MD, FCAP, is internationally recognized for her expertise in clinical chemistry and toxicology, has been named a "Top Doctor" in *Boston* magazine, and was named one of the Top 100 Most Influential Laboratory Medicine Professionals in the *World by the Pathologist*. She is Professor of Anatomic and Clinical Pathology Emerita at Tufts University School of Medicine and the former Chair of the Department of Pathology and Laboratory Medicine at Tufts Medical Center, Boston, MA. She is also the former Chair of the College of American Pathologists (CAP) Toxicology Committee and donates a portion of the proceeds from her novels to help women receive free breast and cervical cancer screening through the CAP Foundation. You can learn more about Dr. Magnani, her work, and her *Poison Blog* at BJMagnani.com, and follow BJ Magnani on X (Twitter), Instagram, Facebook, and LinkedIn.

If you enjoyed this book,
please consider writing a review
and sharing it with other readers.

Many of our Authors are happy to participate in
Book Club and Reader Group discussions.
For more information, contact us at info@encirclepub.com.

Thank you,
Encircle Publications

For news about more exciting new fiction, join us at:

Facebook: www.facebook.com/encirclepub

Instagram: www.instagram.com/encirclepublications

Sign up for the Encircle Publications newsletter:
eepurl.com/cs8taP

Printed in the USA
CPSIA information can be obtained
at www.ICGtesting.com
LVHW041627230524
781008LV00001B/7